THE
TURTLE-JACK
KILLINGS

A
Mitch and Al
MYSTERY

GLENN ICKLER

outskirts
press

Outskirts Press, Inc.
http://www.outskirtspress.com

ISBN: 978-1-9772-7929-3

Outskirts Press and the "OP" logo
are trademarks belonging to Outskirts Press, Inc.

PRINTED IN THE UNITED STATES OF AMERICA

Praise for the Mitch and Al Series

All I have to say is Glenn Ickler needs to keep writing because these Mitch and Al mysteries are unfailingly smart and funny ... they put me in a good mood for days. *–Michael Hartnett, author of "The Blue Gowanus" and "The Blue Rat"*

Readers will be struck almost immediately by the smooth professionalism of Ickler's execution. He lays out the classic elements of a murder mystery—engaging secondary characters, intriguing history, sharp dialogue—in a fast-paced, entertaining narrative. *–Kirkus Reviews*

Also by Glenn Ickler

Dedication

To GMA, who is always right.

And the turtles of course,
All the turtles are free,
As turtles, and maybe, all creatures should be.

-- Dr. Seuss

PROLOGUE

Getting no response when I knocked on the door of apartment 204, I went to the building manager's office, told her that I was checking on the wellbeing of the woman who lived in that apartment, and asked her to open the door with her master key. She asked me for identification, and I showed her my press credentials from the *St. Paul Daily Dispatch*. Apparently assured that I was not a serial killer of women who was seeking my next victim, she said, "All right, Mister Mitchell. Come along with me."

She took a ring of thick metal keys out of her top desk drawer and led me to the antique elevator. It creaked as we got on and it groaned when it responded to the push of the second-floor button. In this complaining carriage, we reached the second floor in about twice the time it had taken me to climb the stairs.

When we reached apartment 204, she unlocked the door, told me that she would go in first, opened the door, and walked in. A second later, I heard her shriek, "Oh, my god!"

I went charging through the door into the living room and was stopped after four quick steps by the reason for Madeline's ear-shattering cry.

1

TWO DAYS EARLIER

The deeply-lined bronze face of the man standing in front of me was topped by a ring of upright eagle feathers that made him nearly eight feet tall. The age lines rippled into a smile as this intimidating figure reached both hands out to me and gently placed a turtle into my upturned palms.

Not a living, crawling, snapping kind of turtle, mind you. This turtle was carved from a block of white pine and painted by the same hand that had carved it. I thanked the donor, whose name was Chief Raymond Hardshell Turtle, and whose title was president of the Minnesota Ojibwe Tribal Council. I promised the Chief that I would continue researching and writing about a proposed nickel mining project adjacent to the western boundary of the Ojibwe Reservation, where we were standing onstage in front of about three hundred Native American residents and a television news crew from Moorhead, the nearest major city.

A month-long investigation by the *St. Paul Daily Dispatch*, where I work as a reporter, had exposed the probability of severe environmental damage if the application for the mining project was approved by state officials. The project would require draining a spidery expanse of wetlands that provided a constant flow of fresh water to a lake abounding with walleyed pike on the Rez, as it is known. In addition, the threatened swamp waters were the home of an endangered species of turtle, which members of the Ojibwe turtle clan revered as a source of strength for the warriors of the tribe.

The remaining lake water would be fouled by the process used for extracting nickel, which is known as sulfide mining. Separating the metal from its sulfide ore leaves a substantial pile of sulfurous waste rock that contaminates any disposal site. Both a news report and an Opinion page editorial had been based on a national environmental study that said that the operation of every known use of the sulfide mining technique has caused pollution of nearby lakes, rivers, or groundwater.

When our managing editor's attention was called to this potential environmental outrage by Ojibwe leaders, four members of the newspaper's staff, including me, Warren "Mitch" Mitchell, were assigned to immerse ourselves in the wetlands story. Although there still was no guarantee that the mining permit requested by Coordinated Copper & Nickel, Incorporated, would be denied, our stories, editorials, and photographs had resulted in a delay in the investigative process, giving the Pollution Control Agency more time to thoroughly examine the potential consequences of issuing an approval.

Now the four of us who'd been submerged in the threatened wetlands story were on the Rez by invitation, being thanked for our preservation efforts by those who lived there. I was at the stage-right end of a line that included photographer Alan Jeffrey, Opinion page editorial writer Ben deLyne, and business reporter T.J. Kelly.

We had spent Sunday afternoon on a guided tour of the Reservation and the turtle-sheltering wetlands that would be drained if Coordinated Copper & Nickel, Inc., was given the requested permit. We saw no turtles, of course, because it was January, and the wetlands had become a sheet of ice covered with a foot of snow. The wetlands' herpetological residents were spending the winter tucked deep in the mud beneath these two frozen layers.

Our guide, Barbara Laughing Turtle, told us that among the varieties of turtles occupying these wetlands was an endangered species known as the northern red-bellied cooter. With guidance from the Division of Fish and Wildlife, a group of Ojibwe school children had been conducting a program to increase the cooters' survival rate by collecting the eggs laid in the spring and nurturing the hatchlings until they were big enough to escape many of the creatures that would prey on them when they were released into the wild.

"Those little critters are only about the size of a silver dollar when they're hatched," Barbara said. "That makes them easy pickings for almost any kind of vertebrate you can think of. They grow up to be ten to twelve inches long, which still leaves them vulnerable to some of their largest stalkers, but they're also quicker and smarter by that time."

She told us that the red-bellied cooters that Rez children were helping to save from extinction are the only cooters that live in the northern states. Several other types have chosen to bask in the warmer climate of the Gulf Coast. "The theory is that it was much warmer here 6,000 years ago and that a small population of the red-bellied cooters survived when this area cooled," Barbara said. "They'd become acclimated to this area, but the population is small and they probably would have been wiped out by predators that were gobbling up both their eggs and their hatchlings if the kids hadn't taken their survival on as a project twenty years ago. Now they'll have no place to live if these wetlands are drained and dug up as a nickel mine."

Appropriately, the awards that we were being given for defending the turtle habitat came in the form of four identical wooden turtles carved by an artist on the Rez. They were about six inches long from the tips of their noses, which were turned slightly up-ward with a look of awareness and attention, to the tips of their tails, and they stood a little more than two inches high.

Before starting to hand out the wooden turtles, Chief Hardshell Turtle had made a short speech about the environmental value of the threatened wetlands, emphasizing the special need to preserve the turtles' habitat, and praising the *Daily Dispatch* coverage of the issue.

Al, the next recipient after me, got a round of applause when he said, "When the full story about this proposed mine has been told, all that nickel won't be worth a dime."

Ben deLyne promised to continue his Opinion page efforts to preserve the Rez's wetlands, and T.J. Kelly went a step further. She reached into a pocket of her navy-blue pants suit and withdrew a tiny object, which she held up between her thumb and forefinger for all to see as she said, "This little thumb drive contains informa-tion that will help me drive this proposed environmental disaster into oblivion when I write my next story. Until then, it will rest in-side this symbolic turtle." With a flourish, T.J. raised the removable shell on the turtle's back, placed the thumb drive inside the turtle's tummy, replaced the shell and held the turtle up high with both hands. This drew another burst of spontaneous applause, along with a couple of war whoops.

I turned my attention to my turtle as the Chief and his entou-rage were leaving the stage. The top of its shell was decorated with a circular painting in various shades of green, brown, white, and blue that depicted the Western Hemisphere of the globe, in accor-dance with Native American fables about Mother Turtle giving birth to the world and bearing it on her back. I gave the shell a quick try. It offered some resistance, but when it came off it revealed an inch-deep hollowed out area where a person could store coins, keys, or candies—or a valuable thumb drive. It was a work of art with a practical use, in accordance with another Native American tradition.

⸺ ∞ ⸺

City Editor Don O'Rourke had ordered all of us to bring our turtles to the *Daily Dispatch* office for a group photo Monday morning. With T.J. Kelly standing on my left and Al Jeffrey and Ben deLyne on my right, we passed our turtles around to each other, looking for variations in the hand-carved, hand-painted figures. The artist had worked with such painstaking skill that when the four were laid side by side on a desk they looked like they could all have been produced by the same mold and painted by the same robotic hand.

Staff photographer Henny "One Shot" Paulson ordered us to hold as still as a turtle sleeping on a rock and took his single shot of us displaying our trophies while smiling the requisite smiles. As the four of us dispersed, T.J. drew me aside. She held the turtle up to her chin and spoke almost in a whisper. "I've still got that thumb drive that I showed the crowd Saturday night tucked in this little guy's tummy. There's some stuff on that thumb drive that's going to blow this whole wetlands wrecking project out of the water, pun intended." She gave the turtle a quick kiss on the tip of its nose and said, "I need to get some confirmations from a couple of places before I can write the story, but once this stuff is out in the open there won't be any danger of the turtles getting dehydrated or the walleyes swimming in sulfuric acid up there on the Rez."

"Our friends up there on the Rez will be glad to see that story," I said. "What have you got that makes you so sure it'll kill the project?"

"You'll see it in the paper after I've made some calls. Probably write the story tomorrow," she said. "This is so good it could put us up for a Pulitzer."

"What kind of a trophy would we get with that?"

"I'm not sure. Probably bigger than a pretty little wooden turtle."

"I can't wait to see that story," I said. "Who do you have to call?"

"EPA and FBI," she said in a whisper.

"I can understand why you'd call Environmental Protection, but why the FBI? Is there skullduggery afoot?"

"You can read all about it in my story," said T.J. Kelly. "Gotta go make those calls." And off she went to her desk, with that pretty little wooden turtle in hand.

That evening, my wife, Martha Todd, pointed to the pretty little wooden turtle sitting to the right of my dinner plate, and said, "That turtle is so beautiful. It has all the colors of that huge mother turtle on the mural in the park."

The mural that Martha was talking about is a 150-foot-long painting that stands in Unci Makha Park, which overlooks the Mississippi River less than a mile from our home. This mural is a representation of the Dakota creation story, and its most prominent feature is a snapping turtle that has trees sprouting from its shell, rivers running across it and the sun behind it. Smaller turtles along the painting lead to this turtle, which occupies fully one-third of the mural. It represents Turtle Island, which is what many Indigenous communities call the North American continent.

Six high school interns from the city's Right Track youth employment program created the mural, which is entitled "As Above, So Below; Seeing Ourselves in the Creation Story." A cultural and artistic consultant guided the artists' work with stories she'd been told by the Dakota Elders. "As above, so below" represents the Dakota belief that on earth there are stars and what's on earth also lives in the cosmos.

"Our little turtle, with all the colors of the earth and the sky on its shell, tells the creation story, just like the huge mother turtle in the mural," I said. "These stories linking the creation of the earth to a turtle need to be preserved, along with the living turtles up there on the Rez."

"We have to find a permanent home for your little earth mother," Martha said. "And some day we should take her to the park to meet her counterpart on the mural."

"You're right," I said. "Mother Turtle deserves to reside in a place of honor, not next to a bowl of mashed potatoes." Martha Todd, who works as a lawyer, is always right. She is also always beautiful, displaying a blend of the best genes of a Cape Verdean mother and a British naval officer father in her coffee-with-cream-colored facial features and a slender, yet enticingly rounded female form.

After dinner, we carried Mother Turtle all around our duplex apartment, placing her in various spots on shelves and tables. We finally settled on a bookshelf about waist high in the hall near the front door. "She can greet us every night when we come home from work," Martha said.

"And give a quiet welcome to any guest who appears," I said. "We don't want her to be shellfish with her greetings."

Martha turned and walked away at triple the speed of a turtle.

2

WHERE'S T.J.?

I wanted to talk to T.J. Kelly about the dynamite story that she'd said she had on the thumb drive hidden in her turtle before I wrote my next story about the nickel mining project, but she was not at her desk when I arrived at the *Daily Dispatch* at 7:55 a.m. Tuesday. Time moved along, as it always does, and when T.J.'s chair was still empty at 8:30, I went to the city desk and asked City Editor Don O'Rourke if this was T.J.'s day off.

"No," he said. "She's late and she hasn't called in. That's not like her, but maybe she's making some calls from home. Yesterday she said she would have a real block buster for me today, so I'm really looking to hear from her."

"I want to talk about that block buster with her," I said. "I'll give her a call."

T.J.'s home number was on a list of staff members on my desk. I called it and got her voice mail. Her cellphone was also on the list, so I tried that next. This also went to voice mail.

I went back to Don O'Rourke. "T.J.'s not answering either of her phones," I said.

"What the hell?" Don said. "She can't just disappear."

"I wouldn't think so," I said. "I'll try again in half an hour."

A half hour later I again got nothing but her voice mail on both phones. This was getting mysterious. The case of the vanishing turtle winner. I reported my most recent failure to Don and got another "what the hell?" in response.

"She only lives six blocks away," I said. "Should I go check on her? Maybe she's sick."

"You'd think she'd call in if she was sick," Don said. "Go ahead and walk down there and bang on her door."

I tried T.J.'s cellphone one more time and got her voice mail one more time. Then I told Don that I was going, and set out for her apartment. She was single and lived alone in a six-story nineteenth-century brick building in Lowertown, just a ten-minute walk from the office.

The address was Apartment 204. Choosing the stairs instead of the open cast iron cage of the nineteenth century elevator, I climbed to the second floor and knocked on the door of 204. There was no response.

I knocked louder. Still nothing.

I pounded with the sides of my fists and yelled, "T.J.!"

No answer.

I'd seen an office for the building manager in the lobby when I'd entered from the street, so I went down the stairs and went to that door. A knock there got a response. "Come in," a woman's voice said.

I opened the door, walked in, and found a short, round, middle-aged woman seated behind a wooden desk that looked as old as the building. A plaque on the desk said "Madeline Webster." I introduced myself and told her that I was trying to visit the tenant in 204 but was getting no response from either calling her phone or knocking on her door. "I wonder if we could check on her," I said. "She's supposed to be at work and our boss is getting worried."

Madeline sighed and said, "Can I see some ID?" I offered both my pictured press credentials and my driver's license. She squinted at them and studied my face for nearly a minute before handing them back.

Apparently assured that I was not a serial killer of women who was seeking my next victim, she said, "All right, Mister Mitchell. Come along with me." She took a ring of thick metal keys out of her top desk drawer and led me to the elevator. It creaked as we got on and it groaned when it responded to the push of the second-floor button. In this complaining carriage, we reached the second floor in about twice the time it had taken me to climb the stairs.

When we reached apartment 204, Madeline unlocked the door, told me that she would go in first, opened the door, and walked in. A second later, I heard her shriek, "Oh, my god!"

3

NO ANSWERS

I went charging through the door into the living room and was stopped after four quick steps by the reason for Madeline's ear-shattering cry. At my feet, T.J. Kelly lay sprawled on her back on a white carpet stained red by a gusher of blood from a wide slash across her throat. Her eyes were open, and her right hand was grasping the gash, as if she'd been trying to hold back the scarlet tide.

"Don't touch anything," I shouted at Madeline, whose eyes and mouth were wide open in the middle of a face that had turned chalky white. "I'm calling 911."

Madeline took a step away from the body, collapsed backward into a leather upholstered armchair, and bent forward until her forehead rested on her knees.

I felt my breakfast trying to make a comeback, so I turned away from the gruesome scene as I made the call to 911 and reported a homicide. "Please remain in place and do not touch anything at the scene, sir," the operator said. "Police will be there in no more than five minutes."

"I'll be waiting for them," I said. Next, I called City Editor Don O'Rourke and, as gently as I could, told him what I'd found in T.J.'s apartment. His immediate response was mostly expletives that I've

Glenn Ickler

rarely heard him use. His follow-up response was, "I'll send your twin over there for pics." My "twin" was Alan Jeffrey. Don had labeled us the Siamese twins, supposedly attached at our funny bones, which, he said, were our skulls. When advised that the modern politically correct term was "conjoined twins," Don said he wouldn't change his label until he received a complaint from the King of Siam. This is not likely to happen, with the former kingdom of Siam having undergone changes in both its name and its form of government.

Two uniformed officers made it to the scene in four and a half minutes, which meant they must have run up the stairs rather than ridden the elevator. I was standing in the open doorway when they arrived. "Right this way, gentlemen," I said. "And it ain't pretty."

"Never is," said one of them as they trotted past me.

I had spent four of the four and a half minutes looking around the room to see if T.J.'s turtle, with the nickel mine killer thumb drive tucked in its tummy, was anywhere in sight. I'd been told not to touch anything, but T.J.'s thumb drive contained information for an extremely important story. It would be foolish to leave that thumb drive sitting inside that turtle for possible discovery and examination by homicide investigators who might very well store it away forever in an evidence locker. Who could possibly make better use of the information on that thumb drive than staff writer Warren Mitchell?

Looking around the room, I saw that some books had been pulled off a shelf, the sofa cushions were on the floor, and the drawers on T.J.'s desk were hanging open. Apparently, the killer had been looking for something. Money? Jewelry? Who knows? The fifty-inch TV was still bolted to the wall and T.J.'s laptop and cellphone were lying side by side on a small wooden desk.

I couldn't spot a pretty little turtle on the desk or any shelf or table in the room. Was it in the bedroom or a closet? Could I slip into the bedroom or open a closet to search for the turtle without being stopped by the officers? While I was looking for an opening,

12

any chance of slipping away vanished with the arrival of the next wave of law enforcement.

Al arrived with his camera in hand simultaneously with this wave, which consisted of the Chief of Homicide, Detective Curtis Brown, who was informally and surreptitiously known as Brownie by members of the news media, and Detective Mike Reilly, who was well known as a hater of all members of the news media. All three were breathing heavily from having run up the stairs. Reilly stopped long enough to order Al and me to keep our distance and Brownie went directly to the object on the carpet.

"Who's that?" Reilly asked me, pointing to the woman sitting with her head in her lap.

"Building manager," I said. "Madeline something. She let me in."

Brownie finished his initial examination of the body and turned to us. "Who found the body?"

"Me and Madeline," I said.

"Okay, I'll take both of your statements later," Brownie said. "Meanwhile, all three of you can clear out while we process the scene."

Al kept shooting pictures while I went to Madeline and put a hand on her shoulder. "We need to leave," I said. "Order from police."

"I don't think I can stand up," she said.

"We'll help you." I called Al over and we each took an elbow and raised Madeline off the chair. Holding the wobbly-kneed woman between us, we walked to the elevator, rode it slowly down, and deposited Madeline in the chair behind the desk in her office. I asked if we could get her some water or anything and she said that she'd be fine. We left her slumped in the chair, pale-faced and staring into space.

Don O'Rourke was full of questions when we got back to the city desk: "Who could have done it?"

"I have no clue."

"Why would anyone kill her?"

"I have no clue."

"Was it a robbery?"

"The room was messed up like the killer was looking for something, but I have no way of knowing if anything was missing."

"Was she raped?"

"She was fully clothed. Wearing what she had on yesterday."

"Thank God for that."

"Amen," I said.

Writing the story was a struggle. How do you objectively describe the blood-splashed murder scene of a person you've known and worked with for almost twenty years? As a business reporter, T.J. Kelly was the ultimate professional. She had well-placed contacts all over the Twin Cities, the state of Minnesota, and Washington, D.C., and any time I had a question pertaining to the business world she always came up with a complete and easy to understand answer.

As for personal details, I knew nothing about T.J.'s life outside the office, other than that she lived alone in that apartment. I didn't know if she'd ever been married, if she had any family nearby, if her social life included a male companion, or if she had any contacts with the sort of person who would resolve an issue by cutting someone's throat.

Al offered Don a choice of photos that included the surroundings in the room, the uniformed cops, Madeline bent over in the chair, and Brownie and Reilly. He offered nothing showing T.J. on the carpet, although I knew he had taken some shots of her lying there. To accompany my story, Don selected a shot of the two homicide detectives together and the one of Madeline with her head on her knees and I wrote a cutline explaining that she was the person who discovered the body. I dug deep into my memory bank and remembered that her last name was Webster.

"You need a statement of some sort from the cops," Don said after he'd read my story.

I called the number known only to reporters for Homicide Chief Curtis Brown, hoping that he'd be back in his office by this time. He answered with one word, as he always does. "Homicidebrown."

I responded with one word, as I always do. "Dailydispatchmitchell." Then added, "I need a statement from you about T.J. Kelly."

"And I need a statement from you about T.J. Kelly," Brownie said.

"You go first," I said.

"We have no information to release about the unfortunate death of Ms. Kelly."

"No persons of interest? No apparent motive for the killing?"

"Nothing. Nada."

"Did you find the murder weapon?"

"Again nothing. Nada. Killer left nothing behind. No weapon, no fingerprints, no boot tracks, no business card. Now it's your turn. Come to the station so I can record your statement."

"I'll be there in about fifteen minutes, soon as I wrap up the story I'm writing."

"I'll tell the desk sergeant to send you straight back the minute you get here."

The best thing about the location of the *Daily Dispatch* building in downtown St. Paul is that it is within walking distance of every key office in the city. The police station, the city hall, the county's official emergency hospital, and even the state Capitol are all within less than fifteen minutes on foot. I was on my way to the police station a minute after sending my amended story to Don, and I arrived within the promised fifteen.

The desk sergeant waved me through to Brownie's office, where I recorded a verbal rehash of what I'd seen in T.J.'s apartment. Brownie asked me what I knew about T.J.'s business contacts, which, I said, were bountiful, and her life outside the office, of which, I said, I knew nothing. "I was hoping you could give me something to start on," Brownie said. "Has she been feuding in the paper with anybody that she's reported on? Does she have any longtime enemies in the business world? Has she had any threats that you know of?"

"I know of nothing along any of those lines," I said. "She's kind of off in her own little world as the business writer; has her own office up front by the managing editor, and she doesn't mix much with the herd of animals in the newsroom. Or, I should say, 'was,' 'had,' and 'didn't?'"

"What about that nickel mining project out near the Rez that the paper's been ripping apart? I saw a scene on the network news from an award ceremony involving the reporting and the editorial campaigning about that project that included Ms. Kelly the other night. Wasn't she the woman holding up a wooden turtle and a thumb drive?"

"Yes, that was T.J. sounding off. That shot went viral all over the country after the Moorhead TV channel put it on NBC. I'm sure that it wasn't appreciated by some of the would-be nickel miners and a couple of politicians who aren't happy with what our stories and editorials and photos have done to screw up their quiet little swamp draining plan. I've heard from some of them myself. They weren't fun to talk to, but I've never been threatened physically in any way by any of them. I can't imagine any of those people sending out a guy with a knife to cut a reporter's throat."

"And there's no ex-husband or boyfriend on the scene? That's who we normally look at first in a case like this."

"As I said, I don't know anything about T.J.'s life outside the office. I don't know if she's ever been married, and I've never heard her speak of a boyfriend. Actually, I'd call it a *man* friend because she wasn't exactly a teenager. She had to have been in her middle forties."

"Forty-eight, according to her driver's license," Brownie said.

"My guess was close," I said.

"You could set up a 'guess your age and weight' stand at the state fair," Brownie said.

"I'll consider that when I retire from writing about murders in our fair state."

"Well, good luck writing about this one. If you find out anything that I should know, give me a call."

"Will you do the same for me?"

"That's not in my job description," said Brownie. "We'll let the chief decide what and when we tell the press about our investigation. Have a good day, Mitch."

I thanked him for his good wishes and returned to my office, where my day actually did get a little bit better.

4

EX ON THE SPOT

The improvement of my day came in the form of Annette Randall, who is in charge of the *Daily Dispatch* library, which isn't called "the morgue" anymore. I don't know why the tradition of labeling newspaper libraries as morgues has been abandoned. (Or why it ever started, for that matter.) Maybe it's another case of political correctness, although I've never heard of any mass protests by either morticians or their clients. And a protest march by a mob of the latter definitely would be newsworthy.

Annette Randall came to my desk and asked me if I'd learned anything about T.J.'s murder from the police. When I replied that they had no leads whatsoever, Annette said, "If I were them, I'd be looking at her ex-husband."

"She has an ex-husband?" I said.

"She does. We sometimes have lunch together, and just last week she said that he was living in Iowa but that he's back in St. Paul visiting some of his family and they'd had a quarrel."

"Did she say what the quarrel was about?"

"It started with something about the guy she's been seeing lately," Annette said. "She also said that it was pretty standard for them to get into some kind of a fight any time they got within speaking distance of each other, which was a major reason why the term 'ex' had been placed in front of the word 'husband.'"

"And they were within speaking distance of each other that recently?"

"They were."

"Do you know the name of the ex?"

"It's Sean. Spelled S-E-A-N. A real authentic Irish Kelly."

"Do you think he's still in town?" I asked.

"I'll bet that he's not if it was him that cut her throat," Annette said. "He's probably back in Iowa. Iowa City, I think she said was where he lives."

"Could you look up an Iowa City directory and see if there's a land line number for a Sean Kelly there?"

"That's part of my job description," she said. "I'll do it right now and buzz your extension if I find anything."

She hustled away and two minutes later my desk phone rang. It was Annette, with an Iowa City number for Sean Kelly. I thanked Annette, hung up, and punched in the number she'd given me. There was no answer, not even from a machine directing me to leave a message.

Something else was ringing a bell. I called Annette's extension. "Did I hear you say that T.J. was currently seeing someone of the opposite sex?" I asked.

"You did," she said.

"Do you know his name?"

"Not completely. His first name is Murray and he runs a hardware store somewhere on Snelling Avenue."

"That shouldn't be too hard to find," I said. "Thanks for the tip."

A hardware store. Mmm. Might a store of that type stock big sharp knives?

I went on the Internet and did a search for St. Paul hardware stores. Up popped Murray's Neighborhood Hardware on North Snelling Avenue.

Now I had some choices to make. I could call Brownie and tell him everything I knew about Sean the squabbler and Murray the merchant, or I could continue trying to contact the former and go visit the latter. No brainer. I told Don O'Rourke that I was off to interview a man who'd been dating our late business writer and Don said, "Go get him."

On the way to the elevator, I met Al, who was returning from an assignment, and told him where I was going.

"No kidding?" he said. "Murray's is just a few blocks from our house. I've been in there several times for stuff. Murray was dating our T.J.?"

"So our librarian says," I said. "You don't happen to know Murray's last name, do you?"

"Nope. The only people I've talked to there are shelf stockers and checkout clerks. Never had a reason to complain to the manager."

At Murray's Neighborhood Hardware, I went to the checkout counter and told a woman whose name tag said "LIZ" that I needed to talk to Murray.

"Is there a problem, sir?" Liz asked.

"Not with the service," I said. "This is actually something personal."

"You're a friend of Mister Hill?"

So, Murray's last name was Hill. "Not exactly," I said to Liz. "I just need to talk to him. Can you tell me where to find him?"

"I'm afraid that he's not in the store today," Liz said. "He called in sick this morning."

Sick? Or worn out from the effort of cutting a woman's throat? "Do you have a number where I can reach him?" I asked.

"I'm sorry, sir. I'd lose my job if I gave that out."

"And I suppose that you can't tell me where he lives."

"Oh, no, sir." She laughed and added, "I'd lose my life for telling you that."

Still wondering if Murray Hill would take someone else's life for some other reason, I returned to the *Daily Dispatch,* where I reported my failure to Don and searched the St. Paul and Minneapolis phone books. If Murray Hill had a land line in the Twin Cities, it was unlisted.

That left the score for the day at Slaying Suspects two and Mitch Mitchell zero. Not a propitious start on Mitch Mitchell's search for T.J. Kelly's killer.

Al came to my desk, bearing two paper cups full of coffee. He cleared one corner of its jetsam and perched there while I told him what had happened at Murray's Neighborhood Hardware.

"His name is Murray Hill?" Al said. "That sounds like one of those prefixes, like Garden View, that the phone company used to use back in the days before they went to all numbers. I can remember calling a number like Murray Hill seven, three-four-five-six when I was in grade school."

"My parents had Glen Vista nine, seven-six-six-six," I said. "You dialed GV9-7666. My mother, the devout Methodist, always hated the triple-six because it supposedly is the area code number combination for hell, so it's one of Satan's favorites. Poor Mom couldn't get it changed when she tried."

"The devil, you say," Al said. "Anyhow, good luck getting up Murray Hill. I'm off to shoot a grip-and-grin in the mayor's office."

I decided that it was time to do the proper thing and share some of my meager knowledge with Brownie. He picked up on the third ring with his customary "Homicidebrown."

"Dailydispatchmitchell," I said. "I have some news for you on the T.J. Kelly case. She had an ex-husband named Sean, and he's been here in town recently."

"Thanks for thinking of me, but it's not news to me," Brownie said. "Sean Kelly came in here an hour ago to put in a claim for Ms. Kelly's body as soon as it's released."

I let that surprise register in my brain for a few seconds before asking how Sean Kelly knew that T.J. was dead and that her body was in police possession. "Said he read about it on-line in the St. Paul paper," Brownie said. "Some local reporter must have written a story about it."

"With great accuracy, I'm sure," I said. "Will Mister Kelly be getting custody of the body?"

"He will unless some other survivor speaks up and contests his claim. So far, we haven't been contacted by any blood relatives of the victim."

"And you haven't tried to contact any blood relatives?"

"Don't know of any. Mister Kelly told us that they'd had no children, that both of her parents are deceased and that she was an only child. As far as we know, as her former husband, he's the only thing close to a survivor."

"Have you questioned him about where he was at the time of the victim's demise?"

"We have no comment on what procedures we have taken at this time."

Ah, the standard police run around. "How about this: do you have any persons of interest?"

"We have no comment on that at this time."

"Can you tell me how I can contact Mister Kelly?"

"He gave us a contact number in Iowa City, Iowa."

"I've got that. But I'd like to have a cellphone number because I assume he'll be staying in St. Paul until you release the victim's body."

"That assumption may or may not be accurate," Brownie said.

"You're not holding him in St. Paul for further questioning are you?"

"Nice try, Mitch. We have no comment on that at this time."

The blank wall thrown up around Sean Kelly by Brownie was so frustrating that I decided to keep what I knew about Murray Hill to myself until I could swap it for something useful.

"Thanks so much for the update," I said. "I'll be in touch."

"Have a good day, Mitch," said Detective Curtis Brown.

Interesting. A man who lives in Iowa City just happens to be in St. Paul when his ex-wife is murdered and shows up at the police department to claim the body—saying that he read about the murder in the paper—within a couple of hours after the story first appeared. What inspires a man who lives in Iowa City to read the on-line edition of the *St. Paul Daily Dispatch* in the middle of the day? And didn't Annette say something about a quarrel involving the victim and her ex? Could the quarrel have escalated into an armed assault, and could the apartment have been torn apart to disguise the attack as a burglary gone wrong?

When I got home at the end of the day, I parked my Honda in the street in front of the duplex because I'd filled my side of the garage with some boxes full of odds and ends to be sorted for possible disposal. I hung my blue blazer in the hall closet just inside the front door, turned around, and saw a new addition to my welcoming committee: the pretty little wooden turtle sitting on the shelf where Martha and I had placed it. I patted Mother Turtle on her little upturned head and proceeded further into the apartment, where I received the traditional greetings from a beautiful wife, with her arms open for a hug and a kiss, and a burly black and white cat named Sherlock Holmes, with an insatiable desire to rub his body against and around my ankles.

5

A LIVE ONE

The next morning, the ritual was reversed. I patted Sherlock Holmes on the head while he rubbed himself around my ankles and hugged and kissed the extremely kissable lips of my lawyer wife goodbye as she left for her work in the downtown office of Linda L. Lansing Associates. Then I patted pretty little Mother Turtle on her uplifted head, closed the front door behind me, tugged at the door to make sure the automatic lock had functioned properly, and headed off to the office of the *Daily Dispatch*.

As I passed City Editor Don O'Rourke, he waved me toward his desk. "Got an assignment for tomorrow morning," he said. "I want you to interview the Winter Carnival's guest of honor."

The St. Paul Winter Carnival, a traditional celebratory event held annually since 1886, was due to start Friday night with the coronation of the Queen of the Snows. Every year the usual cast of Winter Carnival characters is joined by a nationally known celebrity who, as the guest of honor, takes part in some of the major events, including the Friday night coronation ceremony and the Saturday afternoon Grande Parade out on Grand Avenue.

"What shining star of stage, screen or television will I be interviewing?" I asked.

"You haven't been reading our twice-a-day Carnival hyping stories?" Don said.

"Never touch the stuff. The Carnival's too cold to interest me."

"This year's honored guest is Jimmy Kimmel," Don said. "Late night host of Jimmy Kimmel Live. I'm giving you a heads up so you have time to come up with some questions that pertain to his program."

"Never watch Jimmy Kimmel Live, Jimmy Kimmel Dead, or Jimmy Kimmel Resurrected," I said. "I'm afraid that I know zip about his program. We turn off the TV right after the news."

"Well, you'd better watch Jimmy Kimmel Live tonight because he'll actually be broadcasting *live* from the ballroom in the St. Paul Hotel instead of taping the show in the afternoon. He'll be getting into town this morning, but I couldn't get an interview set up with him until tomorrow at nine o'clock. Your Siamese twin will be going with you to do the photo shoot."

"I can hardly wait," I said. "Meanwhile I'll be checking with Brownie on the little matter of the murder of our business writer."

"That's your priority this morning. Get me something as soon as you can," Don said.

My first call was to Brownie, who answered in the usual manner: "Homicidebrown."

"Dailydispatchmitchell," I said. "What's new on our late business writer?"

"I wish there was something new," Brownie said. "All I can tell you is that we're proceeding with the investigation."

"Is that all you *can* tell me or all that you're *willing* to tell me?"

"We have nothing to tell the media at this time."

"Does that mean that you know something that you're not telling us at this time?"

"It means that we are not releasing any information to the media at this time."

"I will quote those exact words in my non-news story this morning."

"Your readers will be most fortunate to find such accuracy in your fine publication. Have a good day, Mitch," Brownie said as he hung up.

That conversation gave me further cause not to say anything to Brownie about Murray Hill until I'd talked to Hill and could swap my information for something we could print. I wrote a whole three paragraphs updating the lack of progress in the T.J. Kelly murder investigation, sent it Don, and told him that I was going to Murray's Neighborhood Hardware for another go at interviewing T.J.'s man, not boy, friend.

Again, the woman named Liz was working at the checkout counter and again I asked her to summon Murray, again using the first name as if we were old chums. Liz said that Mister Hill was in his office at the back of the store and suggested that I go back and knock on the first door on the left. "The one across from the unisex rest room," she said.

My knock on the master's door brought a response of "come in," which I did. The blond, middle-aged man with his elbows on the gray metal desk straightened up, looked at me with obvious surprise, and said, "Who are you?"

I told him who I was and where I was employed. "Sorry I was so abrupt," Murray said. "But I was expecting to see a guy who was supposed to be here ten minutes ago."

"Looks like I beat him to the draw," I said. "I'm here because I'd like to talk to you about the late Ms. T.J. Kelly. I've been told that you've been seeing her, and I wonder if you'd like to say something about her for a story I'm writing."

"Oh, god, poor T.J.," Murray said. "What is there to say? Who'd do such an awful thing to such a beautiful person?"

"We're all wondering that. Do you have any suspects in mind?

Or motives? Did T.J. ever talk to you about enemies or threats or anything about a possible attacker?"

"No, not really. The only adversarial thing she ever mentioned was that some official at Coordinated Copper & Nickel was really pissed off about what she'd been writing. You know, the stories she got an award for last Sunday night. But you don't normally think of a corporate desk jockey as being a vicious killer."

"Were you in the audience at the award ceremony Sunday night?"

"Yeah, I was up there at the Rez to see her get her award. I didn't hear anybody around me say anything bad about T.J."

"How about Monday night? Did you see her Monday night?"

"You mean the night she was killed?"

"I do."

I must have said that too suggestively because Murray pushed his roller chair back and snapped up onto his feet. He was several inches more than six feet tall and was as muscular as a football tight end. His face was turning red as he said, "You're not thinking that I did it, are you?"

He looked big enough and strong enough to have overpowered T.J. with ease, but I chose the path of discretion and said, "Oh, no. I didn't mean to sound like I was accusing you."

"You'd better not be thinking along those lines," he said. "And I think I'd rather not make any comment whatsoever for the story that you're writing, Mister Miller. It's better if my name is not mentioned in your paper at all. The fact that T.J. and I had gone a couple of places together is none of the paper's business. Now maybe you should be on your way. The man I'm expecting should be here any minute."

I chose not to correct him for making a Miller out of a Mitchell. I merely thanked him for his time, assured him that his name would not be included in my story, and took my leave.

Hmm. Big, strong, and quick-tempered. Murray Hill's name would not appear in print, but it would be imprinted on my mind as a possible large knife wielder.

I returned to the *Daily Dispatch* office and reported my failed interview to Don O'Rourke. "You're not having a very productive day," he said. "Why don't you sit down at your computer this afternoon and look up some recent Jimmy Kimmel Live broadcasts on YouTube so that you won't sound like you're from outer space and have never seen his show when you talk to him tomorrow morning?"

"Good idea," I said. "I'll have him thinking that I stay up and watch him every night."

"He'll love you for that. People like him have monstrous egos and they respond best to people who sound like they're spellbound by their superior personalities."

"I don't think I'll go quite as far as being spellbound," I said. "I'll try to keep the ties a little looser."

"Whatever it takes to get a story," my city editor said.

It was mid-afternoon, and I was half-dozing while watching my second YouTube video of Jimmy Kimmel Live when Don yelled my name across the newsroom. I jumped up and double-timed my way to his desk. Don's calls for a reporter rarely sound this urgent.

"Vinny just called from the police station," Don said. "There's a 911 call to an address that checks out to be Ben deLyne's home. Grab your Siamese twin and get a car and get out there."

"Where' Ben?" I asked. "Isn't he here?"

"It's his day off. He should be home, but he's not answering his cellphone," Don said. Off days for most reporters and editorial writers rotate through the week, so that a person will have Monday off one week and Tuesday off the next week, for example, in addition to almost always being off on Sunday. Don handed me a slip of paper with an address on Grand Avenue, not far from the small apartment where Martha and I had lived before moving to larger quarters in the duplex on Lexington Avenue. In less than ten minutes, Al and I were in a company car and on the way.

6

NOT SO GRAND

The Vinny who'd called was Vinny Viola, our police reporter, whose office is in the police station. He monitors the emergency calls as they come in and talks directly to the people who respond to them when they return to the station. He emails or phones in his stories and visits the *Daily Dispatch* office so infrequently that some of our reporters don't even know what he looks like.

What we found on Grand Avenue was not so grand. The house was a well-kept white two-story frame structure built in the 1920 style, but parked in front of the house were two marked police cruisers, one black unmarked police SUV, and an ambulance. All their emergency lights were flashing.

Al and I parked as close as we could get and ran to the scene. We were stopped at the end of the sidewalk that led to the front porch by a uniformed officer whose nose and cheeks were glowing red from the cold. His name tag said MULLENS. We flashed our press credentials, and I asked what was going on inside.

"I'm not authorized to talk to the press, sir," Mullens said.

"I won't print anything you say," I said. "Just give us a quickie on why you guys are here."

"All I know is that somebody came home and found somebody else laying on the floor."

I pointed to the unmarked black SUV. "Is that Homicide?" I asked.

"Yes, sir, that's Detective Brown's vehicle," Mullens said.

"But you don't know who was lying on the floor?"

"No, sir, and if I did, I couldn't tell you. You know that's above my pay grade."

I did know that, but I always ask in hopes that something will slip out. And this homicide scene was especially nerve-wracking because a man we knew and worked with lived here with his wife and two children.

I called Don O'Rourke on my cellphone and told him what we had encountered. He uttered an expletive that he'd never allow to be printed in the *Daily Dispatch* and told me to wait at the scene until somebody who was permitted to talk to the media appeared.

"It's twelve degrees out here," I said. "The wind chill must be close to zero."

"So wait in the car," Don said. "If you run the heater, leave the windows open a crack so you don't get carbon monoxide poisoning. One dead body on the scene is enough."

"This one is more than enough," I said. "It's got to be either Ben or somebody in his family."

"Why do you think I sent you out there?" Don said.

Al and I stood beside Officer Mullens for a few minutes, flapping our arms and stomping our feet to counteract the cold, then retreated to the car. Al started the engine, turned on the heater, and lowered both back windows about two inches.

"Should we invite Officer Mullens to join us?" Al asked.

"He's getting paid to serve and protect," I said. "Freezing his ass is within his pay grade."

"Your heart is as cold as my feet. Have you no mercy?"

"Only when it gets me a story. If Officer Mullens would promise to tell us all he knows, I'd be a veritable Mother Teresa and invite him to shelter with us in this cozy confine."

"There's nothing more chilling than police bureaucracy," Al said.

A car emblazoned with the logo of TV Channel Four appeared and parked on the other side of the street. The reporter who got out was so heavily bundled in a fur trimmed parka that I barely recognized her as Trish Valentine. Trish is one of my favorites among the TV tribe because her warm weather wear always hugs the lines of her splendidly rounded hips and ass and she always leaves the top two buttons of her always too-tight blouse unbuttoned. This combination is always rewarded with the quick and ongoing attention of any male official presiding at a media briefing and Trish always gets to ask the first question.

Trish was followed by an equally heavily wrapped man bearing a TV camera. They, too, were stopped by Officer Mullens and they, too, retreated to their vehicle. Steam billowed from the tail pipe, and I hoped that they'd opened some windows a crack. I decided to go over and check. Wouldn't want Channel Four to lose such a prime asset as Trish.

I tapped on the passenger side front window, which was closed. Trish turned to face me and lowered the window to the level of her nose. "Hey, if it isn't the *Daily Dispatch's* great turtle winner," she said. "What's up, Mitch?"

"Just came over to say hello while we wait for somebody to come out and tell us what's going on inside," I said. "It's personal as well as business with Al and me because the homeowner happens to be another one of our great turtle winners."

"Oh, my, god! Wasn't one of your other great turtle winners just murdered?" Trish said.

"She was. And now we have Chief of Homicide Curtis Brown inside this great turtle winner's house."

"Brownie's here? Do you think somebody's got something against people who win great turtles from the Ojibwe on the Rez? Maybe you'd better send yours crawling back to Chief Hardshell Turtle."

I hadn't thought about the turtle connection until that moment, but if a pattern was developing, I certainly did not want to be woven into it. "Must be just a coincidence," I said, trying to be Mister Cool.

"Whatever," Trish said. "But if I was you, I'd watch my ass."

I wanted to say that I'd rather watch hers, but, not wishing to be perceived as either a sexist or a lecher, I swallowed that comment and said, "That is something to think about. Anyhow, it's been nice talking to you. And maybe you'd want to leave your window down an inch or so after I go. C-O-one and all that."

I was three steps away from the van when I looked back and waved goodbye. Trish waggled two fingers at me out of the still open window.

"Welcome back, Mister Boy Scout," Al said as I slid into the passenger seat. "Have you done your good deed for the day?"

"I have, indeed, done my good deed," I said. "They were buttoned up tight with the motor running. A dangerous thing, indeed."

"I'll have Kevin nominate you for a merit badge at the next troop meeting." Al's eighteen-year-old son, Kevin, was an Eagle Scout.

"I seek no reward for my good deed, other than the continued visibility of a viable Trish Valentine at all media briefings held in the great city of St. Paul."

"Your modesty overwhelms me, but I, too, will be visually rewarded by the continued viability of Ms. Valentine."

We high-fived each other and settled back to wait for someone or something to emerge from Ben deLyne's house. And waited. And waited. And ...

Hark! The door was opening. Something was emerging. It consisted of two EMTs rolling a gurney that contained what appeared to be a human form completely covered with white sheets. They rolled it to the ambulance, collapsed the gurney's legs, and slid the flattened carrier and its contents into the rear of the vehicle.

Al and I turned our attention back to the front door. Two uniformed officers came out, followed by Detective Curtis Brown. We popped out of the car, hustled to the sidewalk, and met Brownie head-on at the foot of the front steps, with Trish Valentine and her cameraman just a step behind us.

"Well, aren't you Johnny on the spot?" Brownie said.

"Actually, it's Mitchy and Ally on the spot," I said. "And we've been on the spot for a long time. Who did we see riding the gurney and why?"

"You saw a person riding the gurney because the person was deceased," Brownie said. "We will not identify said person to any representative of the media until the entire family has been notified, at which time we will notify all the media simultaneously."

"We've been waiting patiently out here in the cold," Trish said. "The fair thing to do is tell us first."

"Nobody said that life—or death—is fair," said Brownie. "Detective Terry Townsend is in charge of the investigation that is now taking place inside the house. We'll be in touch with your offices as soon as it's appropriate. Meanwhile, have a good day, folks." He walked past us, got into the black SUV, and drove away.

Doctor Lyle Lundberg, the county medical examiner, emerged from the house carrying his black leather bag. He greeted us as he passed, declined to comment without slowing down, and departed in another black SUV.

I phoned Don O'Rourke and told him what had happened.

"What could you tell from what you saw on the gurney?" he asked. "Size? Sex?"

"Couldn't tell the gender but it was a really long body."

Former college basketball star Ben deLyne was six-foot-six.

7

JUST THE FACTS

Still looking for an official identification of what I'd seen on the gurney, I called Brownie when I got back to my desk. We exchanged the usual one-word greetings, and I asked my question.

"We are currently in the process of notifying all the appropriate next of kin," Brownie said. "When that process is complete, we will notify all media of the time and place of a briefing by Chief Casey Riley."

"A friend and fellow *Daily Dispatch* writer lives in that house. Can you give me a hint if we go off the record?"

"We have strict orders not to make any statements either on or off the record prior to the chief's press briefing. Have a good day, Mitch."

"It's been really swell so far," I said as I put down the phone with extra vigor.

"Talking to yourself again?" asked Corrine Ramey from the desk closest to mine.

"Might as well," I said. "Nobody I need information from will talk to me."

"Brownie is not cooperating?"

"Brownie is going by the book."

"So, you can't confirm that it was Ben that they brought out on the gurney?"

"Not officially. But I doubt that either his wife or either one of his kids is that tall."

"You didn't see any of them at the house?" Corrine asked.

"If they were there, they didn't show themselves," I said.

It was 4:30, half an hour from my quitting time, when the call announcing the time and place of the media briefing came. It was set for 5:30, perfect for the TV newscasts to put it on live as "breaking news." I told Don that I would stay to cover the briefing and Al also volunteered for the extra time. Together we hiked to the police station where Chief Riley was going to tell all the news to all of us who were eager to hear all the news.

The usual crowd was gathering when we arrived. Trish Valentine, of course, was up front in the lineup of reporters and photographers that was forming in the briefing room. Also on hand were representatives of the other three Twin Cities TV channels, the Minneapolis morning and afternoon papers, and two radio stations. Al and I stationed ourselves behind Trish Valentine, confident that she would be called on to ask the first question.

Chief Riley walked in at one minute past the advertised time, looked us over—with a second glance at Trish Valentine, who had hung her winter wraps on a chair and was displaying her charms in a light blue, low-cut, V-necked blouse—and began reading his statement from a sheet of paper.

"At fourteen-seventeen hours today, St. Paul Police officers were summoned to an address on Grand Avenue by a thirteen-year-old boy who had just arrived home from junior high school and found his unconscious father lying on his back on the living room floor with his shirt saturated with blood. First responders who arrived at fourteen twenty-five determined that the man was deceased and summoned the county medical examiner, who arrived sixteen minutes later and pronounced the man dead. The probable cause of death was a knife wound to the abdomen. The official cause of death will be announced at a later time, following an autopsy.

"The victim's name was Benjamin Donald deLyne, that's with a lower case 'd' and an upper case 'L' on deLyne, age forty-one, who was employed as an editorial writer at the *St. Paul Daily Dispatch*. The victim's son had also phoned his mother at her workplace, and she arrived at the home after the victim's body had been removed but while the scene was still being processed. A fifteen-year-old daughter, who is a student at a nearby high school, arrived shortly after the victim's wife. The investigation of this crime is being led by Detective Curtis Brown, chief of the Homicide Department. Now, are there any questions?"

Chief Riley looked directly at Trish Valentine, who hadn't had time to raise her hand. She raised it and he pointed at her. She leaned forward, aimed her microphone at him and asked, "Didn't the victim recently win an award for his editorials about an environmental threat in northwestern Minnesota?"

"He did," the chief said, with his eyes focused on the area revealed by the lowcut V-neck of Trish's blouse. "The award ceremony was held just last Sunday."

"Any sign of a motive?" asked a man from Channel Five. "Like the victim came home and surprised a burglar or something like that?"

"Some objects in the room were scattered about, as if someone had been searching for something, but it hasn't yet been determined if anything was missing."

"Was the murder weapon found?" asked a woman from the Minneapolis morning paper.

"No. The murder weapon was not left at the scene," the chief said.

"Has his wife been able to give you any leads as to who might have wanted to kill the victim?" asked the Channel Seven reporter.

"No, not as of this time she hasn't. She was understandably distraught, so we did not attempt to question her in detail about any suspicions that she might have. We plan to talk with her again this evening, when emotions are not quite so high."

No other hands went up and no other voices called out. The chief thanked us all for attending and went back to his office. Al and I hustled back to our office to finish our work for the day.

I had just sent my story to the city desk, where Fred Donlin, the night city editor, was now in command, when Al came over to say goodbye.

"I've been thinking about what you told me Trish said about somebody maybe having it in for the winners of turtle trophies," he said. "Do you think there's a connection between T.J.'s murder and Ben's?"

"As an editorial writer, Ben has pissed off a lot of people, but I can't picture a major international business like Coordinated Copper & Nickel, Inc., sending out a hit man to do away with reporters and editorial writers," I said. "I just wish that I'd been able to find T.J.'s turtle with that thumb drive in it before the cops arrived at her apartment. That thumb drive might give us some kind of answer to whether the killings are connected."

"Whatever. I think we'll be keeping the doors locked tight at our house and not opening them for anyone we don't know," Al said.

"Sounds like a good policy for our house, too," I said. "Luckily, our doors both lock themselves automatically when we go in or out, so we don't have to worry about forgetting to lock up. Zhoumaya had them installed as a safety measure when she decided to rent out half of her house." Zhoumaya Jones, who owns the duplex we live in, is both our landlord and our next-door neighbor.

"Better be sure that you're always keyed up when you go out."

"You've got that right. Martha found herself performing off-key one time when she took out the trash. After that, we gave a spare one to Zhoumaya as insurance against ever being out of key again."

"That's the key to success," Al said. "See you tomorrow."

Ah, yes, tomorrow. Tomorrow I'd be interviewing Jimmy Kimmel, hopefully live, when I should be asking Brownie if he had any key suspects for either of the murders and if anyone had seen a pretty little turtle in T.J. Kelly's apartment.

An interview with a late-night comic. Oh, what the hell? Maybe it would be a relief to talk to someone about something other than a homicide.

"What time is my live meeting with Jimmy Kimmel?" I asked Don O'Rourke as I passed the city desk Thursday morning.

"The meeting is at eleven," Don said. "But there's been a slight change in who you're interviewing."

"What's going on?" I asked.

"There's been a last-minute surprise replacement brought in for Jimmy Kimmel. Just announced this morning."

"Why? Is he sick?"

"I don't know why. The carnival PR people didn't give a reason for the sudden switch. They just sent an email saying that a different guest of honor was brought in late last night and that the interview would be at eleven o'clock this morning."

"So, who is it?"

"Someone very big."

"Am I supposed to guess?" I asked.

"You could give it a try," Don said.

"It's somebody in show business?"

"Of course. It always is."

I thought for a moment. Somebody big in show business. "Is it Lady Gaga?" I said.

"Bigger."

"Bigger than Lady Gaga?"

"Way bigger."

"Then it has to be one of the Kardashians."

"Still bigger."

"Wow! It must be Oprah."

"Even bigger."

"You're kidding." Who might be bigger than Oprah? I could only think of one possibility. "Then it's gotta be Taylor Swift."

"Don't you wish?"

"Oh, come on, Don. There's nobody bigger in the American world of show business than Taylor Swift."

"Think broader," Don said. "Think international."

"My knowledge of show biz entertainers ends at the water's edge," I said. "I know of nobody in either Europe or Asia who would surpass the stature of either Oprah or Taylor Swift."

"Yes, you do," Don said. "You've actually met this person."

"When? Where?"

"Think river cruise in Portugal."

"Oh, my god! Not Lady T?"

"The one and only," said Don. "You've got a date with the great Lady in the St. Paul Hotel at eleven o'clock. Suite Eleven-fourteen-A. Take your Siamese twin with you; I want pictures of this celebrity."

This was special! For a couple of reasons. The first reason was that Al and I had met Lady T five months earlier on a river cruise ship in Portugal. She was a Hungarian TV personality who dominated the screen throughout Europe and parts of Asia. Born into a once royal Hungarian family, her full name was Lady T-Khuppschane, with the single "T" standing for a multitude of given names that all begin with that letter.

The second reason was that we had learned that Lady T also served as a secret agent for Interpol. As she'd said to me, it's amazing what people will brag about to an international television star, even if the boast is self-incriminating.

The cruise on which we'd met had been a disaster because of a jewel theft followed by a murder onboard. It was Lady T who explained the whole scenario to Al and me after we'd figured out who'd stolen the jewel and who'd murdered the thief.

The sudden unexplained replacement of Jimmy Kimmel by Lady T, the TV personality, as the Winter Carnival's guest of honor could mean that something very special of international importance was going on in the Twin Cities or in Minnesota in general. The presence of Lady T, the Interpol agent, told me that there had to be a major story to be uncovered here.

What could it be? Sitting at my desk, I could think of nothing in the local news that would have international consequences. I tried to think of any Minnesota businesses that had international connections. First on the list was 3M, of course, but I couldn't imagine that company being a candidate for Interpol scrutiny.

Wait a minute. What about Coordinated Copper & Nickel, Inc.? In the research I'd done on their background and mining projects for my stories about the proposed nickel mine next to the Rez, I'd learned that they had a number of overseas contracts.

T.J. Kelly had told me that the story she was writing about Coordinated C&N's Minnesota plan was big enough to win a Pulitzer. The details were on the thumb drive that she'd hidden in her pretty little turtle. Could there be something of international intrigue tucked inside that turtle? Something big enough and secret enough to bring Lady T to St. Paul as a surprise guest of honor at the Winter Carnival? Oh, how I was wishing that I'd found that turtle with the thumb drive the morning that T.J. was killed. And how I was wishing that now I could somehow go hunting for it in T.J.'s apartment.

Seeing no solution to that problem, I turned my thoughts to a new one. How was I going to learn the real reason that Lady T had become the last-minute guest of honor at the St. Paul Winter Carnival? I doubted that she'd give me even the tiniest of clues.

8

REUNION

"You're shitting me! Lady T is in St. Paul?" Al said when I told him about the switch in the Carnival guest of honor.

"That's what our sainted city editor says," I said.

"What killed Jimmy Kimmel Live?"

"Winter Carnival isn't giving a cause of death. Just saying that the exalted Lady T is now the live guest of honor we'll be interviewing in fifteen minutes."

"That's weird. Bringing in somebody all the way from Hungary at the last minute for no announced reason, like Jimmy is sick or something."

"We both know what Lady T's other job is."

"Ooh! Yes, we do. Do you think that's why she's here? Because a crime at the international level is going down in St. Paul?"

"That's my suspicion."

"What the hell could it be?"

"I'm wondering if it's anyway connected to what's on the thumb drive that's sitting somewhere in T.J. Kelly's apartment," I said. "She told me that what's on it might be big enough to win us a Pulitzer. Could it also be big enough to win St. Paul a visit by an agent of Interpol?"

"I'd sure love to see what's on that thumb drive. Know any way we can get into T.J.'s apartment and look for it?"

"I wish I could think of an excuse to get in there," I said. "Unfortunately, it's locked up extra tight as a crime scene."

"Can we pick the lock?" Al asked.

"Likely to get ourselves picked up and put in lock-up if we try that," I said.

"Can you find an excuse to have the cops unlock it for you? Like maybe you loaned T.J. something that you really *really* need to have back?"

"What could that be?"

"I don't know." Al thought for a moment. "Hey, how about your turtle? Maybe she borrowed your turtle from the award ceremony to let it mate with hers. And you want it back so you can show it to your mom and your grandmother this coming weekend."

"I doubt that the cops would fall for a shell game like that," I said.

"Yeah, they might not snap that up. Anyhow, let's give it some thought."

"I guess thoughts can't get us in any trouble," I said. "Meanwhile, let's go interview the Lady from Hungary."

"Hey, isn't Lady T a Turtle?" Al asked.

"You bet your sweet ass she is." What he'd asked about was membership in an organization known as the International Association of Turtles. In order to join this association and officially become a card-carrying Turtle, a person must solve four riddles, each of which could have more than one answer. The first answers that come to a candidate's mind might not be the answers you would give to your nine-year-old granddaughter. The correct answers are as pure as the water in Turtle Lake, and the riddles are always presented to the candidate with the admonition "think clean."

Also, it is assumed that every member of the International Association of Turtles owns a jackass. Therefore, if one is asked, "Are you a Turtle?" the correct answer is, "You bet your sweet ass I am." Failure to answer properly requires the responder to donate a beverage of the questioner's choice.

At the stroke of eleven, I knocked on the door of the designated suite on the eleventh floor of the St. Paul Hotel. A familiar voice, belonging to Lady T's faithful assistant, a younger woman named Gigette, answered. "Who eez eet?"

"It's Mitch and Al, your old friends from the River of Gold," I said. "We have an appointment for an interview with Lady T."

"One mo-*ment*," said Gigette. One mo-*ment* later, after what I assumed was a consultation with Lady T, the door was opened, and Gigette, looking lovely in a blue sweater and skirt combination that hugged the elegant shape of her body and set off her sky-blue eyes, waved us into the suite.

Lady T was seated in a large armchair near a window that looked out onto Fourth Street. She was a physically imposing woman who reached six feet in height when standing and was built like a female football player, with broad shoulders, a substantial bust, and extra-wide hips. She was wearing a loose-fitting deep purple sweater that must have been made from a hundred balls of yarn and a pair of black pants with bellbottoms as big as the Liberty Bell. Gold loops three inches in diameter encircling molded silver turtles dangled from her ears.

Without rising, Lady T offered her right hand for shaking and we took turns doing the same. Gigette, who was slender with curves in all the right places—the exact opposite of Lady T in stature—retreated to a corner near a wooden desk and stood as stiff as a soldier at attention watching us, with her enticingly kissable lips turned down in a frown.

"Lady T welcomes you both," said Lady T. Her schtick as a performer was always to refer to herself in the third person.

"It's good to see Lady T again," I said. "Mister Mitchell is wondering how she was chosen as the substitute for the Carnival's original guest of honor." I could also play the third-person game.

She smiled just a smidgen, but said, "Lady T refers Mister Mitchell to the officials of the St. Paul Winter Carnival for an answer to that question."

"Doesn't Lady T know the reason? Or is it some sort of secret?"

"Lady T knows only that she was instructed to give that answer when asked that question, Mister Mitchell."

"I ask it because it seems like they reached out an awfully long way for a replacement. Why did they reach all the way to Europe when there are many TV personalities right here in the United States they could have asked to take Jimmy Kimmel's place?"

"Lady T is pleased that she has been noticed at that great distance by people in the United States and has been invited to take part in this unique event in the city of St. Paul."

I decided to play it straight and just begin the interview with the obvious questions. "I'm sure it will be colder here this week than it is in Hungary and there will be an outdoor parade this weekend. Did you bring along the kind of clothing needed for that?"

"Lady T has been assured by St. Paul Winter Carnival officials that sufficient clothing of that nature will be provided for both Lady T and Gigette."

Before I could speak again, what sounded like a "woof" was heard from behind the closed door of the bathroom. "Is that your Corgi, Laddie T?" I asked.

"It is Laddie T. Gigette placed him in the bathroom so that he would not interrupt our conversation."

"You might as well let him out," Al said. "He seems to want to participate."

Lady T nodded toward Gigette, who went to the bathroom door and opened it. Out scurried a little brown Corgi, who stopped long enough to look us over and then ran to me. I reached down and gave his ears a scratch and he sat down with his butt on my left foot.

"Laddie T remembers you and likes you, Mister Mitchell," Lady T said. "That is a very good sign."

"Will he be riding in the parade with you?" I asked.

"Lady T has requested a warm covering for Laddie T and has been assured that one will be provided."

Al shot a picture of the dog sitting on my foot and I resumed asking questions. We talked about what Lady T had done since the ill-fated Douro River cruise and what her future looked like. "It's very lucky that you had an opening in your very busy schedule when the Carnival officials called," I said.

"That's right," Al said. "Timing is everything." That's one of his favorite cliches.

"Yes, it was most fortunate," Lady T said.

"You didn't have to cancel anything?" I asked.

"As Lady T has said, the timing was most fortunate."

Her apparently easy availability seemed suspicious to me, so I decided to take a shot. "Going off the record for a minute, Lady T, is it possible that your reason for making such a sudden and un-explained appearance in St. Paul is something in addition to your duties as an honored Winter Carnival guest?"

With no change of facial expression, she said, "Lady T's stated and obvious reason for being here is that she was invited to St. Paul to act as the guest of honor of the St. Paul Winter Carnival."

"There's no connection with, um, your other means of employ-ment?" I asked.

Still with the poker face, she said, "Lady T's stated and obvious reason for being here is that she was invited to St. Paul to act as the guest of honor of the St. Paul Winter Carnival. Lady T is now ready to end this interview, having answered all of your questions pertaining to her appearance in St. Paul."

I closed my notebook, thanked Lady T for her time and coopera-tion, and twisted my left foot out from under Laddie T. When I got to the door, I turned back and said, "Lady T, I have one more question before I go."

"And what is your one more question, Mister Mitchell?" she said.

"Lady T, are you a Turtle?"

This time the bland expression was replaced by a smile. "You bet your sweet ass I am," she said, breaking her third-person schtick to give the required answer accurately. Gigette covered her mouth with her right hand, but I could hear her giggle.

In the hall, waiting for the elevator, Al said, "I was watching Gigette's body language while you were asking those off the record questions about why Lady T is suddenly in St. Paul."

"I can believe that you were watching Gigette's body," I said. "What did you learn from your keen observation of that lovely form?"

"There's some kind of shit going down here that Lady T can't talk about."

Al's observation confirmed my suspicion. A major switch in Carnival luminaries that brings a normally fully-booked-up international TV star who is also a secret Interpol agent to St. Paul just doesn't happen by chance. But what clandestine operation could be going down here that required the presence of Lady T? Again, I wondered if what she was here to investigate had anything to do with the nickel mining project that had been exposed and opposed by the *Daily Dispatch* in our effort to save the Ojibwe Reservation's turtles. Oh, how I wanted to get into T.J.'s apartment and find that thumb drive.

The driving desire to recover the thumb drive led me to wonder if the crime scene investigators had seen the turtle containing it. If they had seen it in the room where T.J.'s body was found, would they have scooped it up along with all the crime scene evidence and packed it off to the police station? Would Brownie tell me if they had done either?

All I could do was ask. After finishing the story about my interview with Lady T, I punched in Brownie's private number and got his voice mail. Typical. The biggest time waster of a reporter's life is the hours spent waiting for the return of an unanswered phone call. I left a message, crossed my fingers in hope of getting a response before the next deadline, and went to the lunchroom to buy a sandwich and a cup of coffee. I toted them back to my desk and waited for the hoped-for return call while I ate. I was still waiting when the ham-and-cheese on rye was gone and the coffee cup was empty, so I punched in the number again.

Again, I got Brownie's voice mail. As I put down the phone, Don O'Rourke arrived at my side. He plopped a scrap of paper down on my desk and said, "Here's a job for you to tackle. Ben DeLyne's home phone number is on that piece of paper. I want you to see if you can talk to his wife—start by giving her our condolences and get some comments if she's willing to talk."

What could be a worse assignment than talking to the wife of a murdered coworker and friend? I wanted to pick up that piece of paper and hand it back to Don. Instead, I said, "Do we know what her first name is?"

"It's Laurie. It's on there with the phone number, along with her last name. She kept her maiden name when they were married. Like your wife did." Don turned and hustled away before I had a chance to whine about receiving this most unpleasant assignment.

The name on the slip of paper was Laurie Lincoln. Lincoln, I thought. No wonder she wanted to keep it. I opened a notebook, jotted down a couple of questions to ask, took a deep breath, and punched in the number. This time I was hoping I'd get a voice mail, but of course it was answered immediately. "Lincoln and deLyne residence," said a female voice.

"Ms. Laurie Lincoln?" I asked.

"This is Laurie's sister, Lillian," said the voice. "Who's calling?"

I told Lillian who I was and why I was calling. She said to hold on while she asked Laurie if she would take the call. Not sure whether I wanted a "yes" or a "no," I held on.

The answer I got was "yes." A different female voice said, "This is Laurie Lincoln. What can I do for you, Mister Mitchell?"

"I'm calling to convey the sincere condolences of everyone here at the *Daily Dispatch*," I said. "And I'd also like to note anything you have to say about Ben and about what happened to him. And please call me Mitch."

"Thank you, Mitch," she said. "Ben loved his job at the *Daily Dispatch* and talked a lot about the great people he was working with."

"Ben was a great writer and great guy," I said. "We're all going to miss him very much. I was lucky enough to work closely with him for several months while he was doing editorials on the proposed nickel mine near the Ojibwe Reservation. We both won pretty little wooden turtles for our work on that."

"I was there in the audience the night that the turtles were awarded," Laurie said. "Ben was very proud of that turtle, but now I don't know where it's gone to. It's not where Ben put it when he brought it home and I haven't seen it anywhere else."

"The turtle has disappeared?"

"It seems that way. I can't imagine where it could be that I haven't looked."

"I hope it turns up. It's an award to be proud of and it should be on display."

"It surely is. And I also don't know what to say to you about what happened to Ben. It's such a horrible shock to me and our kids that there just aren't words for it. I still can't believe it happened."

"Do you have any thoughts about who might have done it?" I asked. "Do you know of any threats that were made or any people who were extremely mad at Ben about something?"

"No," Laurie said. "The police—Detective Brown—asked me that same question, but I've drawn a complete blank on that. I mean there were people who disagreed with his editorials from time to time, of course. Ben always said that pissing people off is the name of the editorial page game. But he usually laughed it off when somebody complained about what he'd written, and he never said anything about death threats or possible violence of any kind. I can only go along with Detective Brown's theory that a thief broke in and was surprised to find somebody at home."

"Did it look like a burglary? Was stuff tossed around or out of place, like someone had been searching for hidden money or jewelry or things?"

"There were some things moved, like somebody was hunting for something, but nothing is missing that I know of."

"Nothing missing?" I said. "What about the turtle?"

"Why would anyone want to steal that turtle? There's no place they could sell it. I haven't really looked for it very hard, and I'm sure it will turn up someplace."

Why indeed? Laurie was right; it couldn't be sold. But the pretty little turtle didn't crawl away from where Ben had put it of its own accord. What could be a reason to steal the pretty little turtle? Could the killer be someone who just liked turtles? Was it taken as a souvenir of the murderous act? This puzzle was making me even more eager to try to find T.J. Kelly's turtle.

I asked Laurie about some of Ben's favorite things to see and do, about the family members, and about funeral arrangements; repeated my words of condolence; and thanked her for talking to me. I was about to say goodbye when Laurie said, "I read the paper every day, Mitch, and I know that you and Alan Jeffrey, the photographer, have got yourselves a reputation as crime solvers. Please solve this one for me and my kids."

"I'll do my best, and I know that Al will do his best to help me," I said.

Now I was convinced that it was vitally important for me to find out if T.J.'s turtle had been found or could be found. I needed to know if possession of the pretty little Ojibwe turtles by Ben and T.J. could be the motive for either or both of those killings, because I knew of two additional award winning people who possessed pretty little Ojibwe turtles. Their names were Mitch and Al.

My desk phone rang as I was proof-reading what I'd written about my conversation with Laurie Lincoln. I wanted to be dead certain that the story contained no mention of the missing Ojibwe turtle. This tidbit was not for public consumption.

The caller identified himself as "Homicidebrown," and I replied in kind: "Dailydispatchmitchell at your service, sir."

"Didn't you leave a message for me to call you?" Brownie said.

"I did, indeed."

"Then I'm the one who's at *your* service. Let's get the record straight."

"Ah, yes. That's your duty, isn't it? To protect and serve and keep the record straight. Thank you very much for returning my call."

"I assume that you're not looking for protection, so what kind of service are you looking for?"

I had decided to be straightforward and not to play games with my request. "I have a question about the T.J. Kelly case. Is there anything in the investigative report about a little hand-carved wooden turtle that the victim received as an award from the Ojibwe tribe the night before she was murdered?"

"I'd have to review the report to be certain, but offhand I would say no," Brownie said. "I can't recall any mention either written or verbal about a turtle of any kind. Why are you asking about a hand-carved wooden turtle?"

I explained that T.J. had told me that a thumb drive she had hidden inside that turtle contained information that would blow Coordinated Copper & Nickel's northern Minnesota mining project out of the water—pun intended. "I'd really like to get hold of that turtle and that thumb drive," I said. "T.J. told me that the story she planned to write, using the information on that thumb drive, is very important and I'd like to be able to write it."

"Looking to get another award?" Brownie asked.

"Looking to save the planet," I said. "That's the unpublished goal of our editorial page, you know: to save the world. As a gatherer and dispenser of facts, I'm trying to help them achieve that goal, one undrained swamp at a time."

"A modest editorial objective, indeed. But I'm sorry, oh, would be savior of our world, I know nothing about the existence, or non-existence, of a hand-carved wooden turtle in the apartment occupied by the deceased."

"Then I have another question for you. Might it be possible for me to enter the premises and—with a police escort if necessary— conduct a cautious and non-disruptive search for the seed of a potentially powerful mine-busting story?"

"The entire apartment is a crime scene, you know," Brownie said.

"That's why I'm suggesting that an officer accompany me," I said.

After a long moment of silence, Brownie said, "This is even weirder than your usual requests, Mitch. I'd have to run it past the chief."

"Would you please do that? I know Chief Riley has an interest in this nickel mining story. I saw him in the audience at the program on the Rez when T.J. was presented with the turtle."

I had time to envision an assortment of interlocking geared wheels spinning and exchanging places in Brownie's head during the lengthy silence before his response. "Okay," he said at last. "I'll talk to the chief and get back to you. Have a good day, Mitch."

"That's pretty much up to you," I said when I was sure that he could no longer hear me.

"Talking to yourself again?" asked Corinne Ramey, who'd again been eaves dropping from her vantage point at the nearest desk.

"Yes. I always enjoy conversing with an especially intelligent person," I said.

"Does that mean you were thinking about conversing with me?" said a voice from behind me. I spun my chair around and found myself facing Al, who held a paper cup filled with coffee in each hand.

"Only as an afterthought," I said.

"It's afternoon, so let's have an afterthought with our aperitif," Al said. He handed me one of the cups and perched his butt on the only open corner of my desk.

"What I was really thinking about was going into T.J. Kelly's apartment to hunt for her Ojibwe turtle. I'm dying to see what's on that thumb drive she was hiding in it. Want to come along if the police chief decides to let me go into the crime scene?"

"I've got a more immediate crime scene to worry about," Al said.

"What's that?"

"Carol got a death threat on Facebook this morning."

9

BANNERS AND BUMMERS

Al's beautiful blond and blue-eyed wife, Carol, teaches American Literature at a high school in the northern St. Paul suburb of Roseville. During her twenty years of introducing teenagers to the world of adult literature, she has received occasional complaints from some parents about the suitability of certain titles that were being made available to these young people. Recently the complaints had gone beyond the perennial book banners' gripes about such long-standing targets as "The Catcher in the Rye." An organized group of parents who called themselves Guardians of Our Family Standards was clamoring for the expungement of all books dealing with gender, race, and sexuality from the school district's libraries and the students' reading lists.

When writing about this group, *Daily Dispatch* reporters had been forbidden to use its very tempting acronym, which, of course, would be GOOFS. The denizens of the copy desk also have been told to be on the alert for any attempts to sneak this acronym into a story.

Among the books that have been attacked by the Guardians are volumes by such offenders as a famous civil rights leader, a Supreme Court Justice, and a poet who'd read her rhymes at the inauguration of a president. What did these three authors of allegedly mind-damaging works have in common? Skin that was darker than that of the unanimously pale-faced Guardians, that's what.

Carol had also shown Martha and me a list of "offensive and/or inappropriate" books that had been presented to the school board by this group, which was demanding the removal of fifty-four titles from the school libraries in the district. It included such seemingly innocuous titles as "Freestyle," "Hummingbird," and "Parachute Kids." One can only imagine what horrors the Guardians must have found between the covers of these books.

"I assume this death threat came to Carol from an anonymous source," I said.

"Of course," Al said. "The cowards who make these threats never say who they are."

"But Carol has to take it seriously."

"She is taking it seriously. And, thank heavens, so is the superintendent. He's called in the Roseville cops."

"Did the threatener name a specific book or author that he or she thinks is worth killing a teacher who refuses to burn it?"

"Two of them; both dealing with gender identification or homosexuality."

"At least this homophobe is not also a racist," I said.

"Maybe racism is coming next," Al said. "A mind that small probably can't handle more than one form of hatred at a time."

"What are the Roseville cops going to do?" I asked.

"They've assigned a man to sit in Carol's classroom and to escort her back and forth between home and the school every day. They've also made a deal with the St. Paul PD to have a marked cruiser parked in front of our house at night for a while."

"The night watch will be a good thing to have, especially with the Winter Carnival stuff coming up," I said. We'd both been assigned to the crew that would be covering the coronation of the Queen of Snows on Friday night and the Torchlight Parade on Saturday night.

"Yeah, it is," Al said. "Carol is also going to ask her brother to come and stay with her Friday night so that she's not alone in the house while I'm downtown shooting the Coronation fun and frolic."

"Good plan. That cop parked in front of your house could be keeping both of you out of danger."

"Both of us? I wasn't aware that I was in any danger."

"You don't remember talking about possible motives for the murders of two *Daily Dispatch* writers who were honored with the presentation of hand carved turtles by the folks on the Ojibwe Reservation?"

"I do remember talking about that while we were sitting in front of Ben's house. But I also remember that we kind of blew it off as a coincidence. Are you now thinking that the two murders are connected in some way to the two turtles?"

"I'm now thinking that it's possible," I said. "This morning, Ben deLyne's wife told me that his turtle isn't where he put it. She hasn't seen it since his death, which makes me even more concerned about the whereabouts of T.J. Kelly's turtle, which I didn't see while I was in her apartment the day she was killed. I'm really hoping that I can find it, because that would make it less likely that there's a connection. But if it turns out that I can't find T.J.'s …"

"Oh, come on! Why would anyone want to kill somebody in order to swipe those turtles? They have no meaning to anybody but us."

"I don't know why. I can understand someone wanting to swipe the thumb drive that T.J. tucked into her turtle after showing it to the world at the award ceremony. They could have taken it, turtle and all, after killing her. But why they'd want Ben's turtle, which holds no information about the nickel mine as far as I know, is a mystery to me. But, as I said, his wife hasn't seen it anywhere in the house since Ben was killed."

"So, we can crawl away from the connection theory if you find T.J.'s turtle safe and sound in her apartment?" Al said.

"I'll definitely feel much better about the safety of my turtle and my throat, along with both of yours, if I can find her turtle," I said. "I'm just hoping that Chief Riley will give me a chance to search the place tomorrow. Meanwhile, I'm sliding the old inside bolts into place to keep my doors double-locked tonight."

My desk phone was ringing and the caller ID said: "Unidentified caller."

"Probably Brownie," I said. "He masks his calls that way." I picked up the receiver and said, "Dailydispatchmitchell."

"Homicidebrown," was the response. "You're in luck, turtle chaser. The chief okayed your admittance to Ms. T.J. Kelly's apartment, along with an officer who will meet you at the building manager's office at ten-hundred hours tomorrow. You are to wear the gloves the officer gives you, to not handle anything unnecessarily, and to not disturb any neighbors who might be sleeping late."

"Thanks," I said. "That's quite a list of does and don'ts. Anything else I should know?"

"There is one thing. The deceased occupant's ex-husband, who has assumed ownership of all the deceased's earthly goods in the absence of a will or any blood relatives, will be joining you while you are in the apartment."

That gave me a jolt. "Her ex? The guy who might have killed her?"

"The person in question has not been charged with any crime," said Brownie.

"Surely he's a person of interest. Isn't he?"

"We will not comment on that at this time."

"This is going to be really weird."

"Take it or leave it," said Brownie.

"I'll take it," I said. What choice did I have?

"Ten hundred hours at the manager's office. Have a good day, Mitch. Hope you're fast enough to catch a turtle," Brownie said as he hung up.

"What's going to be really weird?" Al asked when I put down the phone.

"T.J.'s ex-husband has taken ownership of everything in the apartment and will be there while I'm looking for the turtle," I said.

"Her ex? The guy who might have killed her?"

"The exact question that I asked Brownie."

"And Brownie said?"

"That the person in question hasn't been charged with any crime and that he couldn't comment on whether or not the person in question is a person of interest in the investigation."

"The person in question could really screw up your search. Or worse."

"He could. But there will also be a cop on the scene, so I'm not worried about worse."

"Cop or no cop, I wouldn't turn my back on the guy if I was you," Al said.

"I wish I had a hard shell on my back, like a turtle," I said.

"I bet your sweet ass you do," Al said.

Sean Kelly was standing outside the door of the building manager's office when I walked into the lobby of the Lowertown apartment complex at five minutes to ten on Friday morning. Kelly looked to be about the same age as his thirty-eight-year-old ex-wife, although he had gained some space on his forehead because the orangey-red hairline had moved upward and backward. As if in response to the hairline's retreat, Kelly had grown a combination of bushy beard and monstrous moustache, which matched the red of the hair higher up. He stood about five-ten and was put together like a middle guard on the Minnesota Vikings defense, with a thick neck and wide shoulders. He was dressed in a dark gray suit, white shirt, and plain blue tie, and his hands were buried in his pants pockets.

"Good morning," I said as I offered my right hand for shaking. "I'm Mitch."

"Sean here," he said. His hands remained entombed in his pockets.

I retracted my hand and said, "Is Madeline in?" I had reviewed my notes from Monday and refreshed my memory on the building manager's name.

"Haven't checked," Sean Here said.

"Let's knock, shall we?" I said, and I did so with the hand that hadn't been deemed worthy of shaking. Madeline Webster's voice responded with, "Come in."

Madeline was sitting behind her desk. The visitors' chair was occupied by a stocky, middle-aged uniformed police officer, who rose, introduced himself as Officer Seidz, and offered his right hand for shaking. Sean Kelly found this hand acceptable. He grabbed it with both of his hands and pumped it three times with enthusiasm before allowing Officer Seidz to retrieve it. As the second-place shaker, I gave the officer's hand one single-handed pump before releasing my grip.

Seidz held up Madeline's ring of keys. "Shall we go up, gentlemen?" he said.

"Let's get it over with," Kelly said.

"Let's take the stairs," I said.

"Good idea," Seidz said. "My shift might be over before that rattletrap elevator got the three of us up to the second floor."

Seidz found the key that unlocked the apartment door, pushed the door open and waved Kelly and me past him into the entryway. I felt goosebumps popping up on my arms as I stopped just a few feet from where Madeline and I had seen the body of T.J. Kelly sprawled on the floor. The blood-soaked rug on which she'd lain had been removed, but my scalp felt like my hair might be standing on end. Neither Seidz nor Kelly made any comments about my hair, so I decided that it was not in any unusual condition.

Seidz held out a pair of elastic rubber gloves in each hand and said, "You'll need these, gentlemen."

"I won't need them," Kelly said. "I won't be touching things. I'm just here to make sure that this guy doesn't walk off with anything that ain't a wooden turtle."

"That's all this guy intends to walk off with," I said as I pulled on the stretchy gloves. In fact, all I intended to walk off with was the thumb drive that was hiding inside the turtle. Kelly could keep the wooden Chelonian replica if he wanted it. I had my own pretty little turtle, sitting serenely on the shelf inside my front door.

Kelly plopped himself down on the armchair, leaned back, and crossed his legs. "Then be my guest, Mister turtle hound," he said. He was looking very comfortable for a man who might have committed murder in this room a few days earlier.

Officer Seidz stood with his arms crossed in the center of the living room, almost on the spot where T.J.'s body had lain, and watched me as I searched, revolving like a Maypole to follow my movements when necessary.

As I began to look around the apartment, I felt like hunching over and tiptoeing about, as if I was a nocturnal burglar who'd snuck in out of the darkness. I had to force myself to stand up straight and walk with a normal step.

First, I walked slowly all through the entire apartment—entryway, kitchen/dining area, living room, bedroom, and bathroom—looking at shelves and furniture tops without touching a thing or opening any drawers or doors. No pretty little wooden turtle reared its head.

Next, I reversed direction and opened every drawer and door and peeked into every corner of every closet. I even opened the door of the walk-in shower and found only a green shampoo bottle and a yellow rubber ducky with a smile on its face on the shelves in there. Kelly watched my moves from his laid-back position and

Seidz continued to stand and turn to follow me as I made the circuit. Again, no pretty little wooden turtle reared its head. The search for T.J.'s prize could only be described as turtle-less.

I looked at Seidz, and then at Kelly. "Doesn't seem to be any wooden turtle here," I said.

"Don't look at me," Kelly said. "I sure as hell didn't take the silly thing."

"That *silly thing* is what might have gotten your former wife killed," I said.

"Nothing I can do about that," he said.

Seidz faced me. "You done?" he said.

"I'm afraid I am," I said. And now, with two pretty little wooden turtles missing, I had a palpable reason to be afraid.

10

CARNIVAL CROWNS

"Any luck?" Don O'Rourke asked as I passed the city desk on the way to mine.

"Yes," I said. "All bad."

"No thumb drive?"

"No nothing. No turtle, no thumb drive, no help from the ex-husband."

"Does the ex-husband look like the kind of guy who could murder his ex-wife?"

"Ex-husband looked very cool for a guy who was sitting in the middle of the scene of a crime that he might've committed. Either he's a very good actor or he's not the killer. I'm thinking that although he's a jerk, he's an innocent jerk."

"So where does that leave us?" Don asked.

"It leaves me thinking that T.J. was killed by somebody who wanted the thumb drive that she made a big show about putting into her turtle. The first somebody with that motive that comes to mind would be someone employed by Coordinated Copper & Nickel, Inc."

"Does that mean that Ben deLyne's murder had nothing to do with his turtle?"

"If whoever wanted the thumb drive got it from T.J.'s apartment,

I can't see any reason for them to also kill Ben. Still, the fact is that Ben's wife hasn't seen his turtle since the visit by the killer. It doesn't make any sense to me."

Don thought for a moment before he said, "Maybe it's not about the thumb drive. Could somebody just be so pissed that our reports and editorials raised so much opposition to the nickel mine that he's knocking off the turtle award winners and taking their turtles as a trophy?"

"I don't like that way of turning turtle," I said. "If that *is* what's going on, there are two more turtle award winners who could be in danger of losing them."

"I think those two should be talking to the cops about getting protection," Don said.

"This one definitely will be talking to Brownie about having the PD covering his ass. The other one already has police protection at his house because of the book banner's death threat to his wife."

"What about the Queen of Snows coronation tonight? Should you both be pulled off of covering that?"

"I don't see any reason for that," I said. "If the pattern holds up, whoever would be coming for our throats would also be coming for our turtles, which would make sitting at home more dangerous than being in the coronation crowd. In fact, if I can't get police protection at our house tonight, I'll have Martha go to Carol's to stay with her and her brother in a house that is being watched while I'm downtown."

"Okay," Don said. "Go talk to Brownie about getting some protection."

Brownie answered on the second ring, and we exchanged the usual one-long-word greetings. Then he asked, "Any luck on your turtle hunt?"

"Yes," I said. "All bad." I described the scene and the events of the morning, told him my theory about the missing turtles and suggested that it would be awfully nice to have a police car parked in front of our duplex until the killer-slash-turtle jacker was out of circulation.

"You don't have an actual written death threat, do you?" Brownie asked.

"No, nothing on paper or a computer or cellphone screen," I said.

"Then we can't justify parking a cruiser in front of your house all night." After a brief pause, he added, "Unless, of course, you tell me where the Treasure Medallion is hiding."

Brownie was referring to the hidden $10,000 Treasure Medallion that is sponsored by the *Daily Dispatch* during every Winter Carnival. A clue to the medallion's hiding place is published every day for twelve days, or until the medallion is found. The treasure hunt sends thousands of scavengers out into the near-or-below-zero cold carrying snow shovels, rakes, and flashlights every year. This includes everyone from avid skiers and outdoor skaters to indoor dwelling couch potatoes who otherwise would never breathe the frigid fresh air of a Minnesota winter.

"Just follow the first clue, and you can't go wrong," I said. "It's in today's paper."

"Oh, right," Brownie said. "That'll steer us directly to the hiding place."

Clue 1, which traditionally offers an extremely broad description, said:

At last it's time for vexatious rhyme
To lead you to fortune and fun
Here's a clue: something old, something new
Off you go! The race has begun

"I can't help you beyond that," I said. "Only the two people who hide the medallion and write the clues know where it is, and no-body on the staff is allowed to speak to them until the treasure's been found."

Brownie sighed. "I was afraid you'd say that. If you can't make me instantly rich, all I can do for you is arrange for a marked car to go past your house at staggered intervals so that anybody who's watching is aware of a police presence in the neighborhood. What about your camera carrying twin?"

"His house has already got police protection." I told Brownie about the death threat to Carol and the fact that the Jeffreys' house would be under surveillance. "I'll park Martha there while Al and I are at the coronation tonight," I said. "Saturday night both of our wives have said they'll come with us to the Torchlight Parade. Maybe by Sunday night you'll have caught the killer-slash-turtle jacker and have everything wrapped up in a tortoise shell package."

"Don't you wish?" Brownie said. "I was hoping you'd find that thumb drive, and that it would contain information that would identify the killer, and that you would, of course, share that information with your friendly local homicide investigator immediately."

"Believe me, I will quickly share any such information I can find," I said.

"That's what a good citizen does," said Brownie. "And for now, have a good day, good citizen Mitch."

"Not likely," I said at a robust volume after putting down the phone.

"Sounds like you're mad at that brilliant self you keep talking to," Corinne Ramey said from the adjacent desk.

"We're both kind of frustrated right now," I said. "Nothing for you to worry your pretty little head about."

"Ooh! Now your brilliant partner is talking like a sexist pig!" said Corinne.

"Pig is just his pen name," I said. With that, I got up and went to the cafeteria to get a cup of coffee. As I entered, I nearly collided with Al, who was on his way out with a paper cup full of coffee in each hand. I suggested sitting at a table in the cafeteria rather than going back to my desk.

"Any luck with the turtle hunt?" Al asked.

"Yes. All bad," I said. I told him about the turtle hunt, and about my opinion of Sean Kelly, while we sipped our coffee.

"So, we've got two dead turtle trophy winners and two missing turtle trophies?" he said when I'd finished.

"Two sets of twins," I said.

"With possibilities of two more," Al said.

"Altogether too true," I said. "With two and two equaling four."

"Which makes one turtle owner, whose house has police protection, almost glad that some dumb-ass book burner sent a death threat to his wife."

"Do you think I could get somebody to send a death threat to my wife so that we could have a cop watching our front door?"

"She's a lawyer. It shouldn't be too hard to find somebody who'd be willing to do that favor for you."

"It would be a process of trial and error."

"If I was judging the case, my verdict would be that you do need more protection than an occasional pass by a cruiser."

"Are you pleading with us to come and stay at your house?"

"I'm not courting you, but that would be a just decision."

"Thank you for that ruling, your honor. Martha and I will be taking it under advisement."

*** *** ***

"No way in hell is any goddamn turtle-hunting, throat-cutting son of a bitch going to force me out of my own bed overnight," was Martha's answer to the suggestion that we spend the night with Al and Carol. Never before, in all the years of our marriage, had I heard my wife reel off such a lengthy string of assorted profanities.

After making her position on intimidation so crystal clear, Martha did agree to join Carol and her brother at the Jeffreys' house while Al and I were mingling with the coronation crowd in search of cogent quotes and color photos. As a result, we did some ride sharing, with me dropping Martha there and taking Al with me downtown to cover the coronation. All the downtown parking lots were full, but I found an empty spot on the street, four blocks from the St. Paul River Centre, and we arrived just as the clutter of the Royal Dinner was being cleared away to make way for the Royal Coronation program, which was scheduled to get under way at eight o'clock.

On our way into the ballroom, where spectators filled every chair, we met the duo who had covered the banquet, reporter John Boxwood and photographer Sully Romanov, on their way out. "Have fun with the stingy Royals," Sully said. "They all loved us when they were posing for the camera, but nobody noticed us when they could have offered a taste of their dessert."

"Fab photo op; flop cake and ice cream op," said John Boxwood, describing the headline that he would suggest putting on the story.

The Royal Coronation ceremony began with the introduction of the Winter Carnival's guest of honor, the illustrious Lady T of European television fame. She was dressed in a flowing green evening gown with her shoulders draped in a six-pointed scarlet cape, which gave her the appearance of a giant poinsettia plant with a colossal blossom. A diamond of horse-choking size, which she had displayed on the river cruise, was nestled in her otherwise bare decolletage and gold hoops the size of silver dollars dangled from her ears. Seated beside the Lady, dressed less flamboyantly in a pale blue off-shoulder evening gown, was the graceful Gigette.

Lady T rose from her chair and acknowledged the applause with a wide smile and a sweeping wave of her right hand. Gigette remained seated with a smile on her lips and her hands in her lap.

"Wonder who's watching Laddie T," Al said. "He could be chewing up the furniture in that fancy suite they're in."

"I'm sure that Lady T will be able to pay for any repairs or replacements," I said.

"I would bet that Lady T could pay for the refurbishment of this whole hotel," he said.

"Just that rock sitting between her boobs would bring in enough to take care of the first two floors," I said.

The program that followed included the introduction and crowning of the new King Boreas Rex, Mighty Monarch of Ice and Snow; the introduction of his group of Royal Guards; the crowning of Aurora, the new Queen of the Snows; and the appearance of four Wind Princes and Princesses. Boreas Rex and Aurora gave short speeches, a band played some wintry tunes and the whole entourage posed for pictures until almost ten o'clock.

During the photo ops, Al and I got close enough to Lady T and Gigette to wave at them and say hello. Al got a shot of Lady T reciprocating with a queenly gesture of recognition, while Gigette pretended that she hadn't seen us. I took a few notes to supplement the information in the printed program, and we left as soon as Al had collected all the pics he needed.

When we got back to Al's house, we found Martha; Carol; Carol's brother, Erik Hanson; and the kids, Kristin and Kevin, gathered in the living room, nibbling cookies and drinking hot chocolate. They were seated around a wooden coffee table, upon which rested a pretty little hand-carved wooden turtle.

"No turtle bandits tonight?" Al said.

"Everything's cool," said Erik.

"If any turtle-jackers came by, that cruiser parked on the street must have sent them crawling away," Martha said. "Let's us go home and see if your little prize is still in his shell."

Twenty minutes later, I parked the car in front of the garage in the alley behind the duplex and we entered our kitchen through the back door. Seeking reassurance, I walked all the way to the front entry, where I was pleased to see that my pretty little hand-carved friend was still resting undisturbed in her appointed place. I patted the tip of Mother turtle's pointed nose and bade her a safe and sound goodnight.

On Saturday morning, I read Clue 2 of the Treasure Hunt aloud to Martha while she scrambled our breakfast eggs.

This is the year of the pioneer
An enterprise first of its kind
An event historic we feel euphoric
Like a park hunter grasping the find
It's been many a year since that newsman came here
With his press afloat he did embark
He's got his own county, a majestic bounty
That he's got in common with the park

"Mangled meter and not much help," said Martha.

"It's only the second day," I said. "They want it to be at least a week before some lucky soul finds the treasure."

Saturday afternoon found us—Al, Carol, Martha, and me—standing in a twelve-degree windchill with thousands of other bundled-up spectators on Grand Avenue, watching the Grande Parade go past. Al and I were standing in the twelve-degree windchill because we had been assigned to photograph and write about the event. I could not understand why all those other people, who were not obligated to be standing in the twelve-degree windchill, were lining the sidewalks along the street on which Martha and I first met in an apartment building near Dale Street.

"It's a spectacle," said Martha. "There's nothing like this any-where else in the whole country at this time of the year. Nobody can even imagine anything like this in Cape Verde."

"It's a lifelong custom," said Carol. "I grew up watching the pa-rade every year with my mom, who loved it, and dad, who thought that mom needed protection in the crowd."

"It's craziness," Al said. "No one in his right mind stands outside in this temperature unless he's on skis or skates."

"It's puzzling. If you've seen one Winter Carnival parade, you've seen 'em all," I said. "Why would anybody do this every year?"

It was, as Martha said, a spectacle, featuring a fleet of profusely decorated floats carrying heavily-dressed members of the Carnival royalty. Between the floats were baton twirlers with fingers too stiff to twirl, horses with riders frozen into their saddles, and march-ing bands with no wind instruments touching any of the musicians' lips. Zigzagging in between them all were uniformed Knights of Columbus members riding on three-wheeled motor scooters. And literally bouncing along the route was the bouncing girl, a light-weight teenager who was repeatedly being tossed high in the air from a blanket borne by six muscular young firefighters.

"Wow! Look at that!" Martha shouted. She was pointing at a float carrying the Carnival's guest of honor, Lady T. The great Lady's body and legs were swathed from neck to boot tops in enough fur wraps to cover a grizzly bear, and she wore a fur hat and heavy scarf combination that covered everything but her eyes. She waved a mittened hand at us as she went by, and Al shot a pic that was destined to dominate the front page.

"Where's Gigette, I wonder?" said Martha.

"Back in the warm hotel room with Laddie-T if she's as smart as I think she is," I said.

"She's not that smart," said Al. He pointed to a smaller figure, clad from head to toe in blue ski jacket, blue ski pants, and blue knit woolen hat, who'd previously been blocked from our view by the bulk of Lady T.

"At her Lady's side in all kinds of weather," I said. "Amazing." I waved to Gigette and called out her name. Gigette pretended not to see or hear me.

After the last unit passed by, Martha went with Carol to get a ride home. Al and I went to the office in my car to write my story and show his pics to Assistant City Editor Ted Gambrell, who sat in Don O'Rourke's chair on Saturdays. It felt really *really* good to be inside a warm office where my fingers could be bent at the joints again.

11

SUNDAY TRADITION

On Sundays, I call my mother and my grandmother, who are both widowed and live together on a farm on the outskirts of Harmony, a small city a few miles north of the Iowa border. After the usual exchange of greetings, Mom launched an attack on Clue 3 of the Treasure Hunt, which was in the Sunday morning edition. I'm not sure why she tries to interpret these clues because during all the years of the Treasure Hunt she has never set foot in the search area.

Not having read the clue, I quickly looked it up.

The search for gold will never get old
This year, add beer can and gnome
Sincerest flattery or idle chattery?
Our treasure sits on top of the loam.

"What's your problem with it?" I said. "There's all kinds of clues there. It's apparently within sight of a beer can, which could be on a billboard or a saloon, and one of those gnome statues like you see in people's gardens, and the last line clearly tells you that it isn't buried under something."

"Beer cans and gnomes are everywhere and the flattery and chattery bit is too vague," Mom said. "Doesn't make sense to me."

"Are you planning to join in the hunt as much as you always do?"

"I would be on my way to St. Paul right now if I could zero in on where it's at."

"You and several thousand other people."

I changed the subject, and we chatted a bit before she called her mother, who we've always called Grandma Goodie because her last name is Goodrich, to the phone. I braced myself for Grandma Goodie's opening salvo, which is always the same.

"Did you go to church this morning, Warnie Baby?" I have been Warnie Baby to her since the moment I was born, and my failure to occupy a pew on Sundays has been of concern to her since the moment I left my Methodist parents' nest.

My response was also always the same. "Couldn't make it to-day." On this day, I added what I believed was a valid reason: "I was out late in the cold last night covering the big parade and I needed to stay warm under the covers this morning."

"It's time that you decided that taking care of your soul is more important than keeping your tootsies warm," Grandma Goodie said. "If you continue on the path that you're on, it could take you down to a place that's a whole lot warmer than your bed."

"I'm counting on you to arrange a cool eternal landing place for me. You've got a head start on that path."

"You can't count on the help of my prayers for your soul much longer," she said. "I'm already way past the age that my generation is expected to live."

"I'm sure you'll be with us at least to a hundred," I said. "And maybe ten years beyond that." I changed the subject to something less contentious than my continuous non-attendance of church services and our conversation continued on a smoother path.

The first thing I did at my desk Monday morning was read Treasure Hunt Clue 4. I'm addicted to these clues, even though I'm not eligible to cash in the Treasure Medallion.

You went out to search, but had to lurch
Because the sunlight had expired
For your hunt to be great, it's okay to stay out late
If you're able to get lights wired.

The "lights wired" bit was puzzling to me. No matter; me wasn't active in the hunt.

The second thing I did at my desk Monday morning was to call Brownie.

After the usual exchange of greetings, I asked if he had come up with any clues on either of the turtle-jack killings.

"I have even less of a clue to those than I've been able to get from reading your so-called clues for the Treasure Medallion," Brownie said. "Are you sure that you don't know where that medallion is?"

"It's a deep, dark secret, as today's clue seems to say," I said.

"Yeah. What's with the line about 'lights wired' for hunting late at night?"

"I'm in the dark on that," I said. "Can you brighten my day with a statement that sheds some light on either or both of your investigations?"

"All we can say is that the investigations of both homicides are ongoing. I take it that you haven't found the turtle with the thumb drive yet?"

"You take it correctly. The killer must have taken it from T.J.'s apartment, and I still can't imagine why whoever it was also seems to have gone away with Ben's turtle."

"Any signs of anybody coming after yours?" Brownie asked.

"All quiet at our house over the weekend. And likewise at Al's, where there's a cop already posted to guard Carol from some kooky book banner who sent her a death threat."

"Too many of those kooks around these days. The Internet makes it too easy for that kind of crap to expand and go on. Ninety-nine percent of the threats are just from some idiot blowing hot air, but enough of them are real that we have to take all of them seriously. Anyhow, have a good day, Mitch."

Sensing that Corrine Ramey had an ear tuned my way from the next desk, I hung up without further comment. If she was disappointed, Corrine said nothing.

Al approached bearing coffee for both of us. He handed me a cup, cleared a corner of my desk upon which to lean his butt, and said, "Big night in Roseville tonight."

"What's up in Roseville?" I asked.

"School board meeting. They're going to vote on a motion to require parental approval of any books dealing with sex, gender change, homosexuality, and whatever else the book burners are torching at any given time," Al said.

"How in hell can a teacher get approval of a book from the parents of every kid in a classroom?"

"The school board will appoint a committee of volunteer parents to rule on all the books in the all the libraries and all the books proposed for use in all the classrooms in all the schools in the district, which is a damn big one. You can bet your sweet ass that every member of GOOFS will be raising their hands to volunteer for that one."

"Ssh!" I said. "Mustn't speak that acronym out loud in the newsroom."

"I'd like to shout it out loud in the newsroom and I might yell it in the school board meeting room. Anyhow, Carol is one of several teachers who are going to speak against the motion."

"Is she looking for another death threat?"

"As you well know, my placid appearing partner is not one to back away from a battle."

"Yes. Both of our wives seem to be afflicted with that condition."

"I'd just like to identify the bastard who made the death threat."

"It's a good bet that he—or she—will be volunteering for the book banning committee."

"That would make everybody on the committee a suspect," Al said.

"Which would be worth mentioning to the Roseville police."

"It would narrow down the list of narrow-minded suspects."

"I take it that you think the motion will pass," I said.

"Judging from what Carol's heard at past meetings, it's a slam dunk."

"Then why bother to speak against it?" I asked.

"As previously noted, Carol is not one to back away from a battle without firing all of her ammunition."

"Let's hope nobody fires at Carol with real live ammunition."

"They have metal detectors at the door, just like the airport."

"What a world we live in," I said. "Metal detectors needed at a school board meeting and journalists apparently being killed over pretty little wooden turtles."

12

HOLY SMUT?

As of eight o'clock Tuesday morning, the Treasure Medallion was still unfound, so I began my workday by reading Clue 5.

A city first, its pride does burst
For our city's all-woman council
We'll observe, for the readers we serve
Of their views we will be ever mindful

The meter was like scrambled eggs, but it was obvious that the writer was bragging about St. Paul voters having elected a City Council composed entirely of women—seven of them, in all. This was a first-in-the-nation achievement that the clue writers thought was worth boasting about, and it also told hunters that the medallion was within the St. Paul city limits.

Naturally my first phone call of the day went to Brownie, and naturally Brownie had nothing to report beyond, "The investigations of both crimes are ongoing."

Al had much more interesting news. He was out on assignments all morning, but we got together in the lunchroom at 12:15 and I asked, "How'd it go at the school board meeting?"

"The motion passed, three votes to two, and they created a

committee to deal with what they called Sensitive Materials Under Trial."

"That would acronym as SMUT," I said.

"Exactly. I don't know if that was an intentional insult or a stupid oversight. Anyhow, the vote was preceded by quite a circus. There actually was a lot of opposition to the motion, both from teachers and parents. We even got a lesson about pornographic verses in the Bible."

"The Bible? Is the SMUT committee going to ban that?"

"The Bible revelation wasn't from anybody on the committee. It was a man who introduced himself as a philosophy and religion professor at Bethel College. He said that in order to comply with the board's apparent literary standards the Bible must be kept out of Roseville schools. He said the Bible could be harmful to children because it has stories that contain incest, bestiality, onanism, prostitution, genital mutilation, fellatio, rape, infanticide, and I think a couple of other fun practices that I can't remember or describe."

"He found all that in the Good Book? Did he name chapter and verse?" I asked.

"He didn't get down to details," Al said. "But he did give us a quote from Song of Solomon that was so good that I wrote it down just so I'd get it right telling you." Al dug into his inside coat pocket and pulled out a sheet of paper. "How about reading this ode to a woman to the kids in your Sunday School class: 'Your waist is a mound of wheat surrounded by lilies. Your breasts are like two fawns, twins of a gazelle."

"Stop. You're making me blush," I said.

"And the professor also told us the story of Jesus and the three eunuchs."

"Jesus and the who?" This was getting more bizarre by the minute.

"He said that Jesus said that there were three types of eunuchs:

eunuchs who were born that way; eunuchs that were made eunuchs by others; and eunuchs who chose to live like eunuchs for the sake of the kingdom of heaven.'"

"This professor had the balls to talk about eunuchs at a school board meeting?" I said.

"The guy was really *having* a ball," Al said. "He had a lot of people laughing. Although I didn't see any of the school board members looking all that amused."

"I assume that Carol's opposition to the motion was on a higher level," I said.

"Yes, it was. She kept her punches above the belt."

"And nobody offered to kill her?"

"She drew a mixture of applause and boos, but nobody lobbed a grenade in her direction."

"Did we have a reporter there?" I asked.

"John Boxwood was there. His story is in the paper this morning, eunuchs, and all. I can't believe you didn't read it."

"I didn't get past the Treasure Hunt clue this morning," I said. "After trying to decipher that I made my routine fruitless call to Brownie about the turtle-jack killings and then Don put me to work writing about some other Carnival crap."

"Read the story. He's got so much about the reasons for banning the Bible in it that SMUT will probably demand burning the print edition that's in the high school library today."

We finished lunch and Al went out on an assignment while I went back to my desk, where I looked through the *Daily Dispatch* for John Boxwood's story. Sure enough, it was on the front page of the local section under a head that said, "Roseville man seeks Bible ban." I read all about the erotica and the eunuchs and found myself wishing that Ben deLyne could see this story. It was perfect grist for the editorial page mill, the kind of issue that would send Ben off on a column filled with wit and wisdom. Why in hell had someone killed poor Ben and grabbed his pretty little turtle when they already had T.J.'s turtle with the thumb drive inside? There had to be a motive beyond the thumb drive. Would that motive drive the man with the knife to Al's house? Or to mine? I silently thanked the police patrols protecting both our pads.

I was shutting down my desk computer at the end of the day when Al came hustling toward me. "All done shooting?" I asked.

"I wish I could do some real shooting," he said. "Carol just called me. She's got another death threat. This one said that she'd sealed her fate with her remarks at the meeting last night."

"She's getting right popular with the wrong people. Any way of telling if it's the same nut cake or a new one?"

"No, not really," Al said. "But I hope it's not a second coocoo nut. I'm cracking up just watching out for one."

"Has Carol relayed this message to the cops?"

"Oh, yeah. They'll have the cruiser parked at our house again tonight, watching every car that comes by."

"That's good. It'll also give you protection from the turtle jacker if he decides he wants your trophy."

"What about your turtle? Who's guarding your place?"

"I believe the occasional drive-by is still on the books, but I'll check that out with Brownie before I go home, just to make sure," I said.

"You and Martha and your turtle are always welcome to occupy our guest room," Al said.

"You couldn't drag Martha there with a whole team of giant Galapagos turtles under these conditions."

"That would be too slow of a drag to save your sweet ass, I'm afraid. Keep your doors locked tight and I'll see you in the morning."

Brownie assured me that cruisers would continue to drive past at odd intervals, and I took that word home to Martha. We threw on the extra locking bolts for insurance again that night, but

I found myself waking up every time the wind rattled the shutters or something else made a sound outside. When I got out of bed and checked my pretty little turtle at 3:00 a.m., it seemed to be at peace, resting on the shelf just inside the double-locked front door.

When I entered the *Daily Dispatch* building Wednesday morning, people were still buying morning papers or looking at their cell phones to read Treasure Hunt Clue 6. I looked it up as soon as I got to my desk.

Seek out a pyramid or even a beer amid
Grasses and shrubbery and trees
Look a bit dusty? Or even somewhat crusty?
It may hide the object to seize

A pyramid within the boundaries of St. Paul? Amid grasses and bushes and trees? This was a scene that I could not place. And neither could Brownie when I made my obligatory call. Neither could Brownie give me anything for a story on either of the turtle-jack killings. "I like the way you've labeled them, though," Brownie said. "Turtle-jack killings has a really nice ring to it."

"Thank you so much for the compliment. Now how about closing the ring around the turtle-jack killer's neck?" I said.

"I'd love to ring him up, but I haven't a clue who he is," he said.

"You're starting to sound like the Treasure Hunt writer."

"Maybe I'm in the wrong job. I'm sure the treasure I'm hunting won't bring me ten grand if I find it."

"But it will make two surviving turtle owners feel grand," I said.

"With two grand in mind, I will do my grandest. Have a grand day, Mitch," Brownie said.

I had an outdoor day, along with Al, going from one Winter

Carnival activity to another for stories and pics. We went first to the ice sculptures downtown, then north to the snow sculptures at the state fairgrounds in the suburb of New Brighton, and finally back into the heart of the city where people were riding tobog-gans down a long snow-filled chute on a street near the Capitol building. Fortunately, the temperature had climbed into the middle 20s and the wind speed had descended to the low single digits. It was really quite a balmy February day for the middle of Minnesota.

At the scene of the snow sculptures, we encountered the Carnival's guest of honor, Lady T, awarding trophies to the artists whose works had been deemed meritorious by a judging commit-tee. Al took a shot of Lady T, whose substantial body was again draped in yards of fur, topped by a Russian-style fur headpiece that made her eight feet tall, towering over the grand prize winner, who was a five-foot-two-inch member of the city's Hmong community, and I got a quote from each of them. After all the trophies had been awarded, Lady T came to me and said, "There was a giant turtle sculpture that Lady T thought should have won one of the prizes, but dumb ass judges did not agree."

"Did you ask the turtle sculptor if he is a Turtle?" I asked.

"You bet your sweet ass he is," said Lady T. She turned and walked away to a waiting black SUV with the Carnival logo on its front door. As she was getting into the middle seat, I saw Gigette sitting in the right front seat and waved to her. Gigette pretended not to see me, but Laddie T rose up in her lap and pressed his wet nose against the window.

All the outdoorsy stuff on Wednesday must have worn me out because I slept late Thursday morning, taking advantage of it be-ing my non-Sunday day off. I vaguely remembered being kissed goodbye by Martha when my eyes opened. It was 8:33 by the bed-side alarm clock.

I couldn't afford to be lollygagging any longer than that because a memorial service for Ben deLyne was being held at 10:30 in a Unitarian-Universalist Church a ten-minute drive away. I was guessing that every seat in the church would be filled so I wanted to get there early. I rolled out of bed, showered, did a quick trim on my moustache, and checked the coffee pot in the kitchen. Martha had left a cup's worth, which I put into the microwave to reheat while two slices of sourdough bread were turning brown in the toaster.

While eating toast covered with blueberry jam and sipping the coffee, I opened the online edition of the *Daily Dispatch* and examined Clue 7 of the Treasure Hunt.

If you're in the pink wait for a link
To a place that's right for wonder
For the bold there's a mystery of old
In this land once cast asunder

Was "land once cast asunder" the writer's way of describing a dump? The medallion wasn't buried under anything, but it could be sitting atop the trash in a landfill. I decided to dump the question and turn my attention to prose that was more easily interpreted. As I turned to the sports page, I was wondering who, if anyone, was checking with Brownie on the turtle-jack killings. I would be very jealous if another reporter got a mystery breaking reply from the chief of Homicide while I was preparing to attend a funeral.

I thought about taking my pretty little turtle to the service with me as a symbolic gesture. It would fit into a pocket on the knee-length topcoat that I weas wearing over my suit. I picked up the turtle, looked it in the eye, and returned it to its safe spot on the shelf. I decided that it might not be in the best of taste to display it at the service, and I didn't want to risk having it damaged by someone applying an overzealous hug to my body at what I was certain would be an emotion-charged event.

My estimate of the attendance proved to be accurate. The church was filled with friends, family, and fans of Ben's editorial page writing. I squeezed into the end of a pew next to a row of people I didn't know fifteen minutes before the starting time.

Ben's body had been cremated, so there was no coffin on display. The décor at the altar consisted of four floral arrangements and a long table covered with a white cloth and rows of photos of Ben that ranged from babyhood to fatherhood.

The service was conducted by a woman minister who seemed to know Ben quite well. After her eulogy, the minister invited family members and friends to step up and talk about their memories of Ben. Laurie Lincoln was first at the lectern with a description of their life together, beginning with an initial meeting as members of opposing college debate teams. She noted that her team won the debate, but that she later lost her heart to the most attractive opposing debater. The line of relatives and friends that followed Laurie to the lectern for the next thirty minutes made it clear that Ben had been a well-loved and popular fellow.

Of course, lunch was served in the fellowship hall following the service. I gathered with a half dozen *Daily Dispatch* staffers who were off duty, including Al, and several others who managed to slip away on a workday, including the entire Opinion Page staff. "We worked double time yesterday, so we could skip out today," said the editor, Robert C.R. Carter.

I managed to capture a minute with Laurie, who asked me if I knew anything about Ben's murder that hadn't appeared in the paper. "I'm sorry to say that I don't," I said. "The cops have nothing for clues other than the missing turtles. What we really need is the thumb drive that was in T.J.'s turtle, but it's nowhere to be found."

"If the thumb drive was in T.J.'s turtle, why would somebody be after Ben's?" she asked.

"I wish I knew the answer to that," I said. "Al and I are both watching our backs."

"Oh, please, God, don't let anything happen to either of you," Laurie said. "This whole turtle award thing that was supposed to be such an honor for all of you has already turned into a nightmare."

"That's a very good description," I said. "I'll let you know immediately if the cop's dream up anything." She gave me a quick hug and I went home, hoping the coast—or at least our half of the duplex—was clear of armed turtle-jackers.

13

ALL CLEAR

Both the coast and the house were clear of everything but a black and white cat that encircled my ankles in hopes of getting its ears scratched. What would a homecoming be like without a greeting from Sherlock Holmes?

Martha phoned to tell me that she'd be working for a couple of extra hours preparing for a trial that was scheduled for Monday morning. She suggested meeting at a restaurant on Grand Avenue for dinner at 7:30 because she would be too pooped to cook when she got home at that hour. We met at the restaurant (she was fifteen minutes late), had a fine dinner of broiled walleye and wild rice, and lingered over a shared chocolate cake and ice cream dessert. When we got home, the coast was still clear, and I settled down on the sofa with a light-hearted book ("Jeeves to the Rescue") in my hands and a heavy-bodied Sherlock Holmes on my lap, feeling relaxed and comfortable for the first time since walking into T.J. Kelly's apartment and finding her bloody corpse on the floor ten days ago. Later, Martha and I engaged in some vigorous lovemaking, after which I drifted away into the longest stretch of undisturbed sleep that I'd had in ten nights. The turtle-jack killings had been pushed completely out of my mind.

On Friday morning, Martha was up and away early to finish prepping for the trial. I was left waiting for the arrival of Sylvia

Valdez, a young single mother who cleans our messy house once a month. With both of us working long hours, there wasn't always time or energy available to dust all the shelves, clean the bathroom and the half-bath, vacuum the dining room and living room rugs, and mop the linoleum floors in the kitchen and the entryway. We'd have gladly paid Sylvia twice what she asked to perform these necessary chores.

While I ate my cereal and toast and drank my breakfast coffee, I read Treasure Hunt Clue Number 8.

Blocks by the passel can raise a castle
Remember when we raised up those pads?
It makes a mind limber, to think of the timber,
"tween our waters bricks shall be had."

Okay, the castles we were supposed to remember would be the grandiose ice palaces lighted in multi colors that were a longtime Winter Carnival feature. They stopped making them big enough for people to go inside several years ago, I think for safety reasons. To have someone slip and fall, or for someone to be hit by a chunk of falling ice could be expensive to the Winter Carnival's sponsoring agency in this era of excessive litigation.

When Sylvia rang the doorbell, I opened the front door and found her carrying the usual house cleaning tools and materials in her right hand and towing a little girl who appeared to be about five years old with the left.

"Valerie came down with a runny nose this morning, so she can't go to kindergarten today, and I couldn't find a sitter on such short notice at this time of day," Sylvia said. "You don't mind if she sits and watches your TV while I work this morning, do you?"

"I'll have to dock your pay for the cost of the electricity that's used while she watches the tube, but otherwise it's okay," I said.

Sylvia laughed as I handed her a check for the usual amount and bid her and Valerie goodbye. Valerie wiped a snot bubble off her nose and waved bye-bye with the soggy tissue.

I heard the click of the automatic lock as I closed the back door behind me, and the turtle-jack killings came back to mind for the first time on the day. I wondered if I should go back in and give Sylvia an extra warning about not opening the door for anyone but Martha or me. Would Sylvia be insulted if I delivered such a message? Or frightened? Maybe she'd want to know why I was giving her a special reminder about keeping the door locked and would be spooked enough to leave the minute I told her the reason. I decided that she was smart enough not to open a locked door for a stranger and didn't need a special alert from me. Call it over-confidence if you will, but I was sure that they'd be okay.

"Still won't tell me where the Treasure Medallion is?" Brownie said when I made my first call of the day.

"Still don't know any more than you do about where the Treasure Medallion is," I said. "Today's clue puts it somewhere around the Ice Castle, I guess. Now, how about you telling me who the turtle-jack killer is and that you've got him locked behind bars?"

"Wish either of those things was possible. We did make another very thorough sweep of Ms. Kelly's apartment to look for the turtle with the thumb drive in its tum-tum, but we didn't' find it."

"That turtle with the thumb drive has to be what got T.J. killed," I said. "But I still can't figure out why they also went after Ben and his turtle, which had nothing in it as far as I know."

"If the killer is a collector of turtle figurines, it's a pretty extreme way of getting them."

"You bet your sweet ass it is," I said.

"What was that?" said a surprised Brownie.

"Nothing," I said. "That just slipped out at the mention of a turtle."

"Sounds like this turtle thing has cracked the shell on your brain. Maybe you should take another day off and you and your turtle crawl into bed."

"Oh, no; I'm still in the swim of things."

"I sure hope you're not going to drown in a bowl of turtle soup. Have a good day, Mitch."

I'd barely put down the phone when Don O'Rourke arrived at my desk. "Guess where you and your twin are going today," he said. He seemed altogether too pleased with what he was going to tell me next.

"Um, could we be spending a day with the Queen of Snows and all her lovely ladies in waiting?" I said.

"You should be so lucky," Don said. "How'd you like to go out to White Bear Lake and talk to the cool guys in the ice fishing contest?"

"I'd rather have a tooth pulled by a dentist who doesn't use Novocain."

"You're welcome to do that on your next day off. Today you're going to White Bear Lake to talk to the cool guys in the ice fishing contest."

"My dad was a crazy ice fisherman," I said. "He would drag me out there with him to keep him company in below-zero weather. I'd watch him chop a hole in the ice and dangle a poor frozen minnow on a hook through the hole. We'd stand beside the hole, stomping our feet to keep our toes from freezing, waiting for the bobber to go down. Ice would form around the bobber sometimes and Dad would skim it off with the little net that he dipped the minnows out of the bucket with. That's how we bonded as father and son—shivering and stomping our feet together."

"Did your dad ever catch anything?"

"Sometimes we'd get a perch or some crappies. We'd lay them down on the ice and they'd be frozen stiff as a board in three minutes flat."

"Nothing better than freezing to keep fish fresh," Don said. "Have a fun time on White Bear Lake."

White Bear Lake is a middle-size lake located in a northeastern suburban city by the same name. Although there are two lakes within the St. Paul city limits, neither is large enough to accommodate the number of nuts who chop holes in the ice and stand out in the cold all day angling for a prize in the annual Winter Carnival Ice Fishing Contest.

"What did we do to deserve this?" Al asked as we drove toward White Bear Lake in a *Daily Dispatch* staff car. "Shouldn't a fishing contest be covered by somebody in sports? I don't know a walleye from a sturgeon unless I'm reading it on a restaurant menu."

"I suggested to Don that he send Hank Green, our outdoors writer, but Don said all of the Winter Carnival events come strictly under city desk coverage and that it is yours and my turn to go out on the ice this year."

"Glad I keep my parka and snow boots in the photo department all winter," Al said. "You're gonna freeze your ears off with just that winter coat."

"Ah, but I have a woolen ski hat in one pocket and warm ski gloves in the other," I said. "Like a Boy Scout, I'm prepared." I was also wearing the boots I keep in my car all winter as part of my survival kit. Native Minnesotans are taught to keep a woolen hat, thick gloves, boots, a blanket, and a coffee can containing a candle and a book of matches in their vehicles as survival gear from November through March. A driver who becomes stuck for a long time in a vehicle that won't start or a snowbank that won't yield can don the gloves and hat, wrap himself in the blanket and draw a surprising amount of heat from a lighted candle in a coffee can. Running the motor to provide heat in that situation is frowned upon because of the possibility of carbon monoxide seeping into the enclosed interior. More than one untrained motorist has drifted dreamily away to that big garage in the sky while sitting toasty warm in a stranded vehicle with the motor running and the heater purring.

When we reached the lake, we found the parking lot crammed bumper to bumper with vehicles and the sheet of ice that covered the lake teeming with bundled up humans. Most seemed to be of the male gender, but it was hard to be certain about some individuals because of the multiple layers of clothing they were wrapped in. They stood little more than a yard apart beside holes they'd chopped in the ice sheet. I wondered how many more holes it would take to turn the ice sheet into a sieve that would sink and let the water spurt through onto the surface.

I pointed out that the numeral 12 was displayed on the dashboard thermometer. "At least there's no minus sign in front it, which means that it's twelve above," Al said.

"That gauge doesn't measure the windchill factor," I said. "That's a lot closer to the big round number."

"Let's pretend we're on skates and do this as fast as we can," Al said. "I can slide through enough pics in five minutes to get everything I need. Are you going to be taking notes of what people say?"

"No way," I said. "I'll take off one glove long enough to write down a guy's name, but what he says will be edited down to what I can remember when we get back to the car."

Al's first shot was of a stout person wearing a dark brown fur-trimmed parka over a khaki snowmobile suit pulling a fish about a foot long up through the hole and letting it dangle on the end of the line. "Is that a small walleye?" Al asked.

Two nearby fishermen laughed, and the catcher of the fish stared at Al and said, "It's a perch. You don't know a perch when you see one?"

"I catch images, not fish," Al said. "I'm afraid I don't know a perch from a porch. Get the name, will you Mitch?"

"Could I have your name, sir?" I asked.

The wind-reddened face inside the parka scowled. "It's Margaret. Margaret McMullen."

"Oh! Sorry," I said. "And thanks." I pulled off my right glove, scribbled the name on a page in my notebook, and quickly pulled the glove back on. Didn't I just say it was hard to determine gender with all that winter clothing?

We slipped and slithered through the crowd for about fifteen more minutes, Al shooting pics and me taking names, without any additional fish or gender identification faux pas. Then it was back to the car, where we both sat blowing on our stiffened fingers until the heater warmed us up enough for Al to grip the steering wheel.

After I wrote my story, I had lunch with Al and made another call to Brownie that produced nothing more than "the investigations of both crimes are ongoing." In mid-afternoon, I saw Al burst out of the photo department, run to the city desk, and, arms waving, say a few words to Don. Then he ran to me, with arms waving, and said, "Kevin just called me. When he got home from school just now, he found the back door window smashed and the house torn apart like it was ransacked. Whoever it was threw my turtle on the floor and apparently stomped on it. The cops are on their way there and I'm going home to meet them."

"Now we have turtle cracking as well as turtle jacking. Looks like the cop who's been guarding your place at night should have stayed on watch for the day. Keep me posted on what happens next," I said.

"I'll call you with all the cracker-jack details," he said. He spun around and went running toward the elevator.

Don walked over to me and said, "Do you want to go and check your place?"

"Not a bad idea," I said.

"Should you maybe call the cops and have them meet you there, in case somebody might be inside?"

"Another good idea," I said. "If I see any sign of a break-in, I'll call for an escort before I go inside."

"This whole thing is crazy," Don said. "What is it with these turtles?"

"Wish I knew," I said. "Hope I don't find out the hard way."

At home, I parked my car in front of the garage in the alley behind the duplex. Martha had said she was going to the YWCA to run on the treadmill after work—she had started training for a spring marathon in Duluth—so I didn't expect her car to be there, especially when I was arriving two hours earlier than usual.

The back door of our unit was locked and showed no damage, and I doubted that anyone would break in the front door that faced a busy street, but I played it safe and stayed as quiet as the proverbial mouse when I let myself in.

I was so mousey quiet, in fact, that I was not even greeted by Sherlock Holmes, who always runs for my ankles when I enter the room. I walked slowly and quietly through the kitchen and dining room and stopped at the entry into the living room. Not a creature was stirring, not even a mouse. And not a black and white mouse catcher, either.

I called for Sherlock Holmes by name and announced that I was home. Being a cat, Sherlock doesn't automatically come when he's called, but when he's in the mood he will respond to the sound of my voice. This time, no cat appeared. I took a couple of steps into the living room and called again. Still no feline response.

Thinking that Sherlock might be asleep on our bed, I went upstairs and checked the bedroom. No Sherlock Holmes. The bathroom was also unoccupied. Did he accidentally get locked in a closet? I opened the two upstairs closets and didn't find him. I looked in the two closets on the first floor with the same results.

Next, I went to the basement and called and walked around looking. Where else could a cat be hiding?

I went back upstairs and sat down on the sofa, trying to think of any other place that Sherlock might be. Our landlord, Zhoumaya Jones, who lived alone in the other half of the duplex, loved Sherlock. She had a key to our front door. Maybe she had taken him for a comfort visit. I took out my cellphone and called Zhoumaya's number. "Do you happen to have a big black and white cat in your house?" I asked when Zhoumaya answered.

"No, I don't," she said. "Are you missing a big black and white cat?"

"I am. I can't find him anywhere, but I don't think he could have let himself out."

"He isn't visiting me. I haven't had my door open all day; it's too cold to even stick as much as my nose outside."

Before coming to St. Paul four years ago, Zhoumaya had lived all her life in Liberia. "You never got to play in the snow and ice when you were little?"

"The very thought of that gives me goose bumps," she said. "I hope you find Sherlock."

"I'm sure I will. If he did sneak out somehow, he'll come home in time for supper," I said. "If you see him, tell him his daddy is looking for him."

I had barely put the cell phone down when it buzzed to alert me to an incoming text message. I tapped the icon and saw that I had a message from Name Unknown. I usually delete messages from people with no names or names that I don't recognize, but this call intrigued me, so I tapped it open.

It was fortunate that I was sitting down because if I'd been standing up the photo that I saw on my screen would have buckled my knees and knocked me flat on my not-so-sweet ass.

14

BAD NEWS AND GOOD NEWS

The image on my screen showed Martha Todd sitting in a straight back wooden chair with her hands pulled around behind her back and obviously held in place by some sort of restraint. She was leaning forward and sticking out her tongue at whoever was snapping the picture. That's my Martha—always making a clear statement that can't be misunderstood.

Beneath the photo was a text message that said : "If you want to see this person alive again follow instructions I give next"

All the air had whooshed out of my lungs, and I was having a hard time replacing it. I felt my face growing hot and all my muscles tightening into knots as the level of my shock and anger rose to the boiling point. My first reaction was to crush the cell phone so tight that the fingers holding it cramped as I started to type a furious reply with my other hand. After typing: "You bastard I will kill you," I stopped and let my brain come into play. I sucked in a long deep breath, let it out slowly, deleted what I had typed, and replaced it with: "Give instructions."

The reply said: "Bring turtle with everything to Kowalski's parking lot on Lexington 7:30 tonight back corner black Lincoln suv and NO COPS"

Kowalski's was a supermarket located only about ten minutes

away. A 7:30 rendezvous time gave me three hours to get there and meet with somebody driving a black Lincoln SUV in a dark back corner of the parking lot. It also gave me three hours to think about what, if anything, I could do to help the police catch Name Unknown, either at the transfer scene or later. And I had time to wonder what the hell Name Unknown meant by "turtle with everything?" My turtle had no accoutrements; it was nothing but an empty box.

My cellphone rang and I saw that the caller was A. Jeffrey. "What's up at the crime scene?" I asked.

"Got some good news for a change," Al said. "A half hour ago, the cop who's been watching our house at night pulled over a car that he's seen going back and forth past us several times every night that he's been here. The driver wouldn't answer any questions, but the cop spotted a handgun in the well between the two front seats. The cop took the driver in on an unlicensed gun charge and suspicion of making a death threat against Carol."

"That's great!" I said. "Is the guy anybody you know?"

"It's not a guy. It's a woman with one of the loudest mouths in the GOOFS organization. As much as she shoots off her mouth, I sure hope they take that gun away from her. Anyhow, that's the good news from here. How's things with you?"

"I have bad news that's so bad that you won't believe it," I said. I told him what had happened to Martha and what I had to do to rescue her.

"You're right. I don't believe it," Al said. "How the hell did he kidnap Martha? I thought she could kick most anybody's ass with her taekwondo."

"That I don't know. I can hardly wait to find out. I just wish there was some way to identify the SUV or the driver when I trade my turtle for my wife."

"Could you take a picture?" asked the man who lives with a camera constantly attached to his hands.

"It might spook him if he saw me with a camera. He might take off with Martha still in the car."

"What if I took the picture? I could get to that Kowalski's before 7:30 and park near the meeting place and wait for him to come in. I could get a shot of the SUV with the numbers of the license plate the minute that Martha steps out of it."

"Have you got time to do that?" I said. "Haven't you got a monster house cleaning project of your own going on?"

"It's worth putting off my house cleaning if we can clean house on the turtle-jacker."

"Let's take him to the cleaners then," I said.

"I'm on the way to Kowalski's," Al said. "Just call me Mister Clean."

Waiting out the time until my rendezvous with Martha's kidnapper was like sitting in a car while a mile-long slow-moving train creeps its way through a grade crossing. I paced. I sat. I paced some more. I thought about eating something, but I had no appetite, so I paced some more. I had decided to get to Kowalski's well before 7:30 and finish the agony of waiting in the parking lot, so at 6:35, still wondering why someone wanted my pretty little turtle so desperately, I went to the shelf in the front hall to pick it up.

The shelf was empty. Bare. Unoccupied. Devoid of all turtles—pretty, little, motherly, or otherwise.

If I'd had any food in my stomach, it would have come up and out.

Where the hell could that turtle be? It had been sitting right there on the shelf when I opened the front door for Sylvia and Valerie in the morning. Had Sylvia picked it up and moved it somewhere when she dusted the shelf? I went turtle hunting, going from room to room, checking every shelf, table, cabinet top, and windowsill. I even looked in the bathrooms on top of the toilet tanks and around the sinks. I did not find my pretty little turtle.

I looked up Sylvia's phone number and called it. It was answered by her voice mail. I left a message, asking if she'd moved the turtle off the shelf by the front door. Tears leaked into the corners of my eyes. Without the turtle, how could I ransom Martha Todd? What would Name Unknown say when I showed up without the prize?

Maybe Al hadn't left home yet and could bring me his turtle if I called him. No, that wasn't possible. Al had said that his turtle had been smashed, maybe by the same goon who was holding Martha Todd, when his house was ransacked. I was, as they say in the Navy, S.O.L.

I decided to text Name Unknown and inform him of my dilemma. Maybe accuse him of already having the turtle and playing dirty little games with Martha and me. I opened the text that he'd sent to me and typed a reply that said my turtle was missing and hit send.

More waiting. No response. It occurred to me that Name Unknown might have used a burner phone and tossed it into the trash after our earlier exchange of messages. The only choice I had left would be to go to the meeting point empty-handed and to try to persuade a dangerous criminal to take mercy on my wife, who had done neither him nor his unknown employer any harm. If all my pleading failed, I would volunteer to take Martha's place as Name Unknown's hostage while she went home and tried to locate my turtle.

It was time for me to go. I put on a jacket, turned out the lights and opened the back door. Before I could pass through the open doorway, I was crushed by a person running full speed toward me. The force of the collision carried us both back inside.

"Close the door and make sure it's locked," said Martha Todd. "One of them is sure to be chasing me."

I pulled myself away from her and did what she had ordered. Then we wrapped our arms around each other, and she kissed my face and lips faster than I could keep up with, more times than I could count. When the kissing finally stopped, I could hear her breathing deeply and rapidly. "How did you get here?" I asked.

"I ran," Martha said.

"How far?"

"From a house on Summit Avenue to here. Must have been at least two miles—probably a little more."

"You ran all that way?"

"Marathon training paid off early."

"And they're chasing you on foot?"

"Most likely by car. I zigzagged over a block to a different street, so they must have lost me, but they'll know I was headed here. If I'd seen them behind me, I'd have banged on the door of the first house I came to."

While this conversation was going on, we were locked together in a slow-moving dance toward the living room. I pulled her down onto the couch with me and we started our own marathon of kissing again. When we came up for air, Martha said, "If they show up here, we should have some police waiting to greet them."

"Right," I said. I untangled my limbs from hers, pulled out my cell phone and punched in 911. I explained to the dispatcher that we were being threatened with a home invasion and would appreciate some police protection. She said she'd have a cruiser on the way in minutes and warned me not to open my door to anyone other than a uniformed officer. Like I needed that kind of warning!

When I returned to the sofa, Martha asked why all the lights were out. I told her I was just about to leave for Kowalski's to trade my turtle for her, but that I didn't have the turtle because I couldn't find it. I asked if she had moved it and she said that she had not.

"What is it with these turtles?" Martha said. "Why is whoever hired these bozos chasing all four of them?"

"I don't know," I said. "The guy who was holding you said something about bringing my turtle and 'everything,' but I have no clue what 'everything' is. The only turtle that had anything inside it was T.J.'s; the thumb drive that she waved at the audience and told them and the Moorhead TV news crew that she was putting into her turtle. They got that turtle with the thumb drive the Monday after the awards when they killed T.J., so I don't see any reason for them to be wanting all three of the others."

"This whole thing is crazy. They'll be after Al's turtle next."

"Oh, god! Al!" I grabbed the cellphone again and punched in his number. "They aren't here yet," he said when he picked up. "Where are you?"

"They aren't coming," I said. "I'm at home and Martha's with me. Come over and welcome her home."

"That's great! How'd she get away?"

"I don't know. She hasn't had time to tell me yet. Or how they caught her. Maybe she'll give us the whole story when you get here."

"I'm on my way to storyland."

"One other thing," I said. "Have some ID ready when you get here. There'll be cops looking for a home invasion waiting out front."

"Never a dull moment for a Turtle who wins a turtle," said Al. "One friendly landing force headed for the battle front."

I put away the phone and told Martha that Al was on his way to hear her tell us about her adventure. I also gave her a quick summation of the events at Al's house, including the smashing of his turtle.

"We should go and help them clean up the mess at their house when you get off work at noon tomorrow. And If Al's coming here tonight, why don't we turn on some lights?" Martha said. Duh! I had been so wrapped up in greeting her and having her safe at home that I was oblivious to the fact that we were still sitting in the dark.

I turned on the lights in the living room and on the front porch, and a few minutes later the doorbell rang. I looked out the front window, expecting to see Al and hoping not to see the bozos that might be pursuing Martha Todd. What I did see was a matching pair of uniformed police officers. The 911 dispatcher had promised that they'd be there and, because she'd said it would be safe to open the door for them, I opened the door for them and invited them in.

They introduced themselves as Officers Wheeler and Diehl and asked me why I was expecting a home invasion. When I'd finished telling the tale of the turtles and the turtle-jacking kidnappers as briefly as I could, they said they'd remain parked in front of the house for at least an hour. Martha and I escorted them to the door and as we stood in the doorway thanking them for their presence a black SUV slowed to crawling speed on the street in front of us, and then took off with a tire-squealing burst of speed.

"That's them!" Martha yelled. "That's their car!"

"I guess seeing our cruiser discouraged them from stopping," Officer Wheeler said.

"No point trying to chase them," said Officer Diehl. "They're out of sight and gone. We can hang around for an hour in case they decide to come back, if you want us to."

"We do want you to. And we're also expecting a visitor driving a gray Honda Accord," I said. "You can let him come in."

"We'll have to check him out," said Officer Wheeler. "What's the name on his ID?"

Three minutes later, Al parked his Honda behind the cruiser and was greeted by the officers when he got out. I was waiting with the door open when they'd finished checking Al's driver's license and waved him toward the porch steps.

"First time I ever had to show ID to get into this place," Al said. "You're becoming very exclusive."

"We're becoming very paranoid," I said. "The bad guys were about to stop here a few minutes ago, but they took off like a NASCAR driver when they saw the cop car sitting there."

"Cops did both of us a major service today," Al said. "Don't ever talk to me about defunding the police."

"What did they do for you?" Martha asked.

"Caught the person who threatened to kill Carol," Al said.

"Big day for Carol," I said. "I'll make us a pot of coffee and then Martha can tell us all about the big day that she had."

When the coffee was ready, I fished some chocolate chip cookies out of the jar and the three of us settled down in the living room, with Martha and me on the sofa and Al on an armchair facing us. "Okay, Goldilocks, tell us how a woman who is an expert at taekwondo was captured by the three bears," Al said.

"There actually were three of them," Martha said. "And one of them was as big as a bear." Al and I listened in silence while she told the story of her capture:

As I said, there were three of them. They were hiding behind cars in the parking ramp, near where I always park, and they came from behind me while I was walking to the elevator. Two of them grabbed my arms and whipped them behind my back and the third one, the really big one, stuck a very large knife in front of my face and ordered me to hold still. I wanted to kick him where it hurts the most, but the knife was so close to my eyes that I didn't dare move while the other two snapped my wrists together with a couple of those awful black plastic snap ties.

They marched me to the black SUV that we saw go past here tonight, wrapped a cloth gag tight around my mouth and blindfolded me and pushed me into a back seat. I tried hard to keep track of the turns they were making and when they went uphill on a curving road I had a feeling we were getting somewhere near Summit Avenue. When I got away tonight, I found out that I was right. It's a huge house, and it is on Summit.

Anyhow, they dragged and pushed me into the house and one of them—a bald guy who needed a shave—kept running his hand

over my ass while we went down a flight of stairs into the basement. We were in a small room when they took off the blindfold
and the gag and unstrapped my hands long enough to peel off my
coat. Then they snap tied me to the back of a wooden chair and one
of them took the picture that they sent to you. Then they all left the
room, and I heard them lock the door behind them, like I was going
to run away with the damn chair strapped to my back.

After what felt like a couple of hours, the three of them came
back. By then my shoulders were aching, my hands were numb, my
butt felt like it was bruised from sitting on that hard chair, and my
bladder was almost bursting. I told them that I needed to use a
bathroom right now and they laughed at me. I said if I didn't get
to a bathroom their chair and the rug it was sitting on were going
to get very wet in about two minutes. They didn't think that was
so funny. They unstrapped me from the chair and took the straps
off my wrists and two of them, one on each side holding an arm,
walked me to a half-bath right there in the basement. For a minute
I thought about locking myself in the bathroom, but I didn't see any
advantage in that, so I came out when I was finished, and they took
me back to where I'd been sitting and the bald guy with the stubble
managed to slide his creepy hand across my ass one more time before they strapped me back onto the chair.

They all left, locking the door again, and I sat there for hours
until the bald guy with the stubble, the one who'd been having so
much fun patting my ass, came back all by himself. He said the other two had gone to get some Big Macs for supper and I told him that
I needed to use the bathroom again. He laughed and said that I was
sure full of piss for a person who hadn't been drinking and I said a
drink would be nice, too. He told me to wait a minute and went off
to the bathroom and came back with a glass of water. He set the
glass down on a little end table beside the chair and made the mis-
take of unsnapping my snap ties.

Now it was just me and only one of them, without a knife blade pointing at my face. I stood up facing him, and he put his hands on my shoulders and said maybe we could have a little fun before the other two guys came back. I said that's a great idea and kicked him so hard that I don't think he'll ever have a family. While he was bent over with his hands wrapped around what was hurting, I gave him a couple of chops to the neck that put him on the floor. I told him thanks, that really was fun, then I grabbed my coat and my purse off the floor where they'd dumped them and started running, up the steps and out the door. When I got to the street, I could see the light of the Cathedral dome shining off to my right, which meant that I had to go left to get home. I never stopped running until I crashed into Mitch when he opened the back door.

When she was done telling her tale, Martha wrapped her arms around me and kissed me on both cheeks and the lips. This flurry of passion kept me from saying anything and Al did not interrupt us. When my lips were free and Martha's arms were no longer squeezing me, I asked, "Do you think the cops could catch these guys if you gave them the location of that house?"

"I don't know exactly which house it is," Martha said. "I only know that it's a big house on a street that has several miles of big houses lined up on it. I was blindfolded when those bozos took me into it, and it was dark when I ran out. I was in such a panic to get away that I didn't take time to look at the number on the house and I never looked back at it, so I don't even have a sense of the shape of the house. I got off of Summit at the first cross street I hit, and I wasn't paying any attention to the names of the streets I was crossing until I got all the way to Lexington. If I'd had my wits about me, I would have counted the blocks while I was running, but all I was thinking about was getting home behind locked doors before the Big Mac buyers came back and found their buddy all battered and bruised from his neck down to his nuts."

"Do you think there's a chance that you might recognize the house if we took a cruise up Summit Avenue?" I asked.

"Probably not. I ran down a wide set of stairs to get to sidewalk level, but just about every house on Summit Avenue has a wide set of stairs in the front. Anyhow, there's no way I want to go cruising anywhere near that house tonight."

"Maybe tomorrow afternoon, before we go to help Al and Carol," I said. Both Al and I would be working until noon on Saturday, and we also would be working Saturday night at the Winter Carnival Torchlight Parade. We'd both have next Monday off as comp time for the Saturday night assignment.

Al said that he'd better be getting back to helping Carol, bade us goodnight, and left. Minutes later, my cell phone buzzed. The caller ID read "SylviaCleans." I answered, thinking that Sylvia Valdez was returning my call asking about the turtle. I got a surprise.

"Oh, Mister Mitchell, I'm so embarrassed about the turtle, and I'm sure that you must also be worried about your cat," Sylvia said.

My cat! With Martha's escape from her kidnappers, I hadn't had time to think about the missing Sherlock Holmes, but I said, "Yes, I am worried about Sherlock. Do you know where he is?"

"He's at our house, Mister Mitchell. He snuck out of your house between Valerie's feet when we were leaving, and the door locked behind us so that I couldn't put him back inside. It was so cold out that I thought the best thing to do was to take him home with us where he'd be warm all day, so that's what we did."

"That's a great relief," I said. "I've been looking all over for him."

"I'm sorry about that," she said. "I meant to call you much sooner, but I had another cleaning to do this afternoon and Valerie's cold got worse at supper time, and it's just been one thing after another here. I'll put the kitty in my car right now and bring him back to you."

I decided to be Mister Nice Guy. "Don't drag poor Valerie out in the cold tonight," I said. "Wait until tomorrow morning. Martha will be home to let you in. I'm sure that Sherlock won't mind sleeping at your house for one night if you have anything at all for him to eat."

"He did a really good job of cleaning out a can of tuna," Sylvia said. "Didn't leave a crumb. Anyhow, I'll bring him back first thing tomorrow morning, along with the little wooden turtle you were asking about. Valerie brought it home from your house to take to show and tell."

I couldn't believe what I'd just heard. Valerie brought the turtle home from my house? To take to show and tell? I took a breath deep enough to suck in the amount of air needed to inflate a truck tire while I fought back the urge to shout my entire lexicon of four-letter words at Sylvia. When I'd regained control of my temper and was able to speak in a normal tone of voice, I said, "Valerie took my turtle home with her?"

"She wanted to take it to show and tell at kindergarten Monday because it was so pretty," Sylvia said. "I didn't see it in her backpack when we left your house, but I saw her take it out when we got home. I took it away from her and scolded her for taking it and put it up in the cupboard out of her reach. I'll be sure to bring it back to you tomorrow, along with your cat."

"Yes," I said. "Do be sure to bring that turtle with you when you bring Sherlock home." When I thought about what might have happened to Martha Todd if she hadn't escaped from her captors and I had not been able to swap my turtle for her release, I again wanted to scream profanities at Sylvia Gomez. Instead, I quietly said, "Thank you, Sylvia, and good night," and quietly put down my phone. Then I let out a primal scream so loud that Martha jumped up off the sofa and stared at me with fright-widened eyes.

15

HOUSE HUNTING

The first thing I did when I reached my desk Saturday morning was the same thing that thousands of others in the city and the suburbs were doing—reading Clue 9 of the Winter Carnival Treasure Hunt.

We had reliance on this man of science
To care for everything in wild and street
He was ever there for the land, water and air
A finer man, some say, you would never meet

The Winter Carnival was in its closing weekend, and this was the penultimate puzzle clue. Sunday's Clue 10 would be the last clue given before everyone was told exactly where the medallion was lying in wait for discovery on Monday morning.

I was still trying to figure out who the man of science might be when my desk phone rang. To my surprise, I saw that it was Brownie calling me. Was he calling with good news? Had he arrested the perpetrator of the turtle-jack killings?

"Dailydispatchmitchell," I said. "What have you got for me?"

"Homicidebrown," he said. "I've got sympathy and a question."

"Why sympathy?" I asked.

"I heard that your wife had a run-in with the turtle jackers."

"That's right, she did. And she also had a *runaway* from the turtle jackers after leaving one of them with a possible long-term reproductive disability."

"The runaway is in the report written by the men who staked out your house last night, but they didn't mention that she'd inflicted heavy damage on one of the bad guys."

"We didn't tell them all the gruesome groin smashing details of her escape. Does the report mention that the bad guys drove past our house and would have stopped if the cruiser hadn't been parked in front?"

"It does," Brownie said. "I'm glad that our officers were at the scene."

"Not half as glad as I am. You said you also had a question," I said. "What is it?

"My question is: can your wife lead a squad to the house where she was held?"

"She doesn't think she can," I said. "She was blindfolded when they took her in, and it was dark when she ran out and took off without ever looking back. We're planning to drive up Summit Avenue this afternoon and see if anything rings any bells."

"Why don't you take that drive in the back seat of a cruiser with a couple of uniforms in the front seat? It might be safer for you if the residents happen to see you going by."

"Good point. I'll accept your invitation for transportation on behalf of both of us. Now I have a question for you. Have you got any leads on who it is that's sending these creeps out after everybody's turtle?"

"I have only one answer for that. The investigation is still ongoing."

"Why am I not surprised?"

"What we really need to get hold of is that thumb drive that you said the killers got when they stole Ms. Kelly's turtle."

"Don't I wish we had that?" I said. "That thumb drive might also explain why they're after all the rest of the turtles. It's like there's something magic about the whole quartet. You've heard about Al's house being ransacked and his poor turtle being smashed to bits I assume."

"That story has been going around the building here," Brownie said. "The report said that a party ransacked the house, found the turtle, and then smashed it. Is that what he told you happened?"

"It is. Which turns the turtle-jacking spree into even more of a riddle. Why did they smash that turtle after tearing the house apart to find it? Why didn't they just take it, like they did with T.J.'s and Ben's? My first thought when I couldn't find T.J.'s turtle was that somebody—most likely somebody at Coordinated Copper & Nickel, Inc.—wanted the thumb drive that she'd put in it with great ceremony on stage the night the turtles were given to us. But now, with another turtle missing and a third turtle smashed, I wonder if it's maybe something about the four turtles and not about the thumb drive at all, which would take Coordinated Copper & Nickel, Inc., off the hook."

"Too many unanswered questions about turtles," Brownie said. "But I have one more question of a different kind for you."

"What is it?" I asked.

"Are you really telling me the truth about not knowing where the Treasure Medallion is?"

"I swear on a stack of newspaper stylebooks that I am. Only the two spooks who hide it and write the clues about where they've hidden it have the answer to that. Believe me, after last night's scare, if I could tell anybody where that medallion is, that anybody would be you."

"Well, thank you for that," Brownie said. "The Treasure Hunt must be running out of time, isn't it?"

"One more clue tomorrow, and if nobody finds it before the

Monday morning edition deadline there will be one last clue that gives specific directions to the hiding place. Then stand back and get ready to unscramble a traffic jam."

"My wife and daughter are out there hunting for a $5,000 prize while I'm wasting my time looking for somebody who has killed two people, kidnapped another person, and trashed a house looking for four turtles carved out of wood that you probably couldn't sell for twenty bucks apiece. It's a crazy goddamn world we live in, Mitch!" He paused; then, in a lower volume, he added, "Whatever. I'll have a pair of officers in a cruiser pick you up at fourteen hundred for a ride up Summit Avenue, if that time is good for you."

"Works for me."

"That's it then. Have a good day, Mitch."

"Uff-da!" I said as I put down my phone.

"What's with the uff-da?" asked Al, who had just arrived at my side with a cup of coffee in each hand. In Minnesota, the word uff-da can be used to express many emotions—surprise, happiness, disgust, fright, and, in this instance, relief.

"Brownie just blew off a kettleful of steam about the craziness of this world," I said. "He's frustrated about disappearing turtles and unfound Treasure Medallions."

"I can add a smashed turtle and a torn-up house to those frustrations," Al said. "When I finish this coffee, I'll be heading out for a couple of Winter Carnival shots, after which I'll be going home. See you at the parade tonight." We were assigned to cover the Vulcan Victory Torchlight Parade, which would get under way at 5:15.

When our coffee cups were empty, I called Martha and told her about the scheduled two o'clock police car ride and asked if Sylvia had brought back our cat and my turtle yet.

"She just called and said that Valerie has a fever of 104, so she's taking her to the emergency room this morning," Martha said. "She promised to bring everything back this afternoon. I'd better call her and tell her not to come before three or so."

At noon, I sent my last copy of the day to Ted Gambrell, the Saturday city editor, shut down my computer, put on my coat and went home for lunch and a Saturday afternoon ride in a police car, which arrived at precisely fourteen hundred.

Our driver introduced himself as Officer Palmer and the man riding in the shotgun seat as Officer Turner.

"Oh, this will be fun," said Martha as she settled into the back seat. "I've never ridden in one of these before."

Officer Turner laughed. "Most people who sit where you are do not consider it to be a pleasure trip," he said. "Usually, they're wearing handcuffs. Would you like a pair of those to make the experience more realistic?"

"No thanks," Martha said. "I've already had that experience. In fact, I was dressed that way without my approval when I was taken to the house that we're looking for."

"Okay, no cuffs," he said. "Sit back and enjoy the ride."

When we reached Summit Avenue, Officer Palmer turned eastward and said he would drive at normal speed so that the occupants of the house wouldn't think we were looking for them if they saw us pass by.

"I think I ran about two miles to get home," Martha said. "I could see the Cathedral dome off to my right when I got to the sidewalk."

We drove the length of Summit Avenue, eastbound, until we reached a Y intersection at Ramsey Street, where Summit turned left and went downhill, with Martha studying the houses on our right. As she had noted previously, all the houses were big and almost all of them had a set of wide front porch steps.

Three times she said, "That might be it!"

And three times she said, "No, I don't think it is."

We turned around at the Ramsey Street intersection because

Martha said she was sure that the house we were looking for was at this level, not on the downward slope of Summit. We went back toward Lexington Avenue, with Martha studying the houses that were now on our left. Finally, she said, "It could be any of three or four of them. I should have taken the time to look for the number last night."

"Which might have given them time to catch you before you got home," I said. "It's better that you started running without trying to make out the number in the dark."

"You don't know how many blocks you ran?" Officer Palmer asked.

"I wasn't counting them like I should have been," Martha said. "And I also zigged over to another street. All I had in mind was getting to our back door as fast as I could."

"I can understand that," he said. "The gentlemen chasing you might not have been too gentle if they'd caught you. Detective Brown said you wounded one of them severely when you made your escape."

"As I told Mitch, I placed a very hard kick where it will affect his ability to become a father. Also, I'm sure that he has a very stiff and sore neck today."

"Her hobby is taekwondo," I said.

"Obviously came in handy," Officer Palmer said.

"And footsie," I said.

Officer Turner parked the cruiser in front of our duplex and both officers got out and escorted us up the porch steps to our front door. "Let us go in ahead of you," Officer Palmer said. "In case you have uninvited visitors waiting for you to return."

That seemed like an excellent idea. "My pleasure," I said.

I unlocked the door and stood aside as the two cops charged in with weapons drawn and shouting, "Police!" Martha and I waited on the porch, listening as they circulated through both the ground floor and the second floor, shouting "clear" as they went. I felt like I was an actor in a TV crime show.

Officer Palmer came to the door and said that we could come in as soon as Officer Turner finished checking the basement. Soon Officer Turner appeared and announced that it was safe for us to enter.

Martha and I thanked them for the ride and their diligence, and they said it was all in the line of duty and departed.

"That was a lot of nothing," Martha said. "There were at least three possible houses in the area where it must have been, but I couldn't be sure about any of them. I certainly didn't want to send a squad of cops storming into a house where some poor innocent owner might have a heart attack."

"That would be front-page news," I said. "All the wrong kind of news."

Martha's cell phone rang. "It's Sylvia," she said before she answered. After a brief conversation, Martha put down her phone and said, "They'll be here with our cat and turtle in twenty minutes. Just time for a quick cup of tea before they get here."

"I hope they're not much later than that," I said. "The parade starts at 5:15, so if we're going to find a parking place anywhere near the parade route we need to be downtown by four o'clock, which means leaving here in full winter wraps by quarter to four at the latest."

The doorbell rang a few minutes before 3:30. I looked out the front window to make sure that the ringer was Sylvia before I opened the door. Sylvia came in with Sherlock Holmes in her arms, followed by Valerie, who was holding my turtle with both hands.

Sylvia put Sherlock down on the floor and without so much as a meow he ran straight to the kitchen where his food and water bowls are always on the floor. Sylvia laughed and I said, "That's a fine how do ya do. I guess we know what Sherlock's priorities are."

"I really didn't starve him," Sylvia said. "He had a full can of tuna."

"I guess home cooking is always the best, even with cats," I said.

Valerie handed the turtle to her mother, who held it out toward me. "As you can see, your turtle has not been damaged in any way. It's just the way Valerie found it, and the thumb drive that you're keeping inside is still in there, safe and sound. Valerie took it out, but I made her put it back in."

Two of the words she had spoken hit me like a hammer blow to the head. All I could do was babble them back to her. "Thumb drive?"

"Yes, the thumb drive you had inside of the turtle." Sylvia said.

16

LOST AND FOUND

Sylvia put the turtle into my hands, much like Chief Hardshell Turtle had done, but now both of those hands were shaking as I placed the right one under the turtle's belly and slowly lifted the shell off its back with the left. Lying there, inside the turtle that had been on display on a shelf beside the front door in my house for a week, was a little blue thumb drive.

I could have exploded. I turned to Martha and yelled, "Oh, my god! This has to be T.J.'s turtle."

"How did you get it?" Martha asked.

"We must have gotten them mixed up during the photo shoot when they were all on the same table together. Somebody who's desperate enough to kill two people, ransack a house and kidnap a woman has been looking for this thumb drive and it's been sitting here all this time. This explains why they kept hijacking turtles after they took T.J.'s. When they found out that the turtle they found in her apartment was empty, they had to keep on turtle-jacking the rest of us until they got the one with the thumb drive in it."

Sylvia was staring at me with a "what the hell's going on here" look in her eyes and Valerie had shrunk back away from me and wrapped her arms around her mother's legs. I needed to do some explaining.

"Four turtles that all look like this one were awarded to four of us at the *Daily Dispatch* for our efforts to stop a proposed nickel mining operation up north near the Native American Reservation," I said. "At the awards ceremony, T.J. showed this thumb drive to the audience, said it had information that would kill the nickel mine, and made a big show of putting it in her turtle. Someone who doesn't want what's on this thumb drive to be published in the paper has been stealing the turtles, which seem to have gotten mixed up during the photo shoot, looking for this thumb drive."

"I read about that in the paper," Sylvia said. "I saw the pictures with the turtles on a table and all of you holding your turtles. And didn't someone in the group get killed after that?"

"More than someone. Two turtle winners have been killed, and another one's home was ransacked when nobody was there. This little guy in my hands is the only one of the four that the turtle jackers haven't either stolen or smashed."

"Who would do such an awful thing?" Sylvia asked.

"Someone who doesn't want what's on this thumb drive to be printed in our paper," I said. "I can't say for sure, but I assume that it's someone who will profit in some way from the nickel mine because T.J. told me that what's on the thumb drive would blow that mine completely away. I'm hoping the thumb drive will tell me who wants it so desperately when I have a chance to look at it."

I looked at my watch, saw that it was close to our requisite four o'clock departure time, and added, "Unfortunately, I don't have time to look before we have to get downtown to cover the Winter Carnival Torchlight parade."

The Torchlight parade, which runs through the heart of downtown, is the climactic event of the Winter Carnival. It marks the end of the reign of that year's King Boreas, the Monarch of Wind, Snow, and Cold, and the ascension of Vulcanus Rex, the King of Fire and Warmth. This is the fulfillment of the carnival legend, in which the imperially-robed King Boreas and his fancily-clad Royal Guard rule over what to them is a winter paradise in Minnesota until they are defeated by Vulcanus Rex and his Mighty Krewe, all dressed head-to-toe in devilish red, so that the warmer weather of spring can return to the frozen northland.

All during the carnival, Boreas and his multitude of followers play host to a series of lavish events, including the appearance of the guest of honor, who currently is Lady T, while Vulcanus and his seven-man Krewe seem to be outcasts, riding about the wind-chilled city in the unenclosed rear half of an antique 1920s fire engine. But, as sure as spring always follows winter, the Winter Carnival under-dogs always emerge triumphant at the end.

Sylvia and Valerie departed after bidding us goodbye and good luck. Martha and I drove downtown, found a parking place six blocks away from the parade route, and went to meet up with Al and Carol near the multiple snowman-carrying float behind which the parade was forming. Before leaving home, we had selected and—in turn—rejected numerous hiding places for the thumb drive bearing turtle, which we now left wrapped in a blanket tucked under the driver's seat on the floor of the locked Honda Civic. If the turtle jackers broke into the duplex while we were away, that precious thumb drive would not be there for them to steal.

"Guess what I've got," I said when we met Al and Carol.

"A very cold nose?" Al asked.

"Well, yes, that, too," I said. "What I was wanting you to guess is shaped more like a thumb."

That got his attention. "Not a thumb drive?"

"Yes. And not just any thumb drive. It's *thee* thumb drive."

"Where did you get it?"

"It was in the turtle that's been sitting in my house for a week. Apparently, my turtle got switched with T.J.'s after they sat side by side to have their pictures taken."

"So the jackers didn't get the turtle with the thumb drive when they killed T.J."

"That's right. That's why they went looking for it at Ben's house and your house. The only question now is why they smashed yours instead of taking it like they did the other two."

"Maybe they were just pissed off because the thumb drive wasn't in it. So what's on the thumb drive that's worth killing people to get?"

"Didn't have time to look at it after we discovered that it was there. I suggest that we go to your house after we file our story and pics and stick it into my laptop for a look-see. I'm hoping it will tell us who hired the turtle jacking crew and why it's worth the hunt."

"My money is still on Coordinated Copper & Nickel, Inc." Al said.

"Mine, too, but the question is: If it is Coordinated C & N, who there is masterminding the job? Whoever it is deserves life in the slammer, along with the bastards who killed T.J. and Ben and kidnapped Martha."

With a shower of fireworks bursting in the air above us and a blast on the siren of the police motorcycle in front of the leading float, the parade began to move. Have I mentioned that I find parades to be boring? This one was no exception until the float carrying Lady T and Gigette came by. Lady T again was draped in multiple layers of black and brown furs, topped with the huge black Russian fur hat that made her look like an eight-foot-tall mate for Sasquatch.

We all waved, applauded, and shouted greetings at the great Lady as the float rolled past. She responded by raising her right hand in the tight-fingered, stereotype salutary gesture of a queen, which reminded me that she was of royal Hungarian blood. At her side was Gigette—again dressed in a blue knit ski hat, a blue ski jacket, blue ski pants, and blue ski boots—standing with her back to us, facing the opposite direction.

"Get a load of La Princess Gigette," I said to Al. "Giving us her backside!"

"At least she isn't mooning us," Al said.

"If she was, I'd eclipse that moon with an ice-coated snowball," I said.

"Gigette's hot stuff. That snowball would melt on contact."

"Did you get a shot of her back?"

"I did. I'll make a big print of it, and you can put it up on a wall and throw big icy snowballs at it the rest of the winter," Al said.

"That'll be cool," I said.

The parade went on ... and on ... and on, the way parades do. This one seemed twice as long as normal because where I really wished I could be at this moment was in Al's house with the turtle dwelling thumb drive plugged into my laptop. I knew it still would be a couple of hours—until the parade had ended, we had driven to Al's house, and I had written and filed my story—before my thumb drive wish would be granted.

It was nearly three hours before we'd finished all those actions. Sitting with my laptop on the dining room table, I described the parade in as few words as possible before sending my copy to the city desk. After all, what can a reporter say about the nighttime parade that he hasn't previously said about the daytime parade, other than that the nighttime parade was illuminated by millions of candle power produced by artificial means?

With one eye on the pretty little wooden turtle that was sitting on the table beside the laptop, I did my best to describe what I'd seen, including Lady T's royal gesture of acknowledgement. Al had an image of that gesture, which he emailed to the city desk. He also showed me the image of Gigette's back, which he did not email to the city desk. I managed to get my mind off the thumb drive by imagining myself snowballing a printed blowup of that image while I was waiting for Fred Donlin, the night city editor, to respond to my email.

Fred responded with a couple of questions that I was able to answer without having to dig through the notes I'd scrawled with cold stiffened fingers. He came back with a thank you and wished me a good night. Oh, if he only knew how good I was expecting this night to be.

With Martha seated on my right, Carol seated on my left, and Al looking over my shoulder, I transferred the thumb drive from the tummy of the pretty little wooden turtle to the proper slot on the side of the laptop and clicked on the icon that appeared. All four of us uttered a simultaneous groan.

On the screen before us was a blue rectangle containing a single two-syllable word: PASSWORD.

Al reacted first. "Why the hell would she do that?"

"Beats hell out of me," I said. "I guess she considered whatever's on it to be super-secret for her eyes only. Who wants to make the first guess at what the password is?"

"We'd better be careful with our guesses," Martha said. "Sometimes there's a limit to how many times you can be wrong before the file gets locked."

"That's right. And that limit is sometimes very tight, like maybe only three or four," Carol said.

Again, I asked, "Anybody want to give it a try?"

"I'm guessing that she'd use her initials, like she does on her by-line," Al said. "Something like TJK, maybe combined with something like 'mine' or 'nickel' after it."

I typed "TJKmine" into the space and clicked on NEXT. The response was a message printed in red: Incorrect Password.

"Anyone else have an idea?" I asked.

"Try nickelmine, all lower case," Martha said.

I typed that word in and clicked on NEXT. The response was a message printed in red: Incorrect Password.

"Wish we knew how many chances we have if there's a limit," I said.

"Wish we had a thousand monkeys typing all at once," Al said.

"What good would Shakespeare's plays do us?" I asked.

"He might have mentioned the password for a nickel mine in one of his plays," Al said.

"Forget the monkey business," I said and turned to Carol. "You haven't had a shot. Want to give it a try?"

"I've been thinking about how T.J. might have been thinking," Carol said. "She'd been writing about the Turtle Clan and trying to save a turtle habitat. Why don't you try the word turtle?"

"Turtle?" I said.

"Turtle," Carol said.

"Very possible," Martha said.

"Would that be with an upper-case T or all lower-case letters?" Al said.

"She wasn't *a Turtle*, so it might be all lower case," Carol said.

"But she was a newspaper writer, so she might have started with an upper-case T," I said.

"Try it with all lower case first," Carol said.

"Okay," I said. "It's your baby." I typed "turtle" into the square and clicked on NEXT.

17

HACKER'S HARVEST

Like the bud of a tulip unfolding its petals, the screen opened from darkness into a lighted presentation. Blossoming onto the screen before us was a display that showed a string of emails. By scrolling down and reading several of the address lines, we learned that the messages were a back-and-forth exchange between two senders: Bigdigger@gmail.com and Actionman@PPower.com.

"Looks like T.J. or somebody working with her hacked into somebody's email," Al said.

"And scooped up a pretty heavy download," I said.

"Could Bigdigger be someone at Coordinated Copper & Nickel, Inc., using a personal email account and not the company's?" Martha said.

"It has to be," I said. "That's who T.J. was investigating."

"That makes sense. But what could PPower.com be?" Carol asked.

"Maybe we can figure it out when we start reading them," I said.

"The time shown on the top message is later than the one below it, so you need to scroll all the way down and start with the bottom message," Al said. "If you don't, we'll be reading them backwards."

"I've always wanted to work my way to the top," I said.

"Getting to the top will make you the cream of the crop," Al said.

"Let's not milk this any further," I said. I started scrolling down and discovered that T.J. had captured a series of messages that the two emailers had exchanged over a period of three months, beginning in November of the previous year.

Actionman started the exchange by asking if there was any new information about the possible discovery of Cd. Bigdigger replied that tests had been ordered. The crew would bore through a thick layer of ice to sample material, which would be collected by the end of the week. Actionman's response was, "My superiors hope Cd will be available for use in very short time. Scheduling is important."

"Will expedite tests and give you results ASAP," said Bigdigger in reply.

Five days later, Bigdigger informed Actionman that "Cd tests positive. Will proceed ASAP." Actionman replied that superiors would be pleased.

"Bigdigger is really big on ASAP," Al said.

"Do you suppose he is one?" I asked.

"I'm pretty sure that he has to be anything but a sap to be involved in whatever the hell it is that they're talking about."

"What do you suppose Cd is?" Martha asked.

"I don't think it's the kind of CD that plays music," Carol said. "Might be a code for something. Or an abbreviation."

The next message was dated five days later. It came from Bigdigger: "Start of Cd production delayed by slow action on permit request."

Actionman replied: "Unacceptable. Must have Cd in time to meet production deadline here."

"Working on it," Bigdigger said. "Some hands must be filled with $$ before we can proceed on permit process."

"He's talking about bribing someone," Martha said.

"Fill hands quickly," wrote Actionman. "How much do you need?"

"Actionman's username is right on the money. He really does want action ASAP," Al said.

"And I'm betting that the money that he's right on comes in huge amounts," I said.

"I wish one of them would say what Cd stands for," Carol said. "It has to be an abbreviation or a symbol of some kind."

Al, who'd been bending over my shoulder to look at the screen, instantly straightened up and yelled," A symbol! That's it, Carol! Think about it. Bigdigger is digging something out of the earth. Think about your high school chemistry class. Think about the Periodic Table that we were supposed to memorize. Didn't Cd stand for something on that?"

I tried to visualize the Periodic Table that hung on the wall of our chemistry classroom. I'd never come close to memorizing it, but I was sure that I had seen Cd somewhere on that chart. Unfortunately, I couldn't come up with the name of a substance bearing that label.

Carol came to our rescue. "Doesn't Cd stand for cadmium?" she said.

"I'll find it in Wikipedia," Martha said, picking up her cell phone. A couple of clicks and a swipe later she said, "That's it! Cd *is* the symbol for cadmium. Atomic number 48 to be exact."

"What does Wikipedia say about cadmium?" I asked.

Martha began to read: "It's under a boldface head that says 'Nuclear fission.' Then it says: 'Cadmium is used in the control rods of nuclear reactors, acting as a very effective neutron poison to control neutron flux in nuclear fission. When cadmium rods are in-serted in the core of a nuclear reactor, cadmium absorbs neutrons, preventing them from creating additional fission events, thus con-trolling the amount of reactivity.'"

"So Bigdigger is goin' fission in the Rez's swamp," Al said.

"Fishin' for cadmium instead of nickel," I said.

"Fishin' with a new kind of bait and switch," Al said.

"Oh, god, listen to this," Martha said. "It says: 'Cadmium is one of six substances banned by the European Union's Restriction of Hazardous Substances directive, which regulates hazardous substances in electrical and electronic equipment.' Further down it says that the European Union's limit on cadmium use in electronics is 0.002 percent. And after that, it says that the International Agency for Research on Cancer has classified cadmium and cadmium compounds as carcinogenic."

"No wonder they're trying to disguise it as a nickel mine," Carol said.

"There's more bad news," Martha said. "It says that cadmium is found in sulfide-bearing rock and is mined using a technique called sulfide mining, quote, after which the mining operator must find ways to dispose of the substantial waste rock, unquote. And it's offering me a link to a Sulfide Mining Fact Sheet. That's the same process that's used in nickel mining, which you've already learned causes serious pollution."

"Dig up that fact sheet," I said. "See if it confirms the story I wrote."

"Got it," Martha said. She read silently for a moment and said, "Listen to *this* paragraph: 'Sulfide mining is different from traditional iron ore mines and taconite mining. Sulfide mines have never been operated safely – no mine of this type has been known to have operated and closed without polluting local lakes, rivers, or groundwater.'"

"Exactly," I said. "That could have come from the same study I quoted in my story."

"That's a pretty efficient round of pollution," Al said. "It would knock out everything on the Rez: turtles, walleyes, and people. Leaves nobody to go fishin' and nothin' to go fishin' for."

"Now I understand why T.J. was going to talk to the FBI before she wrote the story about these emails," I said. "Bigdigger@gmail. com is obviously trying to sneak something through that would never be given a legal permit in that part of Minnesota."

"I can see why the FBI would be involved with that kind of crime," Al said. "But you were thinking that the mining project might be why Lady T suddenly arrived on the scene. She only deals in international crime."

"Could it be that Actionman@PPower.com is located in some other country?" I said.

"Maybe that's it. A country starting with P, maybe? Like Peru or Portugal or ... what other countries start with P?"

"Polynesia? No, that's not a country," I said. "How about Paraguay? Or Panama?"

"I'm Petered out," Al said.

"Let's read the rest of these emails," Martha said. "That might help us figure it out."

We returned our attention to the laptop screen and read a succession of messages:

Bigdigger: "Important palms crossed with $$. Waiting for results."

Actionman: "We don't have time to wait."

Bigdigger: "No option. Can't bring in equipment w/o permit. Indian chief is objecting to swamp drain and nosey newspaper in St. Paul is getting involved with pollution bullshit."

Actionman: "Will $$ to more palms solve problem?"

Bigdigger: "Top Indian boss refused $$. Too many people involved in paper's attack to offer $$ to stop. Might backfire on us."

Al interrupted with, "He's got that right. If he offered anybody here a bribe the story would be on the front page the next day, with the company's name in big headline type."

Several days went by before the next exchange was made. If

started with Bigdigger: "Problem worse. Permit process put on in-definite hold because of newspaper stories and editorials."

Actionman: "Can paper be persuaded to stop?"

Bigdigger: "Doubt it. Pictures and editorials have people feeling sorry for poor little Indians living by swamp."

Actionman: "You need to push harder for permit. Must get started."

Bigdigger: "My people talking with permit agency every day. Indians plan to give prizes to newspaper for causing hold on permit."

Actionman: "Fuck Indians and newspaper. Get Cd plan moving."

Bigdigger: "Can't clean out swamp until we get equipment on site to break up thick cover of ice. Everything frozen solid. Will be like breaking up concrete. Doing everything we can to get permit so we can bring in equipment and get started chopping through ice."

Actionman: "Maybe we need to get new contractor."

Bigdigger: "New contractor would have same problem with waiting for permit. Damn newspaper stirred up everybody. They're getting prizes from Indians next week for trying to save swamp for turtles."

The last message was dated January 18, two days before those of us from the "damn newspaper" were rewarded for our words and pictures with pretty little hand-carved turtles from the "poor little Indians" on the Rez.

I pulled out the thumb drive, put it back into the turtle, and said, "I wonder who exactly Bigdigger is. If he's at Coordinated Copper & Nickel, Inc., what link does he occupy in the chain of command?"

"Must be pretty high up," Al said. "Maybe all the way at the top?"

"We need to find out," I said. "Let's look at their website and see if there's any obvious officer of obfuscation in the pecking order."

I opened the website for CCNI, whose office was in Pittsburgh, and clicked on the button that said Administration. Up popped a row of mug shots, topped by that of a man with a flowing dark brown handlebar moustache who was identified as Chief Executive Officer Kurt S.C. Turner.

"Hey, I've seen that face," Al said.

"How could you? He's in Pittsburgh," I said.

"I swear I've seen him in St. Paul."

"Where in St. Paul?"

"I don't know. Hey, wait a minute! Maybe it wasn't St. Paul. I think I *do* know where it was. Let me get my phone."

He ran to another room and hurried back carrying his cell phone. "I had this in my pocket at the turtle award ceremony and I snuck some pics of the audience while we were waiting to get our turtles," he said while flipping through the images on the phone's screen. He stopped at one and swiped it with his fingers to blow it up to full screen.

"Yes! Here he is," Al said, shoving the camera up to my face. "There's that big brown handlebar perched right there in the second row."

Sure enough, there he was. There was no mistaking the big brown handlebar decorating the face of the man sitting in the second row behind a much shorter resident of the Rez.

"You're right; it wasn't St. Paul. The son of a bitch was at the turtle awards on the Rez," I said. "I'll bet you anything that he's our Bigdigger."

"I won't bet against you on that," Al said. "Now we also need to find out what PPower.com is and where Actionman is located."

"What we *really* need to do is talk to Lady T about these emails the first thing tomorrow morning," I said.

"I'll see you at the hotel at eight o'clock," Al said. "Hope the Lady is up by then after that long cold ride in the parade."

"If not, we'll have Gigette get her up," I said.

"Good luck with that," said Martha.

On the way home, Martha said she was wondering if we'd been visited by any uninvited guests while we were away, and whether they might be waiting for us to join them. I confessed that I'd been wondering the same thing. When we arrived there, I was pleased to see a marked police car parked in front of the duplex as we went past it on the way to the alley that led to the blacktop pad in front of our garage. Unless someone was waiting for us in the dim light of the alley or by the back door, we were safe at home.

18

NEAR MISS

After a peaceful night—there had been no uninvited visitors—Martha and I awoke to the buzz of an alarm clock at seven o'clock Sunday morning.

"Uff da," I said. "Why'd we set this thing so early?"

"Because you and Al have an eight o'clock date at the St. Paul Hotel," Martha said.

"I'd never date Al; he's not my type," I said. "But I would enjoy a visit with Lady T and even with snooty little Gigette."

"You aren't fooling me; you enjoy a chance to look at *cutie* little Gigette, whether she ignores you or not," Martha said. I couldn't truthfully plead not guilty to this charge.

I got up and looked out the window. Big fluffy white snowflakes were falling past it an angle that told me they were being influenced by a moderate wind.

"Are we having a blizzard?" Martha asked.

"No. Plenty of snow but not enough wind for a blizzard. Just a normal Winter Carnival snowstorm, but it's enough to increase my driving time to the hotel."

"Better get going," Martha said from the bed. "Should you give Lady T a call to set up a time for the meeting before you go?"

"That would give her a chance to tell me not to come. If we start with a knock on her door and say we have something that might interest her non-public persona, it will be harder for her to send us away."

"I sure hope she lets you in and can tell you what's going on with the cadmium email discussion. Drive carefully. I'll fix us some breakfast when you get back." With that, she rolled onto her right side, pulled the covers up to her chin and closed her eyes. I leaned down, kissed her on the exposed left cheek, and started getting dressed. No need to wear a suit and tie for today's mission, just jeans, a turtleneck pullover, and a sweater.

I put on my most protective winter storm parka, tucked my turtle into one of the two voluminous side pockets, grabbed my laptop in its case, and went out to my car. Enough snow had fallen to make the streets slick enough to skate on. The drive to the hotel took twice as long as it would on dry streets, but I was parking in the hotel's ramp by 7:58, according to the dashboard clock. Al, whose distance from downtown was about the same as mine, was waiting in the lobby when I arrived. He looked at his watch and said, "What kept you?"

"Slept late," I said. "Mother Nature punished me for being lazy by greasing the streets."

"You can't fool Mother Nature," Al said.

"I just hope we aren't fooled and sent away by Mother T-Khuppschane. This cadmium mining project, disguised as a nickel mine, just has to be the real reason for her surprise trip to St. Paul."

We arrived at the door of Lady T's suite, and I knocked with authority. With a clear tone of annoyance, the familiar voice of Gigette asked, "Who eez eet?"

I told her who we were and said that we had information that we thought would be of value to Lady T.

"Wait one mo-*ment*," was the reply.

I waited, and after one mo-*ment*, Gigette said, "Lady T wishes to know what this information is about."

"Tell her it's about cadmium," I said.

"Wait one mo-*ment*," she said. One mo-*ment* later, she opened the door, stood aside, and said, "Lady T grants you permission to come in."

It was clear that Lady T and Gigette had been awake and active for some time. Both were fully dressed—Lady T in a voluminous heavy green wool sweater and gray slacks, and Gigette in a heavy blue wool sweater and blue slacks. Five suitcases—two of carry-on size and three that would require substantial space in the air-craft's cargo hold—stood on end on the floor near the door. Two winter wraps--one extra-large minky-looking fur coat and one medium size blue woolen coat—were laid out on the bed. A pet carrier containing a Corgi named Laddie T was sitting beside the suitcases.

"Good morning, Lady T and Mademoiselle Gigette," I said. "It looks like you're almost ready to depart from our fair city."

"Good morning, Mister Mitchell and Mister Jeffrey. Lady T and Gigette were ready to depart from this fair city ten minutes ago," said Lady T. "However, Lady T received call from Delta Airlines five minutes before her taxi was scheduled to arrive, informing her that because of heavy snowstorm in eastern portion of United States, all flights into New York City, where Lady T and Gigette are scheduled to board flight to Budapest, have been cancelled. This is most dis-turbing turn of events for Lady T, who has television commitment for Monday afternoon in Budapest."

"Lady T's departure ten minutes ago would have been most dis-turbing to Mister Mitchell," I said. "He ... uh ... *I* have something to show you that I believe will be of interest to you in your non-public line of employment."

"What makes you think that is so, Mister Mitchell?" Lady T asked.

"The mysterious nature of the emails on the thumb drive I want to show you and the fact that the word 'cadmium' got us into this room."

I pulled the laptop out of its case and set it up on a desk that stood in one corner of the suite. Then I pulled the turtle out of my coat pocket and set it on the desk beside the laptop, opened it and pulled out the thumb drive. "What's on this thumb drive has gotten two people killed and has two others, Al and me, needing police protection," I said.

As I started to plug the thumb drive into its socket, Lady T said, "Before you start this ... what do you gentlemen of the press call it? ... dog and pony show? ... why don't you gentlemen take off your coats? It's quite warm in this room."

My armpits were already wet with sweat, so I welcomed the invitation to remove our coats. Al and I both took off our coats and laid them on the bed beside those of Lady T and Gigette. Then I plugged in the thumb drive, opened it with the password "turtle," scrolled all the way down to the first email, and invited Lady T to sit down and read the chain of emails between Bigdigger and Actionman. Al and I stood behind her while she read, and Gigette sat down on the bed beside the coats.

Lady T read the entire exchange without changing her blank facial expression or uttering any comments. When she had finished reading, she rose from the chair, turned to me, and said that as an agent of Interpol she was taking custody of this thumb drive as evidence of an attempted international crime. As she plucked the thumb drive from the slot on the laptop, I mentally patted myself on the back for having the foresight to download a copy of its contents onto the laptop.

"How did you obtain this thumb drive?" Lady T asked.

"Accidentally. It came from a reporter who intended to use the information in it for a story after checking it out with our FBI. She was killed by someone looking for the thumb drive that she'd put into her turtle, but her turtle had been accidentally switched with mine."

"Lady T can well understand why someone would kill for this thumb drive."

"That's what I was hoping. What can you tell me about this series of messages about cadmium?" I asked.

"As an officer of international law, Lady T can tell you very little," she said.

"Can you tell me what international crime is involved?"

She sighed. "Lady T can tell you that she believes Actionman is located in a country to which the sale of cadmium is banned by the American government."

"Can you give me a hint about what country that is?"

"In confidence, and not for publication, Lady T can only tell you that she believes that the first 'P' in PPower stands for Persian."

"Persian Power? That would be Iran," I said. "Selling anything pertaining to nuclear power to them would be a major crime. Can you tell me who Bigdigger at gmail is? Is he an official at Coordinated Copper & Nickel, Inc.?"

"Lady T does not know the answer to that question," she said. "That answer will be next step in investigation. Lady T can only surmise that it is someone in the corporation's administrative structure. Probably someone quite high up."

"Such as the CEO?"

"Lady T cannot be certain at this time. It also could possibly be major shareholder who owns controlling interest in the company."

At this time. The standard law enforcement officer's method of dodging a question.

"If it helps you any, Al has an image on his phone showing the CEO of Coordinated Copper & Nickel, Inc., attending an event on the Ojibwe Reservation last Saturday."

"Lady T would be most grateful for copy of this image," Lady T said.

"Tell me your number and it's yours," Al said. A minute later, the message had been sent and received.

Next came my biggest question. "Would I be accurate if I wrote a story about this exchange of emails for our next edition and attributed the identification of the messengers and the designation of the proposed transaction as an international crime to an unidentified reliable investigative source?"

"Lady T believes that you would be only partially accurate and fully too hasty to publish such a story in your next edition," Lady T said.

"Why do you say partially accurate?"

"Because you do not know name and official position of Bigdigger, and you know nothing about name, official position, and actual location of person identified as PPower. Remember that Lady T has said that word 'Persian' is not for public knowledge at this time."

Again with the "at this time." I thought about what she'd said for a minute before asking, "If I do some bigger digging and can find out for certain who Bigdigger is, would I be in a position to do a story attributing the big digging crime perpetrator and the unidentified foreign location of PPower to an unidentified reliable source?"

Lady T shook her head in a robustly negative response. "Lady T believes that you should leave the, as you call it, digging, to agency she represents and await her identification of Bigdigger."

"What if I go ahead and do the extra big digging and don't wait for your official word? Would that damage your agency's case against either party in any way?"

Lady T frowned, sighed, and looked into my eyes. "Lady T believes that you are an overly ambitious man, Mister Mitchell. She sees trouble for you in your proposed digging, but she does not have the authority to prevent you from doing that digging."

"So it's safe for me to go ahead?"

"No, is not at all safe. You, yourself, have told Lady T that already two people have been killed and that you and Mister Jeffrey are under police protection because of what is on this thumb drive. Lady T believes that any digging that you pursue in efforts to uncover Bigdigger's identity will almost certainly result in attempt to prevent you from publishing that information."

That scenario was worth thinking about. "Can I count on Lady T staying in touch with me and providing information on this case when she ... you ... are back in Budapest?" I asked.

"You may count on Lady T to maintain contact with you from Budapest, Mister Mitchell," she said. "Lady T is most grateful for information you have provided this morning and will be pleased to assist you in accuracy of your eventual story, if there is one, even though Lady T must never be revealed as source of information."

"Then maybe I'll back off and preserve my neck from possible slitting," I said.

"Lady T believes that would be excellent choice, Mister Mitchell."

"One more thing," I said. "I promised our local police that I would give them access to that thumb drive if I found it. Are the local police aware of your secret status?"

"Local police not aware of it, and must not be made aware of it, Mister Mitchell."

"Okay," I said. "I won't tell them where the thumb drive went. In fact, what's on the thumb drive wouldn't be much help to them in their mission, which is solving the two homicides. It almost confirms the suspicion that Coordinated Copper & Nickel was involved in the turtle-jack killings but it doesn't name an individual responsible for hiring those hit men."

"Is excellent observation, Mister Mitchell," Lady T said. "Now Lady T must see about making arrangements for another flight to Budapest. Lady T is still hoping to depart from what you call your fair city sometime today if unfair weather allows flights to resume."

Gigette had our parkas in her hands before Lady T finished that sentence. She nodded to each of us as she handed us our wraps and opened the door to assist in our departure.

"May you have a very boring flight when you're finally able to get one," I said.

"Thank you," said Lady T.

"Au 'Vois," said Gigette as she shut the door behind us.

As we walked toward the elevator, Al said, "That's what's known as a near miss. If their flight hadn't been cancelled by the snowstorm out east, they'd have already been gone when we got to the hotel."

"It's an ill blizzard wind that blows somebody some good," I said.

"I think you snowed Lady T with your little blizzard of fibs. You're not really going to give up trying to find out who Bigdigger is, are you?"

"I did tell Lady T a teeny tiny little white fib about that," I said.

"Let's hope you're not heavily punished for telling that light little lie," he said.

When I got home, I found Martha Todd sitting at the kitchen table drinking coffee and reading the *St. Paul Sunday Dispatch*. "You looked so comfy when I left that I wasn't sure you'd be up yet," I said. I took off my snowy coat and hung it up to dry on the tall rack beside the front door.

"I got to thinking about what was on that thumb drive and couldn't go back to sleep. Those puzzling email signatures kept running through my mind."

"Speaking of puzzling, what's Clue 10 got to say about where the Treasure Medallion can be found?" I asked after a hug and a kiss.

"There's a lot of information in it, but I can't square up any of it with any place that I know," Martha said. She handed me the front page and I read the clue.

Movie stars and candy bars
Plus grain that's sweet to eat
Find them all, and you'll have a ball
And score a great prodigious feat

"You're right. There's a lot there, but it doesn't ring any bells," I said.

Martha fried some bacon and scrambled some eggs, and we ate our Sunday brunch, topped off with some still-warm caramel rolls that she'd put into the oven minutes before I arrived home. Then it was time for my routine Sunday call to my mother and Grandma Goodie on the farm near Harmony.

"Why aren't you covering the big celebration?" Mom said when she answered.

"What big celebration?" I asked.

"The one going on at your paper. I'm watching it on the TV news. Breaking news, as they call it."

"What kind of news is breaking?"

"There's a bunch of people whooping it up because two guys with long hair and beards found the Treasure Medallion this morning and they've brought it to the office to collect the reward."

"Did they say where they found it?"

"Yah, they did. It was somewhere in some park named after somebody who used to be important about something."

"Thanks. That really nails it down," I said.

"Glad that I could give you all the details," Mom said.

"You always were right on the money with the details." We chatted for a couple of minutes about such major topics as the weather and the condition of the roads before the critical moment arrived. She passed the phone to Grandma Goodie, and I knew what the opening question would be.

"Warnie Baby, did you go to church this morning?"

"No, Grandma Goodie, I did not. I actually had to go to work this morning."

"They can't make you do that on the Sabbath, can they?"

"It was sort of an emergency," I said. "I had to catch someone for an interview before she flew away."

"You should be more concerned about your chance for salvation flying away," Grandma Goodie said.

"I'm counting on you to clip my salvation's wings by putting in a good word for me every Sunday while you're sitting in your pew in Harmony Methodist."

"I won't be around, sitting in my pew in Harmony Methodist, every Sunday forever, Warnie Baby. One of these years my soul will be flying away, and you'll be left on your own to save your own."

"I'm confident that you'll be occupying that pew for many more years of Sundays. I'm more worried about the baseball season coming up. Pitchers and catchers will be reporting for spring training two weeks from tomorrow."

That diversionary tactic got us off the troublesome topic of salvation and onto Grandma Goodie's other favorite subject: the seemingly unsavable Minnesota Twins. She's been an avid fan of that team since 1961, its first season in Minnesota. We talked about the Twins for another five minutes and ended by agreeing that the team was in for another mediocre season because the tightwad owners would not ante up the multi-million dollars needed to build a World Series contender. I would have suggested that Grandma Goodie pray for new ownership, but I didn't want to get her going on anything churchlike again.

19

SPEAKING OUT

The snow had stopped falling sometime during the night and the streets had been plowed and sanded by the time I left for work. I was lugging my laptop and was eager to show Don O'Rourke the tale of T.J.'s turtle the minute I got in, but he greeted me with, "Don't take off your coat. You and your twin are going to Roseville High School right now."

"What's happening at Roseville High School?" I asked.

"A big protest," Don said. "Hundreds of students are outside protesting the book ban that the school board just passed."

"Sounds like fun," I said. I put my laptop on my desk and joined Al on the way to the elevator. We picked up a staff Chevy at the *Daily Dispatch* garage and Al drove to the school in Roseville. He said that Carol had called him to report the students' mass protest. "She was happier than a cat with a bowl full of tuna and cream," Al said.

"She didn't instigate the protest, did she?" I said. "That could backfire on her when it's over."

"No, no," Al said. "She was as surprised as the superintendent and the principal were when hundreds of kids showed up with protest signs this morning."

When we arrived at the school building, we found the front

entrance blocked by what appeared to be at least half of the 2,000 teenagers enrolled in the district's ninth-through-twelfth-grade high school. Hundreds of them were waving signs calling for freedom to read and the banishment of book bans. Two police cars were parked on the opposite side of the street and two uniformed officers stood beside each car watching the lively but peaceful throng of protesters. The police presence was merely for show, as the mood among the milling students was more festive than fierce.

Al started shooting pics and I waded into the swarm and started talking to protesters. I chatted with ninth-graders, sophomores, juniors, and seniors, getting quotes about free choice, tolerance of other colors and cultures, and the values of diversity, and asking who had organized the protest. Nobody I talked to could tell me who the organizer was until a senior who said his name was "Charlie Black, not Brown," pointed to a tall girl with waist-length blond hair who was carrying a sign so large that she needed both hands to hoist it above her head. "She's the leader," he said. "She thought this up last week and spread the word though all the classes; got everybody charged up to do it today." I asked Charlie Black, not Brown, what her name was, and he said, "Sarah Nordstrom. Her dad's on the school board."

Great story! "Was her father one of the board members who voted against the book ban?" I asked.

"No, he was one of the members who voted *for* the book ban," Charlie said. "In fact, I think he was the one who made the stupid motion."

Greater story! I had to talk to Sarah Nordstrom and Al had to get a shot of her waving that humongous sign, which said "11th Commandment: Thou Shalt NOT Ban Books." We wove our way through the bodies until we were close enough to call out her name. She smiled and waved the sign with additional vigor while Al shot a picture that was destined for the front page of the *Daily Dispatch*.

I introduced myself and Al, and said, "I was told that your father is on the school board and that he made the book ban motion. Is that correct?"

"Yes, sir, it is," she said. "I told him that he'd be sorry if he made that motion and he said 'no way,' because the majority of the parents were on his side. I told him that he should check on how many of the kids were on his side before he voted."

"How do you think he'll react to what you're doing?"

"Oh, boy, I don't know," Sarah said. "He might be really mad at me for putting this demonstration together, but I was really mad at him for making that awful motion, so I guess we'll be even."

"Is anybody else in your family involved in this demonstration?"

"Yeah, my brother Stan is right over there." She pointed at a slender blond boy about five yards away who was displaying a sign almost as big as his sister's. "He's only a sophomore, so Dad will probably excuse him for being here because he was dragged into this disgraceful demonstration by his big pain-in-the-butt sister, but he actually helped me spread the word about the demo through the classrooms."

I asked her for her father's name, which was Hjalmar Nordstrom, and cell phone number, which she gave me with a questioning look. "I'm going to call him and ask for his reaction," I said. "Is that okay with you?"

"Doesn't matter if it's okay with me," Sarah said. "We're here demonstrating for free speech and open discussions about all topics, so it would be pretty weird for me to ask you not to call him."

"You're a very brave protest leader," I said. "I hope your father realizes that he's got a very smart and courageous daughter."

"Could you please remind him of that when you call him?" Sarah asked.

"Absolutely," I said. "I'm on your side all the way."

"Me, too," Al said. "And, by the way, I'm married to Ms. Jeffrey, the English Lit teacher."

"Oh, my god!" Sarah said. "Ms. Jeffrey is wonderful! Being in her class and talking to her is what got me started on this whole thing. She's one of my favorite teachers."

Al turned toward me. "Better not put that quote in your story. The powers that be might not think that Carol is so wonderful for inspiring a student protest."

"I will yield to your censorship request," I said. "And speaking of the powers that be, we should be finding our way inside and be talking to some of those powers."

I pointed toward the front door and yelled, "We need to go inside, kids." Sarah made a swooshing motion with the sign above her head, and like the Red Sea parting before the fleeing Israelites, a pathway opened in front of us. Uttering "thank you" and "good luck" all along the way, we strode to the front door without obstruction.

The mood changed at the front door, which was closed and blocked by two husky men dressed in khaki coveralls. "Nobody goes in," one of them said, folding his arms across his chest for emphasis.

We both showed him our press credentials, and I said that we were not protestors and that we needed to get a statement about the protest from the principal. "Nobody goes in," the man with folded arms said again.

"How about you asking the principal if he'd be willing to talk to the St. Paul paper," I said.

"How about the St. Paul paper just turning around and going back where they belong?" he replied.

"We are where we belong," I said. "We need to give the administration a chance to comment on the situation before I write my story."

"Maybe they don't have no comment," the gate guardian said.

"Maybe they should be given the opportunity to make that decision," I said.

"All I know is, we've got orders that nobody goes in."

"All I'm asking is that you check with whoever gave that order to see if *nobody* includes a reporter who has at least two dozen comments about the book ban from the protesting students out here."

"All I got to say to you is I ain't going nowhere and nobody goes inside."

Al said, "Thanks to Carol, I've got the school office's phone number on my phone. I'll call it and see if I can get us in." He called the office number, was relayed through a three-link chain of command to someone who finally gave him an answer, and said, "Bingo," when he ended the call. A minute later a woman opened the door behind the blockers and waved for us to enter.

"See ya later, alligator," I said as I passed the man with the folded arms.

"After while, crocodile," Al said as he followed me through the door.

When I looked back over my shoulder, I saw the personification of the cliché "if looks could kill."

Our greeter told us that she was the assistant principal and we followed her to the principal's office. There we met Principal Everett Swanlund, who handed me a sheet of paper with his official comment printed on it and posed rather grudgingly for Al to take a mug shot.

I read the statement, which was noncommittal about his opinion of the protesters but also voiced his approval of the school board's action. I asked, "Off the record, Mister Swanlund, how do you really feel about the kids putting on this massive demonstration."

"Can I trust you not to print what I say to that?" Swanlund asked.

"Absolutely."

He thought for a moment before he said, "I'm very proud of the demonstrators and I happen to agree with them, but as an administrator who reports to the school board I can't condone the fact that they're skipping classes and creating a disruption of the educational process. I do hope that you understand the position I'm in."

"The old 'between a rock and a hard place?'" I said.

"You've got it," Swanlund said. "It's a very uncomfortable place. I expect at least some members of the school board will be demanding that I punish the demonstrators in some way, which will mean punishing the whole school population because I can't very well take roll call out there in front of the building."

"I know what you mean. I'll be calling one of those board members for a comment in a few minutes."

"You're not calling Hjalmar Nordstrom, I hope."

"He's the very one I'm calling. His daughter gave me his cell phone number."

"Oh, brother! I knew Sarah was gutsy but she's even gutsier than I thought she was," the principal said.

"She truly believes in the First Amendment," I said.

"I wish her the best," Swanlund said. "I'm sure she'll be paying for her faith in some way, either at school or at home or both."

We thanked the principal and his assistant and returned to the front door, half expecting to be told that "nobody goes out." We encountered no exit blockade, however, and we gave a cheery farewell wave to the two intrepid guardians of the gate as we went down the front steps and started toward the reopening tunnel of teenagers. The man with folded arms unfolded them and returned our farewell wave, but used only one extended finger to do so.

"Here goes with old Hjalmar," I said as Al started the Chevy.

"Don't forget to congratulate him on raising a really cool daughter," Al said.

"I'll lead the cheers for Sarah and hope they cool off her daddy." I punched in the number and got Hjalmar Nordstrom's voice mail instructing me to leave my name and number and promising to get back to me. Bitten again by the bane of all reporters.

I was back at my desk, almost finished writing my story, when Hjalmar Nordstrom returned my call. "If you're calling about the demonstration at the high school today, I have no comment," he said before I could ask for one. "I do want to know how you got my number. The school isn't supposed to give it out."

"Didn't get it from the school," I said. "One of the demonstrators was kind enough to give it to me."

"Oh, god! I suppose it was Sarah."

"Yes, it was Sarah. She is very smart and very brave, and she believes that the Constitution gives you the right to comment on the students' protest action this morning, whether you agree with it or not."

"You know damn well I don't agree with it."

"Is that for publication, Mister Nordstrom?"

"Oh, damn it, yes, it is! Everything but the 'damn.' I'm going to see to it that every demonstrator is punished for wasting a school day with that nonsense."

Now that I'd received a comment from the man who had no comment, I decided to take the question one step further. "How about at home?" I asked. "Two of your children are involved."

"It's only Sarah that needs to be reckoned with at home. Stan is just following the lead of his loudmouth, disobedient, off-the-wall sister," Nordstrom said. "And you don't need to print any of that as part of my statement. Have a good day, Mister Michael."

"It's Mitchell," I said, too late to beat the beep of his phone shutting off. How about that Sarah? What she had predicted about her father's reaction was right-on, except the pejorative description of herself that she'd expected me to get from him was less volatile than "pain-in-the-butt big sister."

As I added Nordstrom's promise to punish every demonstrator for "wasting a school day," to my notes, it occurred to me that the time spent on whatever was chosen as punishment would waste at least part of another school day. Ah, if only I could be writing commentary for the Opinion page instead of a straight news story.

When I'd finished my straight news story and sent it to the city desk, I turned my attention to the material on my laptop. Before discussing it with Don, I had two calls to make—one to Brownie, offering to email him a copy of what I'd downloaded from the turtle-borne thumb drive, and one to Kurt S.C. Turner, the top man at Coordinated Copper & Nickel, Inc., asking if he was acquainted with anyone employed at his place of business who might identify himself in an email as Bigdigger.

First, I made the phone call to Brownie. Of course he was happy to accept my offer of the tale of the turtle, and of course he said that he would like to have the thumb drive to use as evidence in his two homicide cases. I managed to delay telling him that the thumb drive was no longer available by saying that I would deliver it to him when a suspect or suspects were identified and the need for this evidence arose. This, I hoped, would give me time to prepare an explanation that did not identify Lady T as the present custodian of the thumb drive.

I did not expect an equally cordial response on my next call, which was to Consolidated Copper & Nickel, Inc. I punched in the number and was greeted by the standard recorded menu of numbers to press for half a dozen various offices. Nothing on this list mentioned the CEO, so I tried pressing zero for operator and got a person with a husky voice who said that her name was Madge and asked how she could help me.

"You can connect me with Mister Turner, please," I said.

"Do you have an appointment to speak with Mister Turner?" Madge asked.

"No, I'm afraid that I don't usually deal with phone calls by appointment."

"Mister Turner is a very busy man and gives priority to calls that have been pre-arranged in advance by his secretary."

I subdued the urge to comment on this bit of redundancy and asked, "Can you forward me to his secretary?"

"One moment, please," she said.

A click and two rings later a much more feminine voice said, "Mister Turner's office. This is Caroline. How can I help you?"

"You can connect me with Mister Turner, please," I said.

"What time is your appointment, sir?" she asked.

"I have no appointment. I'm a reporter calling from the *St. Paul Daily Dispatch* with a question about the proposed nickel mine in northern Minnesota."

"The next available time to speak with Mister Turner is 1:35 p.m., Eastern Standard Time. Shall I book you for that hour?"

"I'm afraid that would interfere with my Central Standard Time lunch hour," I said. "How about I hold on and you connect me the moment that Mister Turner finishes the conversation he's involved in now?"

"Sir, that would be most unusual and inconvenient for Mister Turner. Having me connect you with him at 1:35 p.m., Eastern Standard Time, is the earliest option that I can offer you."

"You guarantee me that he will call me at that hour and minute?"

"I will call you and connect you with Mister Turner when you answer my call," Caroline said.

That would, of course, mean missing the next deadline for a story that included answers from the aloof Mr. Turner, but I could see no other option. "I give up," I said. "1:35 EST it is."

"And to whom will I be calling?" she asked.

I gave her my name, occupation, and the numbers of both my cell phone and my desk phone. "You're calling from a newspaper?" Caroline asked.

"That's correct," I said. "You may tell Mister Turner that I have questions about your company's proposed nickel mine in northern Minnesota."

"Minnesota? It's too cold to do any mining there at this time of the year, isn't it?"

"You're right about that. But it's also too hot to do the kind of mining that Mister Turner is planning to do at any time of the year."

"Really?" she said. "I'd never have thought it got that warm in Minnesota." Obviously, she hadn't recognized which definition of the word "hot" I was using.

"Really," I said in confirmation. "There's never a comfortable time for that kind of mining. That's what I want to discuss with Mister Turner."

"I will be sure and tell him that that is the subject of your question, Mister Mitchell. Goodbye now and have a good day."

20

HOT WIRED

I decided that the best way to make it a good day was to put off lunch until after the call from the tightly-tied-up executive in Pittsburgh and use the time between our noon copy deadline and the phone call to discuss the contents of T.J.'s thumb drive with Don. As soon as the last story was on its way from Don to the copy desk, I invited him to join me at my desk to view what was on my laptop.

"How did T.J. get these emails?" he asked after I showed him the exchange of emails between Bigdigger and Actionman and the material about the widespread pollution that always followed in the wake of the sodium mining process for cadmium.

"She didn't tell me what she had or how she got it," I said. "I don't know if she was techie enough to hack it herself or if somebody else hacked it and gave it to her."

"We couldn't print any of this without definite, solid attribution," Don said. "We could get our ass sued big time by Bigdigger and/or Actionman, whoever they might be, claiming that we made it all up. And if T.J. got it by personally hacking Coordinated's email, it might not stand up as any kind of evidence in court."

"Maybe I can find out how she got it. I'll be talking to the man I think is Bigdigger at 12:35."

"Is that someone at Coordinated Copper & Nickel, Inc.?"

"The CEO himself. Mister Kurt S.C. Turner."

"I'm always suspicious of anybody who uses two middle initials, but there's no way a guy in Turner's position will ever admit to being Bigdigger."

If only I could use Lady T as an authenticator, I thought in silence. Out loud, I said, "Maybe I can trick him. At least I can rattle his cage enough to get something started."

"Something already has started," Don said. "Two of our staffers have been murdered and your kidnapped wife came pretty damn close to being the third one killed by these hoodlums."

"Believe me, I'll be asking Turner about that."

"If you're asking on a land line, his answers might melt the wires."

"Whatever," I said. "I'll talk to you before I write anything after my conversation with Mister Kurt S.C. Bigdigger."

I went to the lunchroom early for a sandwich and coffee and was back at my desk, awaiting a phone call from Pittsburgh, by 12:25 CST. With a notebook and pen lying beside my computer keyboard, I watched the minutes tick away on the screen and carried on a silent conversation with myself about how I should approach the man whose company seemed to be secretly mining cadmium and selling it to a forbidden foreign buyer. Should I ease into the hardball questions by starting with a series of softballs, or should I try to catch him by surprise and shock him into admitting his guilt by firing an opening fastball right at his head?

When the number on the screen changed to 12:35, my phone rang. This is really corporate precision, I thought, as I picked up the phone and, precisely and clearly in six distinct syllables, said, "*Daily Dispatch*, Mitchell."

"Good afternoon, Mister Mitchell, this is Caroline at Coordinated Copper and Nickel, Incorporated. I will be putting our CEO, Mister Turner, on the line for you now."

Before I could thank her, I heard a click and a deep male voice said, "Turner here. What can I do for you?"

His tone was brusque, and in an instant I decided to take the proverbial bull by the proverbial tail and look the situation squarely in the proverbial eye. "Am I speaking to the man who sometimes uses the email name of Bigdigger?" I said.

My attempt to knock him off balance was successful. "What?" he said, and he sucked in a deep breath before asking, "What are you talking about?" he said. "This is Kurt Turner, CEO at CCNI. Why are you asking me about somebody's emails?"

"This is Mitch Mitchell, SW at SPDD, and I'm wondering if Kurt Turner, CEO at CCNI, might also communicate on the Internet as Bigdigger at gmail dot com."

"What the devil *are* you talking about? I've never heard of any digger, big or otherwise, and I've never used gmail."

"You've never heard of Bigdigger?"

"Never. Why are you asking me such a crazy question?"

"Because someone who I believe works at CCNI has been emailing messages under the name Bigdigger ever since your recent visit to Minnesota, and I'm wondering if that someone is Kurt Turner."

"It absolutely is not," Turner said. "And I've never visited Minnesota in my life."

"Really?" I said. "What's your email address? I'd like to send you something before this conversation goes any further."

He was silent for a moment before he said, "What are you wanting to send? It better not be some sort of virus."

"Have no fear. It's only a picture taken in Minnesota last Sunday."

"If you're lying, I'll sue you and your paper for everything you've got. My email is KSCT at CNNI dot com."

I was opening my own email while we were talking. I attached Al's image of Turner in the audience on the Rez and sent it. "This photo was taken in Minnesota last Saturday," I said into the phone. "Check out who's in the second row."

The silence was longer as he opened the message and looked at the attachment. "Where'd you get this?" he said.

"It was taken by a photographer who was on the stage in front of an audience on the Ojibwe Reservation in northern Minnesota last Sunday. Why are you denying visiting Minnesota, Mister Turner?"

There was another silence while I assumed that he was searching for a believable answer before he said, "Because I wasn't really visiting Minnesota. I was on a business trip, not a visit, and I was on an Indian Reservation, which is a federal territory in and of itself, separate from the state of Minnesota."

"That's really a stretch, Mister Turner, but I'll let that technicality go and ask why you were on the Reservation and attending that program?"

"I was on the Reservation and attending that program for two reasons. One, I wanted to see for myself what the area that we will be draining and mining looked like and, two, I wanted to get a look at the crew of know-nothing tree huggers that was printing outrageous, over-the-top environmental garbage, and stirring up local and official opposition to our project."

"I'd like to correct your timeline a bit before we continue this interview, Mister Turner," I said. "The local opposition began before we started to write about the project. That local opposition was called to the attention of us tree-huggers and got us started conducting our own investigation, which led us from knowing nothing about digging for nickel to learning all about the unhuggable aspects of sulfide mining and eventually discovering the real object of your so-called nickel mining project."

"Sulfide mining has gotten a bad reputation because it's been done sloppily by miners who didn't care about what they left behind. Our technicians have worked out a much more efficient method of removing the nickel from the mud and leaving a much cleaner remainder behind. Everything you've read or heard about past sulfide mining projects is ancient history, not applicable to our project. This is the story we've been trying to tell your state officials while you've been raising irrelevant, hysterical opposition to the project in your paper."

"Given what you describe as the *ancient* history of sulfide mining, which you, yourself, just admitted has always had terrible effects on the environment, it would require a huge leap of faith by our state's agency to approve your request for a sulfide mining permit."

"We're asking that our innovations and progress be recognized and that we be given a chance to demonstrate their minimal effect on the environment," Turner said.

"Can you offer any previous use of your so-called cleaner method of nickel extraction?" I asked.

"Like I just said, this is new and innovative."

"So the answer is no?"

"The answer is where would the world be if every new technological industrial advance was denied a permit because of problems that occurred in the past?"

"Maybe not in a place where we're dealing with global warming," I said. "But that's a different problem for discussion on a different day. Now let's get back to your project, the site of which is located in the actual state of Minnesota and is adjacent to, not within, the boundaries of the independent Ojibwe Reservation. It seems to me that even if the state takes this scary leap of faith and believes that your new mining technique will leave the area sufficiently clean, the wetlands will still have been drained and the lake will still have been left in a stagnant condition. Is that not correct, Mister Turner?"

"Yes, the stinking swamp will be drained, and a few little old mud turtles will have to find another wet spot, but the demand for nickel is especially strong right now and this project will provide jobs and income for human beings, who I think are more important than any of those mud turtles."

"What do you say to the residents of the Reservation, who think those turtles are of great importance, traditionally and religiously?"

"I can tell those turtle worshippers that many of them will benefit economically from the mining project. Maybe the lifestyle of the whole community will change for the better."

"You're going to drain the wetlands, which provide a home for the turtles and are a source of water for a lake on the Reservation, dig up what you want to dig up and then go away from Minnesota, leaving the Reservation residents nothing but polluted water and tailings from the mine. Please tell me just how you think that this will be a change for the better for the whole Native American community?"

Turner sighed. "There's no use talking economics with you. You're clearly a biased, anti-industry reporter. You should be looking at the project without prejudice, but you're going off on your own mistaken beliefs instead of sticking with the facts. The most important fact is that the world needs nickel more than it needs a swamp full of turtles."

"Ah, but there's the other problem," I said. "It's not nickel that you're really after, is it Mister Turner?"

"Of course we're really after nickel," Turner said. "What else on earth could we be after in a swamp full of nickel ore?"

I couldn't pass up that straight line. "The earthly object that I'm thinking of is cadmium."

"Cadmium? *Now* what are you talking about? Are you out of your mind, Mister Mitchell?"

"I've been sane enough to be mindful of a series of email exchanges between Bigdigger and Actionman, Mister Turner."

His reply was many decibels louder. "Who the hell are they? And what the hell are those emails you keep talking about? And what have those emails got to do with our nickel mine?"

"That's what I was hoping to learn from you, Mister Turner."

"Well, you're shit out of luck, Mister Mitchell, because I don't have the faintest idea what you're talking about."

"I'm talking about an exchange of emails between Bigdigger and Actionman that discuss the urgent need to get your company's request for a nickel mining permit approved so that the real objective—the cadmium—can be dug up quickly and shipped to an anonymous buyer who seems to be in a hurry to get it."

Turner's response was softer, almost a whisper, said in a matter-of-fact way. "You *are* out of your goddamn mind."

"Those conversations are what's on the thumb drive that our business writer held up for the whole world to see at the award ceremony that you personally attended—on Native American Reservation soil that is surrounded by the state of Minnesota's soil. The intended mining and sale of cadmium was recorded on the thumb drive that the business writer made a big show of putting into her carved wooden turtle, the search for which has led to two murders and a kidnapping in St. Paul."

"You really have lost me, Mister Mitchell. I remember that wacky woman waving that thumb drive in the air and saying it was going to kill our application before she stuck it into that stupid wooden turtle, but all this shit about Bigdigger and Actionman and cadmium is way out of my league. You've gone completely off the rails with that shit."

Turner's state of agitation sounded so real to me that I began to wonder if maybe he was telling the truth. Was it possible that someone of a lesser rank at Coordinated Copper and Nickel, Inc., was going by the private email name of Bigdigger and conducting a cadmium mining project that was so secret that it was unknown to the CEO?

"Do you really expect me to believe that you know nothing about the presence of cadmium in the wetlands adjacent to the Rez?" I asked.

"I'd swear it on a stack of Bibles six feet tall," Turner said.

The man's voice rang with sincerity, but I wasn't sure that I could trust that tone of desperation. He could be an accomplished liar pleading innocence to a criminal charge. I've heard some very convincing pleas of that sort in a courtroom before a judge who eventually found the pleader guilty. I didn't want to skewer an innocent man in my next story about the nickel/cadmium mine, but how could I be sure that he wasn't putting on a performance worthy of a Golden Globe nomination?

I thought of a possible way to verify his wail of ignorance, but I realized that it could backfire. If I asked for Turner's help and sent him a copy of the email conversations that I'd downloaded from T.J.'s thumb drive, he might be able (and willing) to identify the real Bigdigger for me. However, if Turner really was the author of the Bigdigger emails, he would know what evidence of a potential cadmium mine we had, and he could continue his denial while seeking a court order challenging the authenticity of the hacked emails. I was on the proverbial horns of the proverbial dilemma.

Once again, I decided to take the proverbial bull by the proverbial tail and look the situation squarely in the proverbial eye. I said, "Mister Turner, I am going to email you a copy of what was on that thumb drive. If you *are* telling me the truth about being ignorant of what you'll be reading there, I will expect you to help me find out the identity of Bigdigger, who has to be someone in your company's chain of command. If you don't take that step, I will assume that you're telling me a fairy tale and that you are, in fact, the real Bigdigger. Does that sound fair to you?"

"I'm willing to go along with that because I am most certainly not the real Bigdigger, and I am also certain that Bigdigger has no connection with Coordinated Copper & Nickel," Turner said. "Send me those emails and I'll look them over."

Now I was being asked to take a giant leap of faith and assume that I'd get a truthful explanation of the emails from the CEO of CCNI. "I'll need a response of one kind or another from you in no more than two hours," I said. "If I don't get it, I'll be writing a story about Bigdigger and Actionman that will thoroughly wipe out your chances for a sulfide mining permit in Minnesota. In fact, I'll have it written and ready to go to press in much less than two hours. The clock will start ticking the minute I hit the send key, Mister Turner. And I'll hang up the phone while you're reading what I send. Have Caroline give me a buzz when you're ready to talk about them."

"Oh, don't worry about that. If this shit you're sending to me is as phony as I think it is, you'll get a response all right, Mister Mitchell," Turner said. "Believe me, you will! And you'll also get a response from a very good lawyer if your paper prints anything that has even the slightest little whiff of libel."

"All you'll be whiffing is the smell of sulfide," I said. "Here it comes, Mister Turner. Flip over your hourglass." I hit send and T.J.'s collection of emails went on its way through the ether to the computer of the man in Pittsburgh. The clock on my computer said the time was 12:47.

21
DOUBTING KURT S.C.

I went to the city desk to consult with Don O'Rourke. When I gave him a rundown of my conversation with the CEO of CCNI, he asked, "Do you think that there's any chance at all that Turner is telling the truth? That he doesn't know what's going on with a crooked cadmium deal right under his nose?"

"It's hard to imagine something that big going on right under his nose without him smelling it," I said. "But he really did sound like he thought I was making up everything I said. I can hardly wait to hear his reaction after he reads what's in those emails."

"Me, too," Don said. "We might have a story within a story: Mining firm's alleged criminal activity is unknown to CEO."

"This could get very tricky to write about."

"Handle it with gloves, like you would real cadmium if somebody dumped a pile of it on your desk."

"The Treasure Medallion writers would call that a vile pile, wouldn't they? What I'm actually hoping is that Turner is telling the truth—that he's not Bigdigger; but also that he can solve the cadmium riddle and tell us who the real Bigdigger is," I said.

"It might be hard for you to get the name out of him. Think about it. Bigdigger must also be responsible for hiring the crew that killed T.J. and Ben and kidnapped your Martha in the search for the turtle with the thumb drive inside. The CEO won't want his company's name to be dragged into a story about those kinds of crimes."

"So you think that Turner might turn turtle to protect CCNI from prosecution?"

Don groaned. "Rather than ducking into a shell, I was thinking that he might clam up."

"Now you're getting into Al's and my territory as staff pundits," I said.

"Whatever. See how much you can fish out of him when he calls you back."

I returned to my desk to write part of the story and wait for Turner's call. My phone rang at 2:25, twenty-two minutes before the two-hour limit that I'd given Turner would expire.

I picked up the phone and said, "*Daily Dispatch*, Mitchell."

"This is Morrie," said a whimpering voice in response.

I almost screamed in anguish. Morrie is a seventyish-looking gray-haired little man who walks through our section of downtown with a twelve-inch-high fluffy white dog on a leash. He is stricken with a psychosis that causes him to imagine that Vladimir Putin and the Russian military are watching him and planning to destroy him. He calls the *Daily Dispatch* at least six times a year to report that Russia's missile targeting radar has him on its scope and begs us to write a story exposing this impending catastrophe in order to save his life. For some unknown reason, he usually asks our receptionist for Warren Mitchell's extension when he calls.

I sucked in a deep breath to control my anger and managed to speak in a calm, helpful manner. "You need to take shelter immediately," I said. "Put down the phone, get into your shower, pull the curtain shut, turn on the warm water, and stay there for at least five minutes. That'll be enough time for the next radar sweep to pass over your building and not see you because of the opaque curtain and the refraction off the running water."

"And you'll write about them looking for me and tell them to stop?" Morrie said.

"First chance I get," I said. This was the truth. Of course, I believed that the first chance I'd get to write about his affliction would be on the day that hell froze over and the Minnesota Vikings won the Super Bowl, but I never told a lie about the timing of my story to Morrie.

"Thanks, Mister Mitchell," he said, and I heard his receiver click off. I had given him this same advice several times in the past two years. I could imagine him getting into the shower and turning on the water. I always wondered if he took off his clothes and his shoes before he got in.

I hung up quickly, hoping that the CEO of CCNI hadn't tried to call while I was shooing Morrie away. I got my answer at 2:45, when the phone rang again and the caller said, "This is Turner."

"You're right on time," I said. "What's your response to what you've just read?"

"My first response was to think that this is a script for some kind of stage play that your reporter dreamed up after drinking too many martinis."

"And what was your second response?"

"To try to think of anybody who works for me who would be damn fool enough to get mixed up in a deal like this."

"Did you, like me, assume there would be a great deal of money involved? Payable electronically to whoever that damn fool might be?" I asked.

"I did think of that probability, but I still can't think of anybody here who would stick his neck out that far, no matter how much money was being offered. He'd have to have the hush-hush cooperation of the crew chief on the site, for one thing."

"I'm asking you to think very hard, Mister Turner, because the next people to see these emails will be the folks at the state

Pollution Control Agency, who already have delayed action on your request for a permit to drain the wetlands and open a nickel mining project on that site because of what they've learned from stories and editorials in the *Daily Dispatch*. Next will come a story about the discovery of the emails that will include your response and the PCA's response to what is in those emails."

"You'll be accusing CCNI of committing a serious crime if you publish an unsubstantiated charge that our company is involved in mining for cadmium. Cadmium production is one of the most highly regulated mining projects in the world and it's nearly impossible to get a permit for it," Turner said.

"The story will also explain that fact and suggest it as a possible motivation for mining cadmium under the guise of digging for nickel. The story will also raise the question of who the purchaser might be. After all, the secret buyer could be located in a part of the world where the sale of such material is banned by the U.S. government, which would raise the criminal charges to an even higher level."

"This is all speculation on your part, Mister Mitchell. Speculation based on a series of hacked emails that could be the fictitious concoctions of the unscrupulous reporter who illegally hacked them."

"Ah, but think of the investigations the story will inspire, Mister Turner," I said. "Our state's Pollution Control officials will continue to sit on your permit request while they ask you and your employees all kinds of embarrassing questions. And because of the cadmium connection, some federal investigators probably will come calling on you as well. It might even go international if the buyer turns out to be in a country that's on the American government's terrorist list." I was pretty sure that it had already reached that level because of the surprise appearance of Lady T in the St. Paul Winter Carnival.

"You're placing an awful lot of faith on those emails being the real thing," Turner said. "You're looking at one hell of a lawsuit if they're not."

"And you're placing an awful lot of faith on those emails be-ing fictitious," I said. "Do you really want to sit by and bet your company's reputation on that chance, or would you rather start an investigation of your own within your own offices?"

"Would you hold off on passing the emails to the PCA and writ-ing that story if I said that I'd conduct an investigation here in the office?"

"I could be persuaded to do that, but while you're investigat-ing, please remember that someone—and that someone must be Bigdigger—hired people here in St. Paul to search for the turtle with the thumb drive, and that those people have committed two murders, a kidnapping and a home wrecking invasion."

"Good God! I don't know anything about any shit like that," Turner said.

"I think that somebody at CCNI does," I said. "Those crimes will be included in my story as well."

"Murders and kidnappings are even harder for me to believe than all the crap about cadmium. There's no way that anybody here could be responsible for those. You're way the hell off base with those, Mister Mitchell."

"You said you would investigate," I said. "I want you to investi-gate everything that has happened here in Minnesota because of your request for a permit to drain a swamp and mine for nickel. That includes some really heavy, as you would call it, *shit*, Mister Turner."

"I don't believe for a minute that anybody here would be in-volved in murder and kidnapping, but I will consider those charges when I start asking questions, just to show you how foolish you are."

"Good. I'll expect to hear from you with a report on your prog-ress before noon, Minnesota time, tomorrow."

"What if I don't know any more than I do now by that time?"

"Call me and tell me that you need more time, and I'll decide how much longer I can wait for some results. If I don't hear anything from you by noon, the emails will go to the PCA before I go to lunch."

I had hung up the phone and was stretching to remove a kink in my back, caused by the tense conversation, no doubt, when Al made his first visit to my desk of the day. "What'cha been doing all day?" I asked.

"Sitting in a courtroom," he said. "The woman the cops arrested Friday night in front of our house made her first court appearance this morning and Carol and I wanted to be there. She's charged with making a death threat to Carol and with being in possession of an unregistered handgun."

"Did she plead guilty and apologize to Carol and throw herself on the mercy of the court?"

"Don't I wish it was that easy? The accused stood up beside her lawyer and pleaded not guilty to both charges and then gave Carol the stink eye when she walked past us on the way out. I don't see any way she can get out of the gun charge; the cops found the pistol in the car that she was driving. But the death threat charge could be pain in the butt if it goes all the way to trial because Carol will have to be there to testify."

"You must admit that that sort of pain is better than the kind caused by a bullet."

"You're right on target there. So, great creator of profuse and powerful prose, tell this flummoxed photographer what you have been doing all day."

After I gave him a summary of my day's activities, he questioned Kurt Turner's veracity. "I wouldn't bet a plugged nickel that what he says about what's going on at that mine is true. He'd have to have a ton of lead in his butt not to catch anybody in his office who was playing Bigdigger and changing the entire mining operation."

"He'll need an iron-clad, gold-plated alibi to satisfy me," I said.

22

TIME FOR DIGGING

Kurt S.C. Turner's story was neither iron-clad nor gold-plated when he called me Tuesday morning. It was, in fact, more like a twisted piece of lead coated with a thin layer of iron oxide, which is commonly known as rust. He had conducted a series of interviews with his managers and department heads, and—can you believe it?—none of them had exhibited any knowledge of either the possible presence of cadmium at the nickel mining site or of an email address labeled Bigdigger.

"I'm at the end of the line here, Mister Mitchell," he said. "I don't think that any of them are lying, so I don't know what else I can do to convince you that Bigdigger is not employed by Coordinated Copper and Nickel, Incorporated."

"I think you need to dig bigger," I said. "I believe that the answer lies somewhere within your organization. Who else would have so much knowledge of the project?"

"There is such a thing as corporate spies, you know," he said.

"You're thinking that a corporate spy somehow learned about the presence of cadmium at the mine site and is somehow planning to ship that cadmium to an unknown buyer?"

"I'm thinking something along that line. Yes."

"How do you think the spy can gain possession of the cadmium in order to sell it?"

"I don't know. He'd have to steal it after it was out of the ground, I suppose."

"Wouldn't the people—your people—know what they were digging up?" I asked.

"Not necessarily," Turner said. "They might think they were digging up nickel."

"Oh, come on," I said. "Yesterday, you said yourself that cadmium is highly regulated as an extremely hazardous material. Your mining crew would be exposed to a suspected carcinogen without any kind of protection if they thought they were mining nickel and were actually digging up cadmium. Is there no one in that crew who would know the difference between the two?"

"I'm not sure about the expertise of the engineer directing operations at the site, Mister Mitchell. That's another thing I would have to check into."

"I'd suggest you do that. Those are your people who'd be exposed if the project ever got started."

"You're right," he said. "How about you give me another day to do some more of that kind of digging before you publish anything about this whole mess in your paper?"

I thought about that request for a moment. On one hand, the whole scenario of an unknowing crew of miners unearthing a dangerous substance that would then be stolen and shipped to an anonymous buyer seemed too ridiculous for me to allow additional time for confirmation. On the other hand, no other news organization was working on this story, so we were not in a competitive rush to publish what I had. In addition, the next day—Wednesday—would be my scheduled day off for this week.

Here was a chance to be magnanimous, with nothing to lose in return. "I'll give you *two* days to do your digging," I said. "Today and tomorrow. I'll have the story written and will need to hear from you by 9:30 A.M., Central Standard Time, on Thursday to keep what I'll have written out of the morning online edition of the paper."

"You'll hear from me, all right," Turner said. "I've booked a noon flight to the Twin Cities today. I'll be in St. Paul today, talking in person with the man I've placed in charge of obtaining the permit from the state, and out at the mining site tomorrow talking with the engineer directing operations on the ground before I call you again."

"Better than calling, come to my office Thursday morning and we can talk about what you find out over a round of coffee and doughnuts," I said.

"You're on, Mister Mitchell," he said. "I'm so confident that nobody in this company is involved in any of this incredible cadmium nonsense that it will be a pleasure to meet you and tell you how wrong you are about us, face to face."

"The pleasure will be all mine," I said. "Have a safe flight."

I went to the city desk and reported this conversation to Don O'Rourke. "I'll write the story about the cadmium mining emails, starting with Turner's denial of his company's involvement, today, so that it'll be all ready to go Thursday unless he comes in that morning with some hard proof of CCNI's innocence."

"Do you think that Turner's lying?" Don asked.

"I'm not sure what to think," I said. "He sounds like he really believes what he's saying; that he knows nothing about what's in those emails. It could be that it's somebody else among the company officials who is doing the lying and is fooling Mister Kurt S.C. Turner."

"I can hardly wait to hear what he says on Thursday," Don said.

"Me, too."

I spent the early part of my midweek day of rest doing just that— resting up from all the extra hours that I'd worked during the Winter

Carnival. Martha kissed me goodbye on my upturned cheek, which was the only kissable spot available, when she left for work at 7:30, and my downturned cheek stayed on my pillow for another two and a half hours. After a plate of scrambled eggs and bacon, a slice of toast covered with blueberry jam, and two cups of black coffee, I opened my laptop and wrote the story that would run on Thursday if Kurt S.C. Turner continued to deny any wrongdoing by anyone connected with his mining company on the wetlands adjacent to the Rez.

My lede said: "Kurt S.C. Turner, chief executive officer of Coordinated Copper and Nickel, Inc., today claimed to have no knowledge of a series of emails that appear to link his Pittsburgh-based company with a mining subterfuge in northwestern Minnesota."

This was followed by a summary of the emails between Bigdigger and Actionman and some facts about the perils of mining cadmium and the polluting potential of the sulfide mining process for both nickel and cadmium. Thursday morning, I would also immediately send a copy of the emails to the Pollution Control Agency and ask for their comment.

Of course, the lede would change if Turner either gave me the name of an underling who was orchestrating the switch from nickel to cadmium or admitted that he was the person who called himself Bigdigger. I didn't expect him to point a finger his own direction and I was skeptical about his finger being pointed at anyone else employed by CCNI. With finger pointing or not, I was looking forward with enthusiasm to the next day's coffee and doughnuts session with the visiting CEO. Maybe he would fool me and come clean. Or maybe he would identify an associate as the perpetrator of the switch from nickel to cadmium. Or maybe he would throw a cupful of hot coffee at me and storm out of the building when I read aloud what I had written. I was thinking that I should wear one of my older shirts to the office tomorrow, just in case the coffee did fly.

I had shut down the laptop and was in a living room chair,

half-reading and half-dozing with a mystery novel in my hands, when Martha arrived home at 5:30. "Big day?" she asked as she kissed me on the lips, which I quickly made available.

"Just work, work, work, even on my day off," I said. "How was your day?"

Before she could answer, the doorbell rang. Martha peeked through the window beside the door and asked, "Did you order pizza?"

"Didn't order anything," I said. "I'm planning to take you out to dinner as my Winter Carnival finale."

"Well, there's a guy wearing a Domino's hat with a pizza box in his hands standing in front of our door."

"Maybe it's for Zhoumaya, next door." I went to the door and pulled it open. There stood a man slightly taller than I am wearing a Domino's hat and holding a pizza box, just has Martha had said.

I started to say, "You've got the wrong door," but my mouth had barely opened when the pizza box was smashed into my face with so much force that I was shoved backward all the way to the living room, where I did a pratfall over a footstool in front of the sofa and landed with my head on the floor and my feet in the air. The pizza box clattered to the floor, and I found myself looking upward into the muzzle of a very impressive handgun held by the man in the Domino's hat. Behind him were two more men, both holding very impressive handguns. They charged into the house and one of them slammed the door shut behind them. The first gunman behind the man in the Domino's hat, whose bald head was practically glowing above a face rimmed with dark stubble, pointed his weapon at Martha and said, "Keep yer hands up and stay back where you are, Pussy, or I'll gladly put a bullet between yer tits!"

Martha raised her hands and quickly took a step back. "Well, if it isn't my three old buddies from my unpleasant visit to the big fun house on Summit Avenue," she said. "Welcome to our humble home."

23

THE VISIT

"To what do we owe the displeasure of your company?" I asked from my ungraceful position on the floor between the foot stool and the sofa.

"You know damn well why we're here, wise ass," said Domino's hat. "Get up off your clumsy ass and get me that thumb drive right now." He backed away far enough to give me room to rise.

When I was up and facing him at eye level across the footstool, I said, "You're too late. I don't have the thumb drive. The law is in possession of the thumb drive, and my story about what's on it has been written." I decided to make my response even more convincing with a little white lie and added, "In fact, the story has been emailed to the city editor of the *Daily Dispatch*. You might as well turn around and haul your worthless ass back to your hidey hole because the cadmium is out of the bag."

"I think that's bullshit," Domino's hat said. "Where's your wooden turtle?"

"You walked right past it." I pointed to the table just inside the front door where T.J. Kelly's turtle was resting. "Take a look inside it. You won't find a thing because the thumb drive is in the hands of an officer of the law, far away from here."

He turned and looked back at the table. "Ahmed, bring me the turtle," he said.

The third gunman, whose bronze face was half-covered by a dark gray hoodie, went to the table, picked up the turtle and carried it to Domino's hat, who ordered him to hand it to me.

"Open it," he said when the turtle was in my hands. I lifted the shell on the turtle's back and tilted the turtle's empty innards toward Domino's hat so he could see that it was empty.

"Believe me now?" I asked.

"Where's the goddamn thumb drive?" he asked. "Where are you hidin' it?"

"I told you, it's in possession of an officer of the law."

"What law?"

"Interpol. You might want to get your guilty asses out of the country before they come for you and the bastard who hired you to go around killing people."

"Bullshit! There ain't no Interpol in Minnesota."

"You'd be amazed at what, or who, was in Minnesota looking for you and your boss."

"Let'em look," he said. "They ain't gonna find neither us or our boss."

"Your problem is that I know who your boss is," I said. "And I bet that when he's arrested, he'll give all three of you up to save his ass from the electric chair." This was a slight exaggeration of what they would face when convicted of murder, as Minnesota has no electric chair and no death penalty in any other form.

Apparently, the threat of the electric chair impressed the bald gunman, who said, "Hey, Gilbert, I think we should undress little Pussy here, have some fun with her while her husband watches with a gun aimed at his head, and then get the hell away from St. Paul as fast as we can."

"I'm in on that idea," Ahmed said, looking at Martha and nodding his head. "I'll bet that she won't be kickin' anybody in the nuts with a gun pointin' at her hubby's head."

Baldy responded to this by covering his crotch with his hands. "You bet your ass she won't be kicking anybody in the nuts again," he said.

I couldn't stop myself from pointing at Baldy and saying, "You must be the one that she emasculated."

"What the fuck does that mean?" Baldy asked.

"It means she made you limp," said Gilbert the phony pizza purveyor. "Like you can't ever get it up."

"Like hell she did," Baldy said. "I'll show you who's limp!" He unzipped his fly, turned toward Martha, and said, "Okay, Pussy, start takin' yer pants off or I'll put a bullet in yer husband where it makes him limp." He swung the muzzle of his gun toward me and lowered it to the level of my crotch.

"Whoa! Slow down!" Gilbert said. "I didn't say you could have a go at her."

"She owes me one for kickin' me that way," Baldy said.

"I know she does, but don't start shooting at people yet," Gilbert said. "Let's do things the quiet way." Then he kicked me in the groin.

As I was bent double from the pain and gasping in an effort to catch my breath, I heard Gilbert say, "Okay, honey bun, get your pants off or I'll give him another one there right now."

"Don't!" I yelled at Martha. "Don't do it!"

"Get those pants off or Maxie will take 'em off," Gilbert said.

"Wouldn't I love to do that?" said Maxie the bald.

Then we all heard: "Bang! Bang! Bang!" Someone was pounding on the front door. Next we heard, "This is the police. Open this door at once and put all weapons down!"

"What the fuck?" yelled Gilbert. He spun and aimed his gun at the front door.

"Well said," I said.

"Shut up!" he said. "How'd the cops get here?"

"Probably in a cop car," I said.

"Shut the fuck up!" he said. He turned back toward me and stuck the gun inches from my nose. "I'll blow your damn head off if you say one more word."

I made a zipping gesture across my mouth with my right hand.

"Open this door at once and drop all your weapons!" again came from outside the front door.

Gilbert turned and walked to the door. "We have two people in here at gunpoint," he yelled. "Go away or we'll start shooting them."

"Drop your weapons and open the door," said the voice outside.

"No way!" yelled Maxie the bald as he trotted over to join Gilbert at the door. This left only Ahmed watching Martha and me. She was staring at him, as tense as a lion about to spring on a baby gazelle, and I could imagine her calculating the odds of a taekwondo attack to grab his gun and get it pointed at Gilbert and Maxie before they could turn and shoot. She gave me a quick glance and I gave her a vigorous negative shake of my head. "Don't try it," I said.

A crash as loud as on-the-spot thunder came from the kitchen, causing all of us to look that way. What we saw was a wide open back door and a room filling with flak-vested policemen with guns in their hands. There were four of them, all shouting the order to drop all weapons and raise all hands.

Maxie aimed his weapon at the mass of blue uniforms and a gunshot left my ears ringing. Maxie flopped to the floor and both Gilbert and Ahmed flung their guns away and fully extended their arms above their heads. Two cops grabbed Gilbert and pulled him away from the door, one cop grabbed Ahmed and snapped handcuffs on him behind his back, and the fourth cop pulled open the front door.

Four more vest-clad officers poured in, almost trampling Maxie, who lay flat on his back with a red stain spreading across the front of his gray sweatshirt.

"Is everyone okay?" yelled the leader of the front door charge.

"Everyone but him," I yelled, pointing at Maxie. "And he's one of the bad guys."

The leader smiled and waved at me and turned back toward his men. "Get on the horn to the EMTs," he said. "Tell them there's a man down."

Within minutes two EMTs had appeared in the doorway, loaded Maxie onto a collapsible gurney and hauled him away to an ambulance parked amid a fleet of police cars on the street in front of the house. While the EMTs were working, Gilbert was handcuffed and escorted out the door, followed by Ahmed and his official escort. The house was emptied of policemen almost as quickly as it had been filled, and, in the sudden silence, Martha and I sat down side by side on the sofa facing the only remaining officer, who hunkered himself down on the footstool. His metal name tag said SGT. WILLIAMS. The pain in my groin, which had been forgotten during the noisy charge of the blue brigade, was throbbing again and my heart was still going at a hundred beats a minute when Sergeant Williams asked, "So, who are those guys? Why were they here?"

I gave him a complete, but as brief as possible, rundown of the events that led to the trio's visit, and asked a question in return. "How did you guys know we needed help?"

"Nine-one-one got a call from a woman who said that there was a home invasion by at least three armed men going on at this address," Williams said.

"A woman called and told you that?" I said.

"Did she give her name?" Martha asked.

"I don't know anything about a name," Williams said.

"Must have been Zhoumaya Jones, our next-door neighbor," I said. "She must have heard some noise from here. But how did she know there were three of them?"

"All I know is that the operator said the caller had a foreign accent," Williams said.

"Zhoumaya has a bit of a British accent, so it could have been her," Martha said.

The doorbell rang. "Now what?" Martha said. She went to the door and opened it. There stood Zhoumaya Jones. "What the heck was all that racket?" she asked. "Did I hear a shot go off?"

"You did hear a shot go off. And we thank you for calling the police," Martha said.

"I didn't call the police," Zhoumaya said. "I was going to call the police and complain about the noise, but then I saw that it was the police that were making all that racket. Banging on doors and yelling about weapons! What kind of party were you having over here?"

"You aren't the one who called 911?" I said.

"Not me," she said. "What was all that ruckus about?"

Sergeant Williams had risen from the footstool. "I'll leave you folks to do your explaining," he said. "But I'd like both of you to come to the station tomorrow and give us your statements in writing. I can hardly wait to hear the details of what this fuss was all about."

Martha and I agreed to give him the entire story and he left us with the requisite closing words: "Have a good day, folks."

"Really?" I said after closing the door. "Have a good day? After all that!"

We gave Zhoumaya a recapitulation of the invasion, explained the reason that it occurred, and asked her again if she'd called 911.

"Nope. Still not me," she said.

"Then who the hell ..."

"I guess we'll never know," Martha said.

Zhoumaya's eyes turned toward the kitchen, where she saw a smashed door lying flat on the floor and a door-size opening to the back steps. "I was wondering why it was so cold and breezy in here. Looks like I need to call my repairman right now," she said.

"The city should pay for that door and the repair work," I said. "It was the cops who broke it down."

"I'll let the insurance company fight it out with the city government," Zhoumaya said. "I'm just glad that it was only a door that got smashed and that both of you guys are in one unbroken piece. I'll go home and call Jerry and get him over here to close that opening. Maybe you can hang a couple of blankets over it until he gets here to keep the winter wind out."

Zhoumaya was barely out the door and Martha had gone upstairs to get some blankets, when my cellphone rang. When I answered, a familiar female voice said, "Mister Mitch-*ell*, this is Lady T's assistant, Gigette. Lady T has asked me to inquire if you and your wife are safe and unharmed at this time."

The identity of the caller and the question that she asked startled me so thoroughly that I stared silently at the phone for several seconds before my mouth could form an answer. "Uh, yeah, yes, we are safe and unharmed," I said when I was finally able to speak. "Does Lady T have a reason to think that we might not be?"

"Lady T was aware of a threat to your safety that occurred a short time ago," Gigette said.

"How in the world was Lady T aware of what was going on here?" I asked.

"Lady T has not authorized me to answer that question, Mister Mitch-*ell*. Perhaps you would like to arrange a time to speak with her in person about that very thing."

"I don't think I can get away from my job long enough to travel to Budapest," I said.

"Lady T is not in Budapest. Lady T is still in St. Paul. You may call here tomorrow morning at the St. Paul Hotel if you wish to speak with her about today's events."

"Can I speak with her now?"

"Lady T is resting at this mo-*ment*," said Gigette. "I do not recommend disturbing her. All I can say is merci for answering the question about your wellbeing and have a good day, Mister Mitchell." With that, the phone went dead.

Martha appeared, bearing two blankets in her arms. "Who was on the phone?" she said. "You look like you're in shock."

"You're not going to believe what I just heard," I said.

"You were right. I don't believe you," Martha said when I finished recapping my conversation with Gigette. "How on earth could Lady T have known that we were being attacked by three goons? She even had the number right!"

"Believe me, I'm going to make that phone call first thing tomorrow morning and get the answer to that question," I said. "This is really spooky."

"Spooky or not, it definitely was a life saver. And I'm not speaking figuratively. Those goons would have killed us both while they were trying to have their so-called *fun* with me."

"I guarantee you that they'd have had to kill me," I said.

"And me," said Martha.

"We owe our lives to Lady T."

"Which certainly is a mystery."

We picked up the splintered back door, braced it up against the frame around the opening with a kitchen chair, and hung two blankets over it, secured with good old duct tape, to cover up the cracks.

"That'll do it until Jerry the handyman gets here tomorrow," Martha.

"He won't be needing a key to get in," I said.

"Now, what about supper?" Martha said.

"Should I call out for pizza?" I asked.

"You touch that phone and I'll break your arm," she said. "I never want to see a man with a pizza box standing at our door again."

We ate scrambled eggs and bacon, with toast and blueberry jam. What the hell? Even if it's the second one, breakfast is good any time of the day.

24

LOOKING FOR ANSWERS

The temperature dropped and the wind velocity rose overnight so that the kitchen was chilly Thursday morning even with the temporary barricade in place. After breakfast—just cereal and toast this time—I took my heaviest coat, the one I'd been wearing throughout the Winter Carnival, off the hook by the front door and put it on for protection as I walked around the house to the alley where my car was parked.

I had two goals in mind when I settled down at my desk in the *Daily Dispatch* newsroom that morning. One was to schedule a meeting with Lady T to find out how she knew about the invasion of our home. The other was to grill Kurt S.C. Turner about his possible role in sending the invaders. Was having the nasty threesome snatch the thumb drive while snuffing us his crude way of stifling the story of the secret cadmium mining project? Would he be able to walk in and greet me with a straight face this morning?

I called the St. Paul Hotel and asked for Lady T's room number. The phone there was answered by Gigette, and after some back and forth chatter between her and Lady T, we agreed to meet in their suite at 11:30, which should give me enough time to finish my 9:30 coffee and doughnuts tete a tete with K.S.C.T., providing he showed up on time.

I was, in fact, wondering if Turner would show up at all. Was yesterday's invasion of my home ordered by him? If it was, had the invaders' mission failure been reported to him? If both of these were true, had he skedaddled back to Pittsburgh to avoid possible arrest in St. Paul?

If Turner did show up, how should I greet him? Should I slam into him head-on with an accusation? Or should I wait until I saw what his reaction to seeing me alive and apparently unmaimed would be and let him make the first move?

While I waited for Turner, I gave City Editor Don O'Rourke a quick description of my Wednesday day of rest and told him that I hadn't decided how to confront Turner about the assault if he kept our appointment.

"Do you think we should have something blunt on hand to conk him on the head with?" Don asked.

"I don't think he'll get violent," I said. "He'll probably fake great anger at being accused of such a thing and stalk out the door with his head held high in justifiable offense."

"You're probably right," Don said. "But I'm going to see if the sports department has a baseball bat or something like that around just to be on the safe side."

"Get somebody with a high batting average to swing it," I said. "I wouldn't want him to miss Turner and hit a home run with my head."

"Charlie Evans once played for the Saints," Don said. "I'll send him up to bat."

"Charlie was a pitcher," I said. "They're notoriously the worst hitters on the team. In fact, they don't even let them bat anymore."

"Whatever. Yell out 'Mayday' if you need help."

At 9:33, I received a phone call from Lynette at the reception desk. She said, "A Mister Turner is here to see you," and I took a deep breath and asked her to escort him to the interview room.

Next, I phoned the cafeteria and asked them to deliver two cups of coffee and an assortment of fresh doughnuts to the interview room. Finally, I picked up a notebook and a ballpoint pen and went off to beard the lion—and to determine if he was lyin'—in that den.

Kurt S.C. Turner was dressed like a millionaire mining executive in a charcoal gray, pin-striped suit that didn't come off a rack at Macy's, a white shirt with a collar starched as crisp as a soda cracker, and a spotless red, white, and blue striped tie. Despite the snow and slush that he'd slogged through on the sidewalk on the way to our building, his black shoes gleamed as if they'd just that morning come off the footwear assembly line, waxed and buffed by a polishing machine. A heavy woolen overcoat was draped over his left arm as he greeted me with a brief and appropriately firm handshake.

We took seats facing each other across a small coffee table and Turner laid the overcoat across his lap. I pushed the plate of doughnuts toward him, and he chose one frosted with chocolate. He might have been an environmental polluter, an aspiring exporter of a banned metallic substance, and the hirer of a band of ruthless killers, but at least he had good taste in doughnuts.

While his coffee cup was in his hand, I decided once again to take the proverbial bull by the proverbial tail and look the situation squarely in the proverbial eye. "I thought you might be surprised to see me here this morning," I said. "I am kind of surprised to see you."

"Why should either of us be surprised?" he said. "This is the time and place we agreed on, isn't it?"

"Yes, it is," I said. "But the three emissaries you sent to my home yesterday seemed to have other plans for both me and my wife."

Now he did look surprised. His hand jerked upward, some coffee sloshed out of the cup and splashed onto the table, and he said, "What are you talking about? Who are these what you call emissaries?" If his tone and body language were phony, his acting skill was worthy of an Oscar nomination.

"You know who I mean. The three rather rough looking gentlemen who you sent to our house yesterday to take away the thumb drive with all the criminal evidence against CCNI on it."

He stared at me, shook his head from side to side, and tapped his right temple three times with his forefinger. "You're talking crazy again. I didn't send anybody anywhere yesterday and I sure as hell have never sent anybody to your house at any time."

"Are you expecting me to believe that the three goons who wanted the thumb drive were not sent to our house by you?"

"You'd damn well better believe it or this conversation is over right now." He undraped the coat, stood up, and stepped around the table, giving himself a clear path to the door.

"Who else would want the thumb drive?" I asked.

"How the hell should I know?" Turner said. "I know nothing about the goddamn thumb drive except what you sent to me from your computer. And why would I want the thumb drive when I know that you've copied it into that computer?"

Now there he had a point. What good would it have done for him to get the thumb drive when its contents already had been copied onto my laptop?

"Okay," I said. "But who else would want it?"

"Whoever is trying to steal a cache of cadmium and frame my company as the thief," Turner said. "I'd give a month's pay to find out who that is."

"Would you give it to me?"

"You or anybody else who can tell me who Big Digger is and where I can find him."

Now this was an additional incentive for me to solve the cadmium puzzle. He probably made more in a month than I made in a year. "It has to be somebody in your company," I said.

"I've grilled everybody on my staff that I can think of who might be in a position to make the switch and sneak the sale of the cadmium to whoever Actionman is," Turner said.

"Maybe you need to make the grill hotter."

"Maybe I will. But first of all, I want you to believe that I personally had nothing to do with whoever it was that threatened you in your home yesterday."

I was beginning to believe him. "I'll drop that charge for now," I said. "But I won't turn my back toward you."

"Turn your back any way you want to. I don't know who sent those people and I hope to hell that it wasn't anybody from CCNI."

"Can you think of where else they'd have come from?" I asked.

He hung his head. "I'm afraid that I can't. But I'll do everything I can to prove that it wasn't one of our people."

"If you can't prove that, we've both got a problem. Yours is that my story, with your denial of any knowledge of the crimes that have been committed in the lede, will be in the next online edition of the *Daily Dispatch* and mine is that whoever wanted to stop it by stealing the thumb drive might come after me looking for revenge."

"Even if you start with my denial of knowing anything about all that shit, that story will totally destroy our chances of getting the nickel mining permit," Turner said.

"It will," I said. "Convincing the PCA to deny that permit was the original intent of our news stories and editorials about your company's plan to drain the wetlands and kill the turtles with a sulfide mining project for nickel. We will have achieved our original goal of saving both the environment and the resident turtles, which have a deeper meaning to the resident Native Americans than tons of nickel have to the rest of the world. And the discovery of plans to extract the illegal cadmium, plus the murders of two of our writers, add up to an even greater reason for the state to deny that permit."

"I'll wager another month's pay that whatever organization is behind the cadmium plan won't take this lightly, Mister Mitchell. You might not outlive any of those turtles that you're so nobly saving."

"Believe me, I plan to ask for police protection until we find out what that organization is, Mister Turner. I hope you're correct when you say it won't have CCNI in its logo."

"I will continue my efforts to make sure that it does not." He put on the heavy woolen overcoat and went out the door without even telling me to "have a good day."

"I see that you survived without any obvious physical damage," Don O'Rourke said as I approached him at the city desk.

"He professed complete surprise at my accusation, pleaded total ignorance of the invasion of my dwelling, denied everything connected with the thumb drive and stalked out of the interview room without any punches having been thrown," I said.

"Do you believe his claims of ignorance and all of his denials?"

"I do sort of believe part of it. For instance, he knew that I had a copy of the thumb drive in my laptop, so his claim that he had no reason to take the thumb drive by force does make sense."

"So, are you thinking that your visitors might have been sent by someone else? Someone who doesn't know that you've copied the thumb drive into your laptop?"

"That's a logical possibility. But I have no idea who the hell that might be, and neither does the nickel mining king, who says he will do his utmost to prove that it was not any of his subjects."

"But it's his crew that was going to be doing the digging for the nickel or the cadmium or whatever they were after, isn't it?" Don asked.

"It is! That's what doesn't make sense," I said. "That's the problem that still needs to be solved."

"What's next on your plate this morning?"

"Next, I need to find out what the police have gotten out of our visitors, and after that I have a date at the St. Paul Hotel with the lady who rescued Martha and me by mysteriously phoning the cops yesterday."

"You're meeting with Lady T?"

"I owe her a personal thank you and I have a batch of questions to ask her."

"My first one would be why is she still in St. Paul now that the Winter Carnival is over."

"I'm pretty sure that I know the answer to that," I said. "My first question will be how in hell did she know that we were being attacked in our home. She even knew that there were three attackers."

"That is a good number one question," Don said. "I'd be damn curious about that if I were you. But tell me, what do you think is the answer to my question?"

"I'm sorry to have to say this, but that's a question that I can't answer," I said. "Now I have to go talk to Brownie for a while." I felt like I was walking on a tightrope strung high above the newsroom by Lady T as I hustled away from my scowling boss.

"Homicidebrown," said Brownie when he picked up the phone on the third ring.

"Dailydispatchmitchell," I said. "What revelations do you have for me on the Turtle-jack killings this morning?"

"The same brand of revelations you gave me when I begged you for the Treasure Medallion hiding place last week," said Brownie.

"You were seeking information sealed behind an impermeable wall. I am seeking information from a public service source that should maintain a modicum of transparency."

"That kind of gobbledygook will get you nowhere, just as the search for the perpetrators of the crimes in question has gotten this investigator nowhere. But I hear from the troops that you had some excitement at your house yesterday."

"I'm most grateful for the arrival of the troops," I said. "Our visitors had a very unpleasant program planned for us. Has anyone there been discussing yesterday's incident with them?"

"One of the best interrogators we have has been chatting with them, one at a time," Brownie said. "All of the chats have been strictly one-way, I'm sorry to say."

"They're not answering any questions?"

"They're maintaining what might be described as radio silence."

"No name of who might have sent them?"

"No names of nobody. None of them carried any identification and none of them has spoken a word since they were brought in."

"Has the interrogator tried a more vigorous means of interrogation? Hanging them up by the thumbs, for example?"

"All the department's hangers are at the dry cleaner's," Brownie said. "And the body stretching rack is out for repairs."

"Most unfortunate," I said. "I'd certainly like to know where my visitors came from and who sent them to my humble abode. If first names will help you get started, they called each other Ahmed, Maxie, and Gilbert. Gilbert seemed to be the head hoodlum."

"That might help us crack the nut. We'll keep working on it, but so far they haven't even opened their mouths enough to ask for a lawyer so maybe the cat did get their tongues, as the old saying goes."

"What about the car? Who's that big black SUV registered to?"

"To a very well-heeled man who reported it stolen late last week. The plates had been switched with a car that's no longer on the road, but we found the registration in the glove box. That's how we found out that it was stolen."

"Not finishing the paperwork will mess up an otherwise clean job every time. They must have stolen that thing just before they kidnapped Martha with it. If only we knew where they'd parked it then."

"It would have been very helpful if your wife could have identified the house that she was held in. Knowing the ownership of
that house would give us something to work with in identifying our
three stonewallers."

"Now that those three are safely ensconced in your sturdy hotel, maybe we could take another run up Summit Avenue and test
Martha's memory again."

"That's up to you and Martha," Brownie said. "I can't offer you
another escorted tour."

"I'll run it past Martha and let you know what she says."

"You do that. And in the meantime, have a good day, Mitch."

At precisely 11:30, with Al beside me, I knocked on the door
of the hotel suite occupied by the great Lady T Khuppschane, the
faithful Gigette, and the Corgi named Laddie T.

The faithful one's voice asked, "Who eez eet?"

"It's Mitch and Al," I said. "You're favorite reporter and photographer team."

"One mo-*ment*," was her reply.

One mo-*ment* later, the door opened, and Gigette, wearing a
snug blue sweatshirt with a Paris Olympic Games logo on the left
breast and skin-tight blue jeans molded to her hips and butt, beck-
oned us into the suite.

Lady T, clad in a similar combination of blue Olympic sweatshirt
and jeans of a much more extravagant size, was seated in her customary armchair. Circular gold earrings three inches in diameter
hung from her ears, but the glittering assortment of jewelry that
usually adorned her neck and breasts was missing. Like a queen,
she slowly stretched her right hand out toward Al and me. For a
second, I considered grasping it by the fingers and kissing the back
of it, but opted to shake it instead, and Al did the same. "Please

remove your coats and be seated, gentlemen," Lady T said, waving us toward a desk chair and a smaller armchair. We both removed our coats, dumped them onto the bed and took our seats like school children obeying their teacher.

"As you might guess, I have a huge question to start off this interview," I said.

I could tell from Lady T's smirk and Gigette's hand-hidden giggle that they knew what I was about to ask. However, Lady T said, "Lady T does not presume to guess what that question might be, Mister Mitchell, but Lady T will do her best to answer whatever you may ask of her."

"Okay," I said. "Please tell me how Lady T ... uh ... *you* ... knew that my home was being invaded by three men with weapons."

"Lady T will respond with a question of her own," Lady T said. "When was the last time that you put your hand into the pocket on the left side of that large coat that is lying over there on the bed at this moment?"

"That's a very strange question," I said. I went to my memory bank for a couple of seconds and found it empty before I said, "I can't remember the last time I put my hand in either pocket of that coat. I make a habit of never putting keys or anything of value in a coat pocket because I've had coats accidentally switched on me at parties and in restaurants."

"Lady T suggests that you put your hand into the left pocket now."

How weird was this? I got up, picked up the coat and stuck my hand into the left pocket. My fingers encountered a small, square, hard object. I grasped the object and pulled out a two-inch-square black cube made of almost weightless metal. I held it up and asked, "What in the world is this thing?"

"This *thing* is an extremely sensitive, long-range, voice-activated wireless listening device," she said. "The very latest advance in international intelligence work technology."

I was still puzzled. "How did this very latest technological advance get advanced into my coat pocket?"

"It was placed in there the last time that your coat was resting on that bed."

I looked quickly at Gigette, who just as quickly looked away from me. I remembered that she had been sitting on the bed beside our coats while I was interviewing Lady T.

"Gigette snuck this thing into my coat while you and I were talking?" I said.

"That is correct, Mister Mitchell," said Lady T. "She did so at Lady T's direction. As you can see, Gigette is capable of being very discreet."

"That coat has been hanging next to my front door ever since then," I said. "And you've been listening to everything that's been said in my house all that time? Everything my wife and I have said to each other?"

"Not everything that was said in the entire house, Mister Mitchell. Lady T and Gigette have heard only what has been spoken within a fifteen-foot radius of your coat rack. Your private conversations with your wife beyond that space have remained completely private."

"Why would you put such a bug into the coat of someone who's not a suspected criminal?"

"Lady T was concerned that the threat of you making public the information on the thumb drive would inspire the type of action that occurred in your home that day. Lady T's hope was that you would not find the device before the persons seeking the thumb drive were in the custody of your local police."

"Well, you lucked out there," I said. "Or maybe I should say that Martha and I lucked out. That coat was hanging right where you were able to hear those men when they came in the door."

"It was actually Gigette who heard them. She informed Lady T of what was occurring, and Lady T directed her to alert your local police."

I turned toward Gigette and said, "I thank you with all my heart, Gigette." She blushed, and looked away, but I saw the beginning of a smile before she turned her head. "You are welcome, Monsieur Mitch-*ell*," she said so softly that I barely heard the words.

I turned back to Lady T and asked the obvious question. "Do you know who sent those three goons to my home?"

"Lady T has more than one suspected source in mind," she said. "However, Lady T is not able to discuss her suspicions with any member of the news media at this time."

Again, the standard "at this time" dodge. "What can Lady T ... uh ...what can *you* discuss with this member of the news media about this case at this time?"

"Actually, Lady T believes it would be wiser for Mister Mitchell to limit his reporting to evidence that he already possesses than to continue seeking additional information before it becomes available from an official source."

"Would that official source be Lady T?" I asked.

"It would be a person who was authorized by Lady T's employer to release information to the media," she said. "Lady T is an investigator, not a spokesperson."

"So, I'm on my own until your employer issues a statement?"

"Lady T suggests that you refrain from conducting any further pursuit of information on your own, as you put it. Continuing investigation on your own could lead to further danger for you and possibly your wife, Mister Mitchell. This could be danger from which Lady T would be unable to intercede on your behalf."

"Are you thinking that Bigdigger would send more goons to stop me?"

"Lady T believes that Bigdigger will use any resource or any method available to prevent your newspaper's publication of any additional evidence of criminal plan involving mining of cadmium."

"If I'm willing to take that risk, can you give me any advice?" I asked. "Is there anything you could suggest as a starting point?"

"Lady T firmly suggests no further investigation on your part," she said. "But if you stubbornly persist, as Lady T knows that you will, Lady T suggests investigating citizenship or nationalities of individuals involved at every level of nickel mining project."

"Does every level include people who do not work in the corporate office of CCNI?"

"Lady T will say no more, Mister Mitchell, other than to repeat her suggestion that you wait for information from official source before proceeding with report." She rose from the chair, indicating that our conversation was over, and Gigette moved to the door and opened it.

Al picked up his coat and stepped out through the opening and I retrieved my coat and followed, pausing in the doorway long enough to thank both Lady T and Gigette again for rescuing Martha and me from the three turtle-jacking goons. Both said, "You're welcome," and Gigette shut the door within half a second after I had vacated the opening.

"Gigette almost hit you in the ass with that door," Al said.

"If nothing else, Gigette is very efficient," I said. I put on my coat, reached into the left pocket, pulled out the little black box of advanced crime detection technology, and said, "I wonder how you shut this thing off."

"Why bother?" Al said. "They're going back to Budapest. They'll never hear you talking from there."

I put the black box back into my pocket, put my index finger to my lips, and whispered, "They could be listening to us right now."

"Spooky," Al whispered. We talked in very low tones all the way back to the *Daily Dispatch* garage.

25

ALL-AMERICAN LINEUP

B ack at my desk in the *Daily Dispatch* newsroom, I sipped a cup of coffee and thought about Lady T's advice on how to proceed if I "stubbornly persisted" in trying to identify Bigdigger. Investigate the nationalities and citizenship of CCNI employees at every level, she had said. This was confirmation that she believed that Bigdigger was connected with Coordinated Copper and Nickel, Inc., and it gave me the impression that Lady T was pointing at someone who'd been born in or was a citizen of a country other than the U.S.A. It also left me wondering where to look for this information. I doubted that Google would be of any assistance in such a project.

I decided to start with the CCNI website, hoping to find biographical information about the people in the company's chain of command. In a couple of clicks, I had found a page containing the organizational chart, with mug shots and—was this my lucky day?—brief bios of all of the corporate officers.

At the top, of course, was Chief Executive Officer Kurt S.C. Turner. Under his mug shot, I found a resume of his corporate accomplishments, a summary of his education that included a master's degree from the Massachusetts Institute of Technology, and a sentence saying that he'd graduated from high school in Canton, Ohio, where he was born and raised. Okay, the top guy was a native

American and therefor an American citizen. Maybe he really was telling the truth when he said he knew nothing about the secret cadmium deposit or the orders that led to the turtle-jack killings.

Lady T had advised checking the backgrounds of officials at every level, so, with Turner possibly off the hook, I looked at the bio beneath the photo of the man immediately below the CEO on the organizational chart's pecking order. His title was assistant executive officer, and his name was Robert R.U. Redding. Good grief, I thought, must you have a minimum of two middle names in order to make it to the top at CCNI?

Redding's bio included administrative positions with two previous employers, a degree from Georgia Tech, and a hometown of Toledo, Ohio. Here was an all-American boy, all the way back to his birthplace.

Next after Redding came a photo and bio of the chief administrative officer, who was a black woman. After silently applauding CCNI for this act of diversity, I read that Shirley White Harrison had grown up in Sandusky, Ohio, (I was detecting a trend toward Ohioans in the upper ranks at this point of my investigation) and held degrees from Ohio State University and Colorado School of Mines. She was clearly another naturally born American citizen.

The chief financial officer was pictured with a bald dome, a ring of white hair at ear level and a Mark Twainish mustache and goatee. His name was Raleigh D. Deusie, and his bio listed Lexington, Kentucky, (not all that far from the Ohio border, I noted) as his place of boyhood and pre-college schooling. His higher education degrees were from the University of Kentucky and Harvard Business School. Another all-American dude operating in the upper echelons of CCNI.

And so it went with the next two levels that were shown on the website—all the way down through the deputies to the whatchacallits and the assistants to the whatchacallits. There were faces from Pennsylvania, Tennessee, Alabama, Arkansas, along with more from Ohio, but none that would belong to employees from outside the borders of the U.S.A. working with a green card.

"How goes it?" Al asked when he arrived at my desk bearing a mid-afternoon cup of coffee.

"Frustratingly," I said. "I've gone through all the levels of people who would seem to have any kind of authority at CCNI and haven't found anybody with a questionable place of birth beyond the borders of middle America. I can't imagine what level Lady T could have found a potential Bigdigger at."

"Could it be at a more practical level?" Al said.

"What do you mean by more practical?" I asked.

"Could it be someone at a hands-on level? Someone directly working with getting the cadmium out of the ground and loaded onto a boat to Persia or wherever Actionman wants it to be delivered."

"You mean someone like a supervisor at the mining site?"

"Yeah, somebody who's right there chasing the turtles away."

"Uff-da!" I said. "How do we check those people out?"

"How about we mosey on up to the Rez and talk to some of the miners in person while they're sitting around waiting for official permission to start draining the turtles' bathtub?"

"Sometimes you actually make sense," I said. "I'll run it by Don and see what he says."

At that moment, Don said something else, and he said it in a very loud voice. "Yo, Al! There's a big house burning near the east end of Summit Avenue. Get a car and get out there."

"How about me, too?" I yelled.

"You might as well tag along with your twin," Don said. "I haven't seen you producing anything sitting over there."

26

BLAZING TIMBERS

We could see the tower of smoke from six blocks away, which was where we had to park our *Daily Dispatch* staff car because access to Summit Avenue was blocked at every corner by police vehicles and every legal parking space on the side streets was occupied. We covered the distance at a gentle trot, figuring that there would be plenty of time for Al to catch pics of roaring flames and clouds of dusky smoke.

Organized chaos would best describe the scene when we came within sight of the burning house. We saw fire trucks of all description—tankers, ladders, SUVs—and I counted five police vehicles with flashing lights parked at various angles in front of the house, which was a sprawling three-story wooden structure with a long, wide staircase that led from the front porch pillars to the sidewalk. Crews of firefighters were spraying water from an array of hoses on flames that could be seen flickering through every window and billowing through a hole where they'd eaten through the roof. A ring of uniformed policemen was keeping a growing swarm of onlookers from getting too close to the action. Many of these onlookers were watching through cellphone cameras, recording the death of an expansive and expensive structure that had stood in that spot for more than a hundred years.

"She's a goner for sure," said a tall, skinny, gray-haired man beside me. "Tall Timbers is a goner."

"Tall Timbers?" I asked.

"That's what she's called, on a count of she's taller than most of the houses on Summit and she's one of the few that ain't made out of brick."

"Do you live near here?" I asked.

"You're standing in front of my house," he said. "Been here for thirty-four years."

How lucky can you get, I thought. Here I was, by sheer happenstance, standing next to a close neighbor who could be a handy source of information. "So you must know who owns Tall Timbers," I said.

He shook his head in the negative. "Used to," he said. "Place changed hands about a year ago. Family sold it for big bucks after old Charlie kicked the bucket and the new owner is some foreign business corporation that rents it out. Some of us old-timers ain't too happy about that rental thing, by the way."

"Are the renters here? Do you see you see them in the crowd?"

"Nope. Don't hardly ever see 'em."

"Is it a small family? Or what?" I asked.

"Nope, don't look like a family. Just three guys who come and go in a big black Caddy SUV. Kinda creepy looking guys, if you ask me."

"Creepy looking? In what way?"

"They're all built like Vikings linemen for one thing, and they always wear black clothes and they're always looking around like they're scared of something when they come out of the house and go to the car."

"You ever talk to them?" I asked.

"No way. They don't look the kind of folks that a guy could chat up. One of 'em's kinda dark skinned, like he could be an Arab or something like that, and none of three of them ever crack a smile."

"How long have they been living there?"

"Oh, I'd say … four … five months or so."

"Do they ever have company?" I asked. "Does anyone else ever come there?"

"Not that I've seen," he said. "Why you so interested anyway?"

I told him my name and showed him my press card. "I'll be doing a story about the fire and it's great to get some information like this on the occupants. Can I use your name as my source?"

"Oh, god, no," he said. "Those guys might not like what I told you about 'em. I wouldn't want 'em coming after me."

"I understand," I said. "I'll refer to you as an anonymous resident of the neighborhood. Is there anything else you can tell me about them?"

"Nope. Don't know anything but what I've seen through my front window. Like I said, they ain't never talked to me—or to anybody else in the neighborhood as far as I know. Anyhow, I think I'll head on into the house now and get outta the smoke. Nice talking to you, Mister Reporter."

"My pleasure," I said. "Thanks for all the info."

I wound my way through the crowd toward Al, who was as close to the burning house as the cops would allow and was still shooting pics of the flames and the firefighters. "Hey," he said. "Did you get anything from the crowd for a story about this mess? One neighbor told me that the place is called Tall Timbers."

"I was told the Tall Timbers name, too," I said. "And I also was told some very interesting stuff about the three big as Vikings linemen, creepy looking men who rent this house and come and go in a big black Caddy SUV."

"Holy shit!" Al said. "Do you think it's the three goons who grabbed Martha and crashed your house?"

"The description sure fits," I said. "I'm wondering if maybe this fire is not an accident."

"Be a good way to destroy evidence," Al said.

"Especially if you thought that the law might be hot on your trail."

We stayed and watched the entire roof fall in with an explosive burst of smoke and flame, followed by the dominoes-like collapse of all the walls. When the flames had subsided to flicker and a glow, I tried to catch the eye of one of the fire department officers in hopes of getting a statement about the probable cause of the blaze. After ten minutes of futility, I gave up on this, but as we were turning to head back to the car I saw a lieutenant I recognized from a previous conflagration talking to Channel Four's Trish Valentine, who was broadcasting live with breaking news. "Let's scoot back and get next to Trish," I said. "Maybe I can squeeze in a question while the lieutenant is admiring Trish."

I got there in time to hear Trish ask my most urgent question: "Does anyone have any thoughts about the probable cause?"

The lieutenant replied that it was too early to answer this question. "You'll have to wait for the investigative report on that one," he said. "Can't start looking for the cause until the ashes cool down a little."

"Was anybody in the house when the fire started?" Trish asked.

"No," he said. "There was nobody home. A next-door neighbor made the 911 call when he saw smoke pouring out of the house and saw that the residents' SUV wasn't sitting where they usually park it."

"And no one who lives there has shown up while you've been fighting the fire?" I asked.

"Not to my knowledge," the lieutenant said. "If any of the residents have come home, they probably went to the chief. He'll probably have a statement for the media later on, when we've made sure that this thing isn't cooking anymore."

The fire chief's statement came long after Al and I had returned to the office, and I'd gone home after writing a story for the evening online edition. Fire Chief Edward Edwards spoke to reporters just in time for the seven o'clock segment of the local TV news, which Martha and I were watching in our living room.

After describing the location and intensity of the fire, and the valiant but unsuccessful battle by the firefighters to save the home known as Tall Timbers, the chief discussed the investigation and the probable cause.

"Signs of an accelerant were found in three separate places within the structure," he said. "Leading us to believe that the fire was intentionally set."

"Have you spoken with any of the people who live there?" asked Valerie Stafford, who'd relieved Trish Valentine at the scene.

"None of them have appeared at the house, nor have any of them contacted fire or police officials in any way," said Chief Edwards. "The house is owned by a rental agency, and a spokesman for the agency said the agency has heard nothing about the fire from the tenants. They seem to have abandoned Tall Timbers."

"Do you know who the tenants are?" Trish asked. "Or should I say were?"

"A neighbor told us that the house was occupied by three very large young men who kept to themselves and never spoke to anyone in the neighborhood."

"You have no names?"

"The rental agency declined to give us the name of the leaseholders because of privacy issues," the chief said.

"What's the name of the rental agency?"

"Top o' the Line, Incorporated. They're located in Dublin, Ireland, would you believe."

The interview ended and went to commercial, whereupon I turned off the TV and said, "We know why the residents haven't shown up, don't we? Two of'em are in jail and third one's in a hospital bed."

Still staring at the dark screen, Martha said, "Why didn't I remember that? Why didn't I think of it?"

"Think of what?" I asked.

"Tall Timbers," she said. "It said Tall Timbers on the logo on the glass that they gave me to drink out of. Why didn't I think of that sooner? Why didn't I make that connection? We might have helped the cops catch those three killers before they almost killed us."

"That would have spared us one very unpleasant evening. But now it's water over the dam."

"I'll drink to that," Martha said. "Strictly water, of course."

My first call at eight o'clock Wednesday morning went overseas to Top o' the Line, Inc., in Dublin, Ireland, where it was one o'clock in the afternoon. A woman who spoke with a delightful lilt answered and passed me along to the agency's public relations director, whose name was Kevin O'Shea.

"I'm sorry, but I can't be givin' out any names of our customers to the press, Mister Mitchell," O'Shea said after I'd explained the reason for my call. "Privacy rules and all that, you know."

"These particular customers aren't likely to complain," I said. "They were being held in police custody while someone associated with them was torching the house."

"You're thinkin' that it was a case of arson, are ya, Mister Mitchell?"

"I'm thinking that it was a case of arson because the fire chief announced that an accelerant was found in three separate places, Mister O'Shea."

"That announcement hasn't made it to our ears here in Dublin, Mister Mitchell. Accelerant in three separate places, did'ja say?"

"That's what the fire chief told us last night. By withholding the names, you're protecting three criminals who lived there and worked with whoever set the fire that destroyed your property, Mister O'Shea."

"And owed us two month's rent to boot," he said. "You needn't put that in your report, Mister Mitchell."

"The rent is not my concern," I said. "My concern is that your renters are in jail as murder suspects in St. Paul, and I'd like to put their names in print. I believe one of them is Ahmed something, one is called Maxie, and the other one is known as Gilbert."

"It bein' a case of arson, the privacy rules might be open for a bit o' bendin'. I'll have to be talkin' to my higher ups about it and then be callin' you back, Mister Mitchell."

I gave O'Shea my number and said that I'd be expecting a call within an hour.

The return call came within half of that time. "There's three names listed on the lease, Mister Mitchell," Kevin O'Shea said. "Those names are A. Smith, B. Jones, and J. Doe."

"Shit!" I said.

"I hear ya," said Kevin O'Shea. "And I'm wishin' ya the best o' luck, things bein' the way they are."

I thanked O'Shea, slammed down the phone with more than necessary vigor and stared off into space. Well, not quite into space. My eyes met those of Corinne Ramey. "You said a naughty word," she said.

"Like you've never said that word," I said.

"Not at a hundred decibels in the newsroom," she said.

I shrugged and turned my gaze to the phone that I'd just punished. If I'd been a character in a comic strip, a light bulb would have gone on above my head as I thought of a way to share my frustration.

I picked up the phone and punched in a familiar number. "Homicidebrown," said the voice that answered.

"Dailydispatchmitchell," I said. "I've got some news."

"Isn't that what you get paid for acquiring?" said Brownie.

"Don't be a smartass or I won't share it with you."

"I eagerly await your report."

"Kevin O'Shea, the PR director at Top o' the Line, Incorporated, has ditched the security clause and shared the names of the lease-holders who torched the house formerly known as Tall Timbers. I thought you, as chief of homicide, might like to have these names, seeing as how they probably also are the killers of two residents of our fair city."

"Your thoughts are commendable. I'm standing by to copy."

"It's a threesome," I said, and rattled off the trio of names in the same order that Kevin O'Shea had given them to me.

"Shit!" said Brownie.

For the first time that morning, I was able to smile. "Funny," I said. "That's exactly what I told Kevin."

27

HEADING NORTH

Dressed in our warmest clothes, Al and I hit the road for the Ojibwe reservation at 8:30 the next morning, after getting a grudging go-ahead from Don O'Rourke.

Don was dubious about the value of interviewing the members of the mining crew while they were doing nothing but sit in a motel all day, waiting for the Pollution Control Agency to take action, one way or the other, on CCNI's request for a permit to start draining the wetlands and digging for nickel.

"What's the rush?" Don asked. "Why do you need to go up there now, while there's nothing going on? The turtles don't need your help right this minute."

"If the PCA denies the permit request, which seems like a no-brainer after the members have read my story about the secret plan to dig for cadmium, those guys will immediately be sent back to Pittsburgh, and I'll lose my chance to talk to them."

"Why do you have this great need to talk to the mining crew?" Don asked. "What's the story angle?"

I had to think fast and devise a viable reason because I couldn't tell him that Lady T had advised me to look for immigrants or foreign nationals at every level of CCNI. "It's about the miners and what they're thinking while they're sitting around with nothing to do but twiddle their thumbs in the motel all day," I said. "How are they keeping their heads together with day after boring day of not being able to work? How do they feel about being away from their homes and their families when there's no reason for them to be stuck in Minnesota all winter?"

"Do you really think any of our readers give a damn about what those guys are thinking and doing?" Don asked.

"I think I can put together a story that will be interesting to a lot of our readers," I said. "I'm guessing that I'll get quite a variety of answers—from guys who are dying to get home to the wife to guys who are more than happy to be getting a paycheck every week while sitting on their butts in a warm motel room instead of chopping the ice out of a frozen swamp." The ice that I was skating on here was extremely thin because of the need to protect Lady T's secret work for Interpol.

Don rubbed his chin while he thought about that statement. "Okay," he said after a moment of silence. "I guess I can spare you two for a couple of days now that the Winter Carnival is over. Go on up there and stay no more than two days, and talk to as many miners as you can in that time."

"Thank you," I said. "You shall be rewarded with a story of great interest accompanied by great action photos of mine workers engaged in their leisure activities."

"While you're up there talking to people who are being paid to do nothing, could you take time to go out on the lake to catch some walleyes, and reward me with a couple of those?" Don said.

"Not likely," I said. "When I was a kid, my dad dragged me out onto frozen lakes for all of the ice hole fishing I ever want to do in this lifetime."

"Don't look at me," Al said. "The only walleyes I've ever caught were grilled and laying on a platter."

The small hotel on the Rez, where we'd been presented with

our pretty little wooden turtles, would have been the ideal place to stay, but when I called its number I got a recorded message saying that the hotel was closed for the season and would reopen on May 1. The motel nearest the proposed nickel mining site had no vacancies because it was filled with members of the idle mining crew, and the next two closest motels were closed for the winter. I'd finally been able to make a reservation for a cabin at a shabby little resort twenty miles away and we had no problem checking in early because we were almost the only guests in sight. The chubby, white-haired man at the check-in desk said that there were permanent year-around residents occupying two of the larger units, which was the only reason that this facility was staying open all winter. "If it wasn't for them, we'd pull the plug on the electric and switch off the propane and hunker down with the little woman by the wood stove in the kitchen back home in the village," said Cornelius Johnson, who identified himself as the owner, manager, caretaker, and desk clerk of Corrie's Charming Cabins. Charming? They might have been the last time they were freshly painted, which I estimated to have been around 1945.

"You boys up here to catch some walleyes on the Rez?" Johnson asked. "I hear they been bitin' pretty good this winter."

That sounded like a good excuse for our visit, so I said, "Yes. We got the word from a guy we know on the Rez, so we're taking a couple of vacation days to get some fresh walleye."

Johnson wished us good luck with the fishing, and we asked about a place to get lunch. He gave us directions to a small diner that stayed open all winter, where we each downed a cup of wild rice soup and a deep-fried walleye sandwich with French fries before heading toward the mine site. We decided to take a quick trip onto the Rez and pay a courtesy call to Chief Raymond Hardshell Turtle before dropping in on the members of the mining crew. We passed their motel on the way to the Rez and saw no signs of life.

"Nothing moving on the outside," Al said. "Think there's anybody awake on the inside?"

"We'll knock on some doors later on today and find out," I said.

The four of us had met with Chief Raymond at his house an hour before the turtle award ceremony, so we knew how to find it. His face lit up with surprise when he opened the door in response to my ringing the bell. "Boo-zhoo!" he yelled, giving us the traditional Ojibwe greeting. "You gentlemen are from the St. Paul paper, aren't you?" he said. "I remember handing turtles to both of you."

We complimented him on his memory of faces and refreshed his memory of names. He ushered us in, and when we were seated in his kitchen-dining area, he said, "What brings you here in the middle of winter?"

"A serious complication with the proposed nickel mine," I said. "We have obtained evidence that there is also a deposit of cadmium there, and that the cadmium is to be mined and sold to a buyer in an off-limits country. The big boss in Pittsburgh says that neither he nor any of his associates know anything about the presence of cadmium in their proposed nickel mine. We need to talk to the mining crew and see if they've heard any word about cadmium, and if they'll let anything slip about how they can possibly sneak it out of here. They can't just throw a load of cadmium into a dump truck and haul it away to a ship somewhere like a load of gravel."

"The state has got to put the kibosh on this whole mining project," the chief said. "That stuff would mess up our water even worse than the crap left over from a nickel mine. The turtles would all be dead for sure, and maybe we would be, too, in a real short time."

"Stopping this whole project—cadmium, nickel, whatever they're after—is what we're working on," Al said. "If the company's big cheese is telling the truth about the higher-ups not knowing anything about secret cadmium, we're thinking that maybe the chief thief is on the lower end of the pecking order—maybe whoever is leading the production crew."

"That's very possible," said Chief Raymond. "But it's terrible to think that somebody in that crew is willing to risk the health—the lives, even—of the rest of the men in the crew."

"Some people will do any kind of terrible thing if the price is right," Al said. "I'm sure that the buyer, the one who calls himself Actionman in the emails, is shelling out very big bucks to have your turtles killed by whoever calls himself Bigdigger."

"And Bigdigger could actually be here, doing the digging," Chief Raymond said. "I hope you guys can find the bastard, whatever his position is."

"Our editor gave us two days to find him if he's here," I said. "Which means that we'd better get our butts in gear and start talking to people at the motel where the diggers, big and small, are sitting on theirs."

"Stay in touch, gentlemen," the chief said as we went out the door.

"I've got your number on my phone," I said. "I'll give you a status report if we make any progress." We went back to the car and drove to the motel where the mining crew was staying.

"All quiet at the miners' digs," Al said as we pulled into the parking lot.

"Hope the miners are in there and not out chopping through the ice in the wetlands to dig for cadmium," I said.

We parked in front of the office door of the L-shaped two-story building, which was big enough to have about twenty units on each floor. The reception desk was unoccupied, but there was a little bell on the counter beside a hand-written sign that said: "Ring bell for service." I dinged the little bell, and we stood there and waited for the promised service. And waited. And waited … so long that I was about to tap the dinger again when a door behind the desk opened and a portly, fiftyish man with a gray-streaked black beard, wearing a maroon wool bathrobe and bulky tan fleece-lined bedroom slippers, walked in and came to the counter. "Help you gents?" he said.

"Yes, you can," I said. "We'd like to talk to some members of the nickel mining crew who are staying here. You can help us by giving us some of their room numbers."

"Pick any room number you like," said the man. "All's we got here is them nickel miners."

"There are miners in every room?" I said.

"I didn't say that," he said. "Some of the rooms are closed off."

"But there's nobody but miners staying in the whole motel? So we won't be disturbing anybody else if we knock on any of the doors?"

"You got it," he said. "Knock on any door you like and if somebody answers, it'll be a miner, less'n a bear snuck in during the night."

"Your bears should still be hibernating," Al said.

"You can't ever trust a bear around here, Mister. So, why'd you wanna talk to any of those guys?"

I explained that we were from the St. Paul paper and were planning to do a feature on the men who were sitting idle in northern Minnesota, waiting for permission to attack the snow-covered ice in the wetlands bordering the Rez.

"Good luck with that," he said. "Some of 'em don't even speak English."

"We'll look for some who do," I said. "Thanks for your help."

"No problem," he said. He turned and went back to where he'd come from. I hate it when a person says "no problem" after I've thanked them. I much prefer the good old-fashioned "you're welcome" response.

"Real chatty host," Al said. "Dresses well to greet his prospective customers, too."

"We might have disturbed his mid-morning calisthenics," I said. "Probably doing push-ups or jumping jacks in a T-shirt and jock strap when I rang the bell, and had to run to the closet to get that robe."

"Yeah, I can see him doing jumping jacks in those slippers," Al said.

"Let's us slip around the corner into the hallway and knock on the first door that we come to," I said. With me bearing my reporter's notebook and Al carrying his camera, we set off on a knock-knock expedition. We went into the hallway, turned right and I knocked on the first door we came to.

Door number 116 was opened by a six-foot-tall, wide-shouldered man wearing a checkered red-and-white lumberjack shirt and blue bib overalls. He stared at my face in obvious surprise. "Who are you?" he asked through a thick black handlebar mustache and beard.

I told him who we were and gave him the make-believe reason for our mission.

"You want to write about what us miners are doing to pass the time away while we're sitting here on our asses?" the man said. "Well, Mister Reporter, you can tell your readers that nickel miner Jimbo Jordan is reading Plato's *Odyssey*." This was followed by a loud round of thigh-slapping laughter that almost blew me out of the doorway.

"Getting a little culture while you wait?" I said when the roaring subsided.

"Very damn little," Jimbo Jordan said. "The truth is that mostly I'm watching daytime TV, which ain't got a thing to do with culture, and nighttime TV, which has ten huge guys dunking a basketball or a couple guys slugging each other in what started out as a hockey game, in order to keep from going crazy."

"Not much night life up here?" I said.

"Nothing but the casino on the Indian reservation and I ain't got the kind of money that I can risk losing any of it there."

"Do any men in the crew go to the casino?"

"Just a couple of the boss guys who get the big paychecks."

The boss guys were the ones we were looking for. "What are the boss guys' names?" I asked.

"That would be Andy Wheeler and You Turn Boch."

"His first name is You Turn?" I asked.

"Yah. His name starts with the letter J, but he pronounces it like it was a Y. I think it's spelled J-U-T-E-R-N."

"And the last name is B-O-C-H?"

"Yah. He's a foreigner. In fact, he's an immigrant from some-where. Talks with an accent."

"I'd like to talk to those boss guys," I said. "Do you know what rooms they're in?"

"Yah. They've got the big suites at the end of the hall up on the second floor, across from each other. I think Andy is on this side and Jutern is on the other side, but I ain't sure of that. Us peons don't get to spend much time with those two."

"Are they the captains of the ship, so to speak?" I asked.

"Yah, come to think of it, that's what it's like. Captain and execu-tive officer. I think Jutern would be the captain and Andy the exec."

"Thank you, Jimbo," I said. "I think we'll go knock on the cap-tain's cabin and see which way the wind is blowing up there on the second deck."

"No problem," said Jordan. "Just don't tell him that I gave you the number. He's not the sociable type."

Grr! Another "no problem." What did their parents teach these guys?

"Wasn't it Homer that wrote *Odyssey*?" Al asked as we climbed the stairs to the second floor.

"It was," I said. "But if I'd have corrected Jimbo on that, he prob-ably would have just said 'no problem.'"

At the top of the stairs, we turned left toward the tip of the

'L'. We'd decided to start with the so-called executive officer, so I knocked on the door of number 201. "Who's there?" asked a deep male voice.

I told him who was there and why we were there and waited for the door to open. "Stand in front of the peephole," the voice said. I placed my face in front of the little glass circle and said that I was Mitch.

"Now the other guy," said the voice.

Al put his face in front of the glass circle and a moment later the door was pulled open by a much smaller man than the voice had suggested. He stood only about five-foot-six and couldn't have weighed more than a hundred and forty pounds. His face bore a two-day growth of coal black whiskers, and he was dressed in a baggy black sweatshirt and blue jeans. "I'm always careful who I let in when I'm away from home," he said.

"A very good policy," I said. "Might save you a lot of trouble some day."

"So, you say that you're doing some kind of a story for the St. Paul paper?" he said.

"That's right," I said. "We're doing a story on what nickel miners do while they can't do what they're waiting for permission to do."

The man wrinkled his nose. "Don't sound very interesting to me," he said. "I can't imagine that anybody in the big city gives a damn that I'm playing solitaire and watching soap operas on the tube all day while a bunch of do-nothing donkeys in St. Paul are letting our permit request lay in a pile of paper on a desk somewhere."

"Can we come in and talk about it?" I asked.

"Oh, sure, why not?" he said. The suite consisted of a sitting room with two armchairs and a desk, and a separate room with a bed and another chair. He waved each of us toward an armchair and plopped himself down on a swivel chair in front of a desk.

"I'm Mitch and this is Al," I said when I was settled into the armchair. "And you are Andy Wheeler?"

"That's me," he said. "How did you know who I am?"

"We were told by one of the men down on the first floor that you are one of the foremen running the nickel mining crew," I said. "Is that correct?"

"Who told you that?" he asked.

"We promised not to tell," I said.

"Huh! Probably Gus. Was his name Gus?"

"No, it wasn't Gus. I can tell you that much."

"Well, it don't matter. And what my job is supposed to be and what I'm doing while we're waiting for those donkeys in St. Paul to make up their minds really don't matter either. It ain't like I'm getting rich sitting on my ass in a motel room when I should be working in a mine up here in this godforsaken part of the world."

"Haven't you been winning anything at the casino?"

"Who told you that I've been going to the casino?"

"The same unidentified person who said you're one of the two men in charge of the actual mining operation."

"Well, that person don't know shit!" Wheeler said. "I've only been to the casino once in all this time, and that time I lost my ass on a slot machine. I think that sucker is rigged to only pay off once in every ten million spins."

"The odds are always with the house in any casino," Al said. "You just have to be lucky enough to be the one who's there for that ten millionth spin. Timing is everything." Again Al was dispensing one of his favorite bits of wisdom.

"I was unlucky enough to be there for a whole shitload of unlucky spins. Other than that, there ain't much I can tell you gents about life in the slow lane up here."

I needed to get Wheeler talking about digging for nickel, or maybe even cadmium, so I asked him what the crew would do first if the permit was approved. "What's your job, exactly?" I asked.

"I'm actually You Turn's right-hand man," Wheeler said.

"You Turn?" I said, playing dumb.

"His name looks like it would be Jew Turn, starting with a J, but he pronounces it like it was a Y. He's originally from somewhere in Europe or Asia or maybe Arabia—God knows where. Talks with a funny accent when he talks, which ain't all that often. Hard-nosed kind of guy."

"He's the captain of the mining crew?" I asked.

"Yeah, I guess you could put it that way. He's the boss and I'm the guy that he relays the orders through and sees that they get carried out."

"What will his first order be when the permit is approved and you can start working?"

"Depends on what the weather is by then. If the swamp's still froze, his order will be to chop away the snow and ice and get the ground uncovered. If it's not until later, when the swamp's already thawed and turned to mud, his first order will be to get rid of all the water and mud."

"And the turtles?" Al asked.

"Fuck the turtles!" Wheeler said. "We'll scoop them out right along with the muck." He noticed that I was taking notes and added, "You maybe shouldn't put that part of what I said in your story. I guess the Indians are pretty pissed about us killing off the turtles."

"Will the turtles be the only thing that your mining kills off?" I asked.

"What else is there?" he asked.

"The lake that the swamp drains into is the best walleye fishing lake on the Rez. Won't your nickel mining process pollute that lake and kill off the walleyes?"

"Yeah, come to think of it, it probably will. Guess they'll have to settle for catching smaller fish in the other lakes."

"Once you're down to the nickel and get it out of the ground, will you be finished?" I asked. "Will that be the end of the mining operation?"

"Yeah, that will be it. We can all go back to civilization."

"There's nothing other than nickel to dig for in that swamp?"

"What else would there be?" Wheeler said.

"You tell me," I said. "That's what I'm asking."

"As far as I know, we're here to dig out the nickel and nothing else," he said. "I don't think there's any gold or silver under that muck if that's what you're thinking."

He sounded sincere, like he was telling the truth, so I decided not to tell him what I was thinking of. "You never know what might turn up while you're digging, do you?" I said.

"I'm pretty sure I'd know if we were after something like gold or silver," Wheeler said. "It would be damn hard to keep that a secret from the crew."

If you only knew what secret apparently was being kept from the crew, I thought. "Okay," I said. "Thanks for your time and your comments. Now I think we'll go and visit Mister Jutern Boch and get his take on the situation."

"No problem," Wheeler said. "But I don't think you'll get a whole lot from Jutern. Like I said, he ain't the talkative type."

"We can only try," I said. "Maybe we'll catch him in a rare chatty mood today."

"Timing is everything," Al said.

"All I can say is good luck to you," said Andy Wheeler. "Getting a complete sentence out of Jutern is almost as hard as getting a quarter out of that goddamn slot machine."

28

JUTERN'S TURN

We waved goodbye to Andy Wheeler and walked across the hall, where I knocked on the door of number 200. Getting no response for at least two minutes, I knocked a second time.

"Hold horses," commanded a strong male voice from inside. When the door finally opened, we were confronted by a man who exceeded my height, weight, and girth, with a swarthy complexion, a shaggy beard that hid his neck behind a curtain of straight black hair that fell almost to his shoulders, and a prominent hooked nose that appeared to have been broken in at least one place. He was dressed in a red-and-black checkered woolen shirt and heavy weight khaki pants with multiple pockets, and he held a cellphone in the extra-long fingers of his left hand. "You the newspaper guys?" he asked.

"How'd you guess?" I asked.

"Little birdy tell me," he said without changing the somber expression on his face.

"Would that be a little Andy birdy?" Al said, pointing at the cellphone.

"Don't matter what birdy," said Jutern Boch.

"May we come in?" I asked in my most jovial and persuasive tone of voice.

"Don't know why you come in," Boch said. "Jutern got nothing to say to paper." Oh, great! Another interviewee speaking in third-person.

"We're curious about what the mining procedure will be if you finally get to start doing it," I said. "How you're going to dig, what you're going to be digging for. Stuff like that."

"You know is nickel mine," he said. "What else you think we dig for?"

I wanted to say "cadmium," but bit my tongue and said, "Might there be anything else in the ground here, in addition to the nickel?"

"You think gold? Silver?"

"Either one of those, or maybe something else," I said.

"No gold. No silver."

"But maybe something else?"

He paused a moment before he answered. "What else you think could be?"

"You tell me," I said. "What else, if anything, is sometimes found near nickel deposits?"

Al whispered, "Empty Coke bottles," and I jabbed him in the rib cage with an elbow. Jutern Boch stared at us without changing expression and said nothing.

After a silence that felt like a ten-minute intermission, I said, "Why don't you tell us about yourself, Mister Boch? The Andy bird said that you're an immigrant. What country did you come here from?"

"Is no business of yours where Jutern from," Boch said.

"How long have you been in the United States?"

"Is no business of yours how long Jutern be in United States."

"How long have you worked for Coordinated Copper and Nickel, Incorporated?"

"Is no business of yours how long Jutern work for this company."

"How many men do you have in the mining crew here?"

"Is no business of yours how many men here. Jutern think you go now." The door moved rapidly toward my nose, which was poking into the doorway, and the big toe of my right foot, which was resting on the threshold. I managed to yank both nose and toe out of extremis a split second before that door slammed shut with a bang that echoed down the empty hall.

We looked at each other and shrugged our shoulders in unison. "That went well," Al said with a sarcastic half-smile.

"Oh, yes, really an exciting and inciteful interview. And I came within a split second of losing a nose and a toe," I said.

Al nodded. "Timing is everything."

"And a barrel of empty Coke bottles to you," I said. "Where did that dizzy comment come from?"

"Aren't pop bottles what the stores put a nickel deposit on?" said Al.

"We're lucky that Jutern Boch didn't put us as a deposit in the trash instead of just turning us back out the door."

"He didn't deposit much information for you to put in a story for Don," Al said.

"We'll have to talk to some of the lower-level *peons*, as Jimbo called them, to get more of a story," I said. "If we knock on enough doors, we might find something more poignant—like a newlywed who's yearning to go home to his bride or a proud father who's itching to see his son play on the high school soccer team. We've still got a day and a half to work on that phonied-up story idea while we stay tuned for hints of buried cadmium."

"Right. Timing is everything," said Al.

Our timing on the next door knock was poor, as the shaggy haired man who opened the door said, "No Englais," and slammed it shut as soon as I started to introduce myself.

"The desk clerk warned us about that," Al said.

"All we can do is keep on knocking," I said. "I wish I could tell

Don that our real reason for being here came from Lady T instead of having to try to cobble together a story that nobody who takes our paper is ever going to read."

"Maybe you could whisper Lady T's suggestion into Don's ear," Al said. "After all, she's back entertaining her audience in Budapest and would have no way of knowing that you'd spilled the Interpol beans."

"Let me try to talk to a few more miners before I resort to giving up Lady T's deep, dark secret."

"It's your call. My camera is multi-lingual so I can go on shooting pictures of people who don't speak English all day."

The next man we encountered did speak English. He was in his early twenties, looked as muscle bound as a weightlifter, and answered the door wearing only his tighty-whitey undershorts. He did a double take and asked, "Who are you?"

I told him who we were and what our announced mission was, and asked if we could come in. He opened the door and stood back, and we marched into his room, which was decorated—in addition to the usual items—with a set of barbells and weights that were scattered across the floor. No wonder he looked as muscle bound as a weightlifter.

"Y'all su'prised me. I was expectin' one of the fellas who likes to come over and do some liftin' with me," he said with a soft Southern drawl.

"How much can you lift?" I asked as an opener.

"I can clean and jerk two hundred," he said. "Wanna see me do it?"

"How about you doing it on camera," Al said.

"Sure thing." The young man's muscles rippled photogenically as he grunted through the process of hoisting a bar with a hundred pounds on each end and steadying it above his glistening shaved head, within an inch of a glass ceiling light, while Al snapped a quick series of shots.

"Very nice," said Al. "I'll make sure you get a copy of my pics of your pecs in action."

"What's your name?" I asked the man as he was lowering the bar to its resting place on the carpet.

"Michael Maxwell. My mama calls me Michael, but the guys here call me Muscles Mike," he said.

"Your mama isn't into nicknames?"

"She hates'em. That one anyhow. My mama makes my brothers and my sister call me Michael, which she says is a beautiful, poetical name, and never Mike, which she says is a common guttersnipe nickname."

"I wonder what she'd say about Mitch versus Mitchell," Al said.

"Be careful or Mitch will snipe at you from the gutter," I said. Then, remembering why we were watching Muscles Mike show off his lifting power, I asked him where he lived when he wasn't out digging for nickel.

"I come from a li'l ol' town in south'n Kentucky, name of Pembroke. Started liftin' weights when I was at Jefferson Davis High School. Comes in right handy sometimes when we needs to be liftin' heavy stuff out'n a hole."

"What do you do besides lift weights to pass the time here while you can't be working?"

"I done brung a laptop with me, and I been watchin' a lot of movies on it."

"What kind of movies do you like best?"

"I guess that would be action movies, with a lotta chases and noise. And pone."

"Pone?"

"You know. Po'nographic. Nekked folks screwin' in front of a camera. But I wouldn't want you to go puttin' that in the paper, Mister Mitchell. Might git back to my mama, and she would give me a right strong talkin' to."

"I will be discreet." I promised this even though I was quite sure that we had no subscribers in Pembroke, Kentucky.

"You can be whatever you wants to be, long as you don't mention me lookin' at pone in your write-up."

"Thanks," I said. "Do you know what you will be doing here after all the nickel has been dug out?"

"Goin' home, at least 'til the next job comes along," Muscles Mike said.

"You won't be digging for anything else here?"

"Nothin' else here to dig for, far as I know. Less'n there's a secret gold mine in that swamp that the boss ain't told us about."

"The boss hasn't mentioned any additional safety measures of any kind?"

"Just the usual stuff we always do when we's doin' sulfide minin'."

I thanked Muscles Mike for his time and comments, Al got his email address and promised to send him images of his strong man demonstration, and we left him to his weights and his pone.

"I wonder how many pounds Muscles will be lifting after he handles a cache of cadmium without the proper protection," I said.

"He might really appreciate having the pics I'll send him," Al said. "He can look at them to remind himself of what he could do in the good old days. After he watches his favorite bit of pone, of course."

It was on to the next, and the next was a door opened by a stubby blonde-haired man with a crew cut and a scraggly blonde beard that was so pale it was almost transparent. I guessed his age to be around nineteen or twenty. He looked at us from left to right, and then again from right to left before he said, "Yah?"

I told him who we were and why we'd knocked on his door. He did the double facial scan again and said, "What I do is read books on my I-pad. It's great to have all this free time to do that because I'm going to be a Literature major at Penn State next fall."

This was quite a switch from Muscles Mike. "Why aren't you in school now?" I asked.

"Taking a year off between high school and college to put away some money." He told us that his name was Sven Odegard, that he lived near Pittsburgh, and that he wanted to become a high school English teacher. "The money is really good on this job," he said. "The work is lots harder than waiting tables or scooping ice cream, but the pay is lots better than most of the other jobs you can get right out of high school." I quietly wondered how much of that good money would go for medical expenses if he was exposed to scoops of cadmium without the proper kind of protection.

I asked Sven what he'd been reading, and he rattled off a list of non-fiction titles that suggested a strong interest in history and politics. I asked what he thought his next job would be after all the nickel had been removed from this site.

"Don't know," he said. "I guess we'll all be sent to wherever the company is working its next mine."

"You haven't heard about doing anything more here after the nickel is gone?"

"No, sir. Nobody has said anything about there being diamonds or gold or anything like that at the bottom of the pit. Be nice if there was. I could make some extra money without having to move out of here."

I wanted to tell him that what was purportedly at the bottom of the pit wasn't so nice. I couldn't do that, so after Al took Sven's picture, we thanked him for his time and his comments and went on our way to look for another prospect.

"Think young Sven will ever make it through Penn State?" Al asked when we were out of the room.

"He will if the PCA denies that permit request," I said. "I can't imagine what is taking them so long to do that even without any knowledge of the cadmium scheme."

"I'm sure your buddy, the CEO, is arguing like hell and telling the PCA that all of your stories about pollution are fake news, and that the world is waiting desperately for that nickel. We'd better find some solid information up here if we're going to kill this project before it kills all the turtles and maybe a few people along with them."

"I'm afraid the key might be the guy who told us that what Jutern does is none of our business. I'll ask the next guy we interview about what kind of vibes the crew gets from him."

The next guy we interviewed was a husky man whose shaggy hair and six-inch beard were both pure white. He was smoking a brownish-colored cigarette in a non-smoking room, and he invited us in to enjoy the second-hand fumes. He said that his name was Rodolfo, and that he was from Hungary. I jumped right on that ethnicity ride.

"Have you ever watched Lady T on television?" I asked.

His eyebrows soared upward as his eyes opened to full width. "Lady T!" he said. "Oh, my god, yes! Lady T! She is wonderful! Beautiful! So much fun! How you know about Lady T here in America?"

I told him that we'd met her on a river cruise in Portugal and that she'd been as close as St. Paul just a few weeks earlier. "You didn't see her in the Winter Carnival on the news?" I asked.

"No, don't watch American news," Rodolfo said. "Ask anybody; is all fake news in this country. Even American presidents say it is all fake news."

"American presidents don't always tell the absolute truth," Al said. "Especially if it's news they don't happen to like."

"Ah, then is like Hungary," he said. "News can't say anything bad about bigshot leaders there."

"Fortunately, we in America can still say those things," I said. "The problem here is getting American people to believe what we say if they don't want to believe what we say."

"So, what can poor Rodolfo tell gentlemen of American press?" he said. Oh, no. Was this going to be another third-person discussion? Was that the standard method of communication in Hungary?

"Rodolfo can tell us what he does to fill the empty hours while he's waiting for a chance to dig for nickel," I said.

"Rodolfo entertains himself," he said. "Rodolfo plays with himself … on this." He reached into a large pocket of the bib overalls he was wearing and pulled out a harmonica. He laid his cigarette in an ashtray, put the harmonica between his lips and produced a string of notes that I didn't recognize as any familiar tune. "You know that song?" he said.

"I'm afraid I've never heard it before," I said, and Al shook his head in the negative.

"Is Lady T's theme song," Rodolfo said. "You never hear it played?"

"Never have," I said.

"Me neither," Al said.

"I thought you say you know Lady T," Rodolfo said.

"We've only seen her in person," I said. "We shook her hand, but we've never seen her perform on her TV show."

The expression on Rodolfo's face turned to open-mouthed awe. "You shake Lady T's hand?" he said in a whisper.

"Both of us did," Al said.

Rodolfo gasped and thrust out both of his hands. "Can Rodolfo touch hands that touched hand of Lady T?"

"Of course," I said. I grasped his right hand and Al reached in and took his left.

"Rodolfo never wash his hands again!" he shouted. After we let go and backed away, he held his hands at eye level and stared at his palms the way a jeweler gazes at a million-dollar diamond-studded tiara. "Never wash these hands again."

We thanked Rodolfo for his time and commentary, and let ourselves out, leaving him to admire his anointed-by-proxy hands.

"What a Lady T fan!" Al said. "If he was a teenager, I think he would have swooned when you said we've shaken her hand."

"Hope his breath gets back to normal so that he's able to keep playing her theme song on that harmonica," I said.

"His notes will sound even sweeter, played on an instrument held in those hallowed unwashed hands," Al said. "Are we going to knock on any more doors?"

"Maybe one more," I said. "What I'd really like to do is find out more about the mysterious Mister Jutern Boch. In his position, he could be the key to this whole cadmium thing."

"Have you tried googling him?"

"I have. He has somehow escaped the all-seeing eye of the Google."

"You mean he doesn't really exist?"

"It seems that way. Let's talk to one more peon and ask him if he knows where his foreman comes from."

The next door I knocked on was opened after some delay by a short, heavy-set, forty-something man with curly red hair on top of his head and a flowing red beard on his chin. He looked up at me with half-open eyes and said, "What do you want?" in a sleepily angry tone. Apparently, I'd awakened him from an afternoon nap.

"A few words with you," I said, and explained my identity and my reason for disturbing him. "May we come in?"

He scowled and said, "I suppose." He waved us in and pointed to an armchair and a swivel chair at a small desk. "Might's well have a seat." He perched himself on the bottom edge of the queen-size bed.

I asked the usual question about what he did to pass the idle hours, and he pointed to the TV set facing the bed. "The boob tube and an occasional nip of scotch keep me quiet and halfway sane," he said. "I'd a whole lot rather be working than laying around here on my ass."

"Can't say as I blame you," I said. "Where are you from?"

"Right next door. North Dakota. Wish I could go back there."

"Very boring, sitting here?" I asked.

"Boring doesn't begin to describe it," he said. "Daytime TV is really the shits, but I suppose you can't print that, can you?"

"You're right; I'll have to censor that a bit. But how do you like working for Coordinated Copper and Nickel otherwise? Do they treat you okay?"

"I guess you could say that. Paychecks come on time, even when we're not working."

"How's the boss? Jutern Boch, I mean?"

"Very quiet man. He doesn't say much of anything to me or anybody else that I know of. Seems to be a very private person."

"Does he have any friends that he confides in?"

"Not that I know of. He's kind of got a wall around him."

"Where's he from?"

"I don't really know. He's never said, and nobody else seems to know, but he's not from anywhere in this country, that's for sure."

"He never talks about home?"

"Like I said, he never talks much about anything. Never any small talk about where he's been or what he's done before he got this job."

"Does he ever talk about what's next, after the nickel is all dug out?"

"Nope. Not a word."

"Nothing about a special project or anything?"

"What do you mean by special project?" he asked.

"Like mining for something in addition to the nickel," I said.

"What would we mine for? I'm pretty sure that there ain't no gold in this here swamp."

I swallowed the urge to say that all that glitters is not gold and asked him for his name.

"Wheeler," he said.

"And your first name?"

"That is my first name. I was named after an ancestor—a rich uncle, I guess. Didn't do me much good monetarily. Anyhow, my last name is Rowned. Wheeler Rowned."

We thanked Wheeler and left him to his (expletive deleted) daytime TV, occasional nip of scotch, and afternoon napping.

"Didn't get much to spin into a story from Wheeler," Al said.

"Just that nobody seems to know where Jutern Boch is from," I said. "Seems odd that an immigrant wouldn't sometimes talk about home."

"Maybe old Jutern has a reason not to talk about home," Al said.

"That's what we need to find out."

29

GOING TO THE TOP

Having struck out with Google, I decided to go the next most obvious source in my search for Jutern Boch's native land. When we got back to our deluxe living accommodations in Corrie's Charming Cabins, I sent an email to the CEO of CCNI, Kurt S.C. Turner, asking for personal information on his onsite boss at the proposed nickel mine in Minnesota. "What country does he come from?" I asked.

The man with two middle initials replied about ten minutes later with a question: "Why you want that?"

"Checking him out," I replied.

"Surely you don't think he's involved with cadmium accusation."

"Checking all possibilities."

"Wasting your time and mine. Name looks German. Will check personnel files and get back to you."

Ten supposedly wasted minutes later, I got the next email from Turner. "Boch lists home of record as Frankfurt, Germany."

"Hot dog! A Frankfurter," said Al, who was reading over my shoulder.

"I assume he has a green card," I replied to Turner.

"Of course. Wouldn't hire without."

"How long with your company?" I asked.

"Three years and seven months."

"Must be fast learner to be in charge of mine project here."

"Resume lists previous mining experience in Germany and Austria."

"Did you personally assign him to this job?"

"No. Department head does that."

"Who is department head? How do I contact?"

"He is not cleared to talk to media," Turner replied. "And he definitely is not your so-called Bigdigger."

"I need more facts about Boch to confirm that," I said.

"Can't help you there."

"I will keep interview with dept. head off the record."

"How can I trust you on that?"

"I can give references." I was thinking about Homicide Chief Curtis Brown, who had worked flawlessly off the record with me on dozens of questions.

"Give me one," Turner said. So, I gave him Brownie's name and the police department's phone number—but not Brownie's confidential number. How ironic would it be to give Turner the confidential number to use to ask Brownie if Mitch Mitchell can be trusted not to break a confidence?

"I'll get back to you," Turner said for the second time.

"Be looking for it," I replied. The wheels of journalism were turning as slowly as the wheels of justice are said to revolve.

I was left looking for nearly an hour. The sun was going down when Turner's next message popped up in my email.

"Brown hard to catch. Said I can trust you. Name you want is Bryce Thoreau," he said. He added a phone number and an email address. I thanked him and said I'd let him know if I found Bigdigger.

"You won't find him working for our company," Turner said.

I was sure that he was wrong, but I didn't reply. He'd already promised me a month of his salary if I identified Bigdigger. Who could ask for anything more?

I called the number that Turner had given me for Bryce Thoreau. True to form, I got only his voice mail after seven rings. I left my name and number as instructed and added that I'd been advised to call him by Kurt S.C. Turner. It was back to the waiting game.

This time the game was shorter than usual. Thoreau's return call came only four minutes later. I suspected that it had taken him that long to check out my message with his boss. "How can I help you, Mister Mitchell?" Thoreau asked.

I told him that I was looking for background information on Jutern Boch for a story I was writing about what his company's nickel miners were doing to while away the days while waiting for permission to mine nickel. "Boch is in charge of crew, is he not?" I said.

"He is," Thoreau said. "But he's not authorized to speak to the media."

"He made that quite clear," I said. "That's why I'm talking to you. For one thing, I'd like to know what country he's from and how long he's been in the United States."

"I think he's from Germany, but I'd have to look up his personnel file to confirm that and to find out when he immigrated."

"Please do that and call me right back," I said.

A few minutes later, Thoreau was on the phone again, telling me that Jutern Boch was a native of Hamburg, Germany, had immigrated five years ago, had acquired a green card in the quickest time possible, and had been hired by CCNI three and half years ago.

This all jibed with what Turner had told me earlier. Now came the most relevant questions. "What are his qualifications for leading your crew here in Minnesota? Why did you choose him for this job?"

Thoreau explained his choice by saying that Boch had previous experience in nickel mining in Europe and had shown leadership qualities on previous projects with CCNI.

"Do you consider him to be completely trustworthy?" I asked.

"What a nasty question," Thoreau said. "Of course I do. I wouldn't have given him the assignment if I didn't have complete trust in his ability to carry it out."

"I'm thinking of his character. You're satisfied that he is honest and would never lie to you or anyone else about his job?"

"I can't imagine where you're going with this, but yes, I'm satisfied that he is an honest man of good character. Again, I wouldn't have given him the assignment if I didn't believe in him completely."

"Have you had much personal contact with Mister Boch?"

"I'd say the usual amount of back-and-forth between worker and supervisor. We've never gone out for a beer together, if that's what you're looking for."

"I'm just wondering how well you really know him. Has he ever talked about his life in Germany with you?"

"Not really. He's said that he lived in Frankfurt, but he's never talked about what it was like there or what he did there before he got into mining."

"No talk about family in Germany, or anything personal?"

"It's always been strictly business talk with Boch, Mister Mitchell. We don't get into anything else with our employees."

I thanked Thoreau for his time and his insight and ended the call.

"Obviously Boch's boss hasn't listened to him talk," I said to Al. "He accepts what's on Boch's personnel record, that says he's a native of Germany, but if that man's accent is German, I'm talking Ojibwe to you right now."

"Boo-zhoo, Chief Mitch," said Al. "I'm with you. The few words that Boch deigned to bestow upon us didn't sound very Germanic to me, either."

"That leaves us with the question of where is Boch really from."

"How do we get an answer to that?"

"We could go back to his room and beat him with a rubber hose."

"Probably be frowned on if this case ever went to court."

"You're right. I think we're up the proverbial stream without the proverbial canoe. Let's beach the canoe for now and I'll write a story about the characters we've met to send to our city editor along with your incomparable pics."

"Sounds good to me," Al said, as he stretched out on the bed. "Wake me when your story is done, and we can send our offerings together."

By the time I finished polishing a story that I was certain would be of very little interest to most readers of the *Daily Dispatch*, City Editor Don O'Rourke had finished his workday and gone home. Fred Donlin, the night city editor, who was in charge when my copy reached the city desk, responded with: "Looks like you two are having a nice vacation up there by the Rez. Are the walleyes biting?"

"Walleyes not biting," I replied. "And neither are the mosquitoes."

"Hope you're home before the black flies bite," Fred replied.

"We will be," I said. I was thinking that we had no reason to stay any longer unless we could confirm our suspicion that Jutern Boch was Bigdigger, which appeared to be impossible.

I woke Al, who had dozed off, and we both decided that it was time to call our wives.

Martha Todd was sympathetic when I told her that we'd hit a roadblock in the search for Bigdigger, but she had no magic method for debunking Jutern Boch's claim that he was German. "Anyhow, what difference does it make?" she asked.

"If he's lying about his nationality, he might be lying about his knowledge—or lack thereof—of cadmium deposits," I said. "He's in the perfect position to be Bigdigger but there's no way to flush him out."

"The best answer is for the PCA to deny the permit for nickel mining," Martha said. "What in the world is taking them so long to do that? They have plenty of reasons to act."

"That's another good question for which I have no answer."

"All you can do on this mining story is keep digging," she said.

"Very funny," I said. "Ha, ha, L-O-L, and all that."

"Couldn't resist, and you, of all people, have no right to complain about a cheap pun."

We made kissy sounds to each other and hung up. Al finished his conversation with Carol a minute later, and after he'd put down his phone, he grinned and said, "Big doings in Roseville tomorrow night."

"What's up?" I asked.

"The question of the school board's stupid book ban is what's up. The published agenda shows that they're planning to reopen the subject at tomorrow night's meeting."

"Have they changed their minds? Are they going to rescind it?"

"Carol says that the huge student protest, lots of negative public reaction, and the threat of a lawsuit from one of publishers whose book is among those banned may have convinced some of the ban supporters to rethink their votes."

"Wouldn't that be a hoot? Wonder if one of them is Sarah Nordstrom's daddy."

"Great story: Progressive youth triumphs over stuffy old-time prejudice," Al said.

"We gotta get back and cover that meeting," I said. "Let's hit the road first thing tomorrow morning."

"Got'cha! Up early and out."

If only we'd been aware of how early and how far out it would be.

30

KNOCK! KNOCK!

It was still dark when we were awakened by loud knocking on the cabin door. "Did you leave a wake-up call with Corrie?" I asked.

"Not me," Al said.

I got up, went to the door, slid aside the locking bolt and opened the door. For the second time in less than a week I was slammed back into a room by an onslaught of intruders, this group consisting of six large men dressed in heavy cold-weather coats, hats, and boots. They charged into the room like a football team's defensive line rushing the opponent's passer. I was pushed back and pinned against a wall by two burly men and Al was dragged out of bed and slammed to the wall beside me another substantial pair.

"Get clothes on," said Jutern Boch, who was the only attacker I recognized. He held a shiny black revolver in his right hand. "Coats, hats, mittens, too."

"Where are we going?" I asked.

"You go ice fishing," Boch said. "Have very bad luck."

"How bad?" Al asked.

"Ice break. You fall in. Nobody awake, nobody hear you yell for help. Very bad luck for you."

"Is this your version of a German *Blitzkrieg*?" I asked.

"What you mean German *Blitzkrieg*?" Boch asked.

"Aren't you from Germany?"

"Fuck Germany," said the supposed native of Frankfurt. "You two get ass in gear; get dressed."

The men holding Al and me against the wall released us, and while we were getting dressed as slowly as possible, I said, "What country are you really from, Mister Boch?"

"None of reporter's business what country Mister Boch is from," said Boch. "Get into coat and hat. Twenty degrees outside. You dress warm to go fishing."

This did not sound like a fun fishing trip no matter how we would be dressed. If the ice on the lake broke, as Boch had told us that it would, and we fell into deep cold water wearing thick wool coats and heavy rubber boots, we would be zooming toward the bottom at close to warp speed.

"What's this all about?" Al asked. "Why are you doing this?"

"My boss say reporter man ask too many questions. Reporter man too snoopy. Want to know too much about what we dig for. Boss say reporter man have to go fishing and because you with reporter man you go fishing, too."

"Is your email name Bigdigger?" I asked.

"Jutern's email name is no business of yours," said Boch. "Reporter man get coat on *now!*" He swung the revolver around in a circle so violently that I flinched in fear that he might accidentally squeeze the trigger with the muzzle pointed toward me. He laughed at my defensive movement and swung the gun around again, but this time I caught myself and maintained a steady pose, even though my legs were trembling.

As soon as we'd buttoned the last buttons on our coats, we were hustled out the door by two pairs of escorts who grabbed us by both arms firmly enough to cause pain and dragged us along like little children. They pushed us into the second seat of a three-seat black Suburban with tinted windows and piled into the seat behind us. Boch took the wheel and was joined in front by the sixth member of the attack force. Off we went, onto the Rez and onward toward the lake we were trying to protect from nickel mining runoff pollution. If Boch's scenario went as planned, we'd soon be polluting the lake ourselves as decaying organic waste wrapped in sheaths of thick fabric and leather footwear.

"You won't fool anybody into thinking that this was a fishing accident," I said. "We've got no fishing poles and no bait to leave beside the hole you push us into."

Boch was smarter than I'd given him credit for. "We have two poles and bucket of bait," he said. "We make it look like big city dumb guys fish on ice too thin to hold two fat newspaper snoops."

"I beg your pardon," said Al. "Who are you calling fat?"

"He might be right about dumb," I said. "I'll never open a door again without asking, "Who eez eet?""

"You'll never open a door again *period*, if this fishing trip goes the way it's planned," Al said.

"You're right. I'll be fat and dumb, but definitely not happy."

"Since we won't be around to tattle, will you tell us who you're working for?" Al asked. "Is it Coordinated Copper and Nickel, Inc.?"

"Why you care?" Boch said. "You not able to tell nobody."

"Just curious," Al said. "I'd like to know who I can thank for this unexpected fishing trip."

"Who you can thank is none of your business," Boch said.

"Knowing who ordered this fishing trip *is* our business," I said. "If you let me go back and get my laptop, I can send them a thank you note."

"Oh, shit!" Boch said. "Forgot laptop. Better we make that go away after you fall through ice and never come up."

Another dumb move on my part: reminding him of the laptop, on which I had entered all the notes taken during the previous day's interviews. If that and the reporter's notebook that was sitting on top of it weren't found by authorities after our demise, there would be nothing in writing to link us to Boch or any of the nickel miners.

"We here," Boch said like a tour guide as he parked the big SUV beside a short stretch of snowy beach that led to the ice-covered lake. "We go chop hole in ice. You come with us. Watch how to chop." I wondered if he thought that knowledge of an ice-chopping technique would be useful in our existence beyond this world.

Al and I were dragged out of the Suburban and into the pre-dawn lakeside darkness by our escorts, who again gripped our arms firmly enough to hurt. With Boch bearing the bait bucket and the sixth man carrying the ice fishing lines, we started moving toward the lake.

Our feet had just left the snow-dusted beach sand and were slip-sliding on the snow-dusted lake ice when the predawn dark-ness was shattered by an array of flashing lights—red, blue, and white—approaching rapidly from behind the Suburban.

All eight of us turned to face the oncoming light brigade. We saw that the lights were attached to three Reservation Police vehi-cles, one of which stopped behind the Suburban, another of which stopped in front of the Suburban, and one of which slid to a stop less than ten feet from our group of eight astonished faces. From this third vehicle came an amplified male voice that said, "Stop right where you are and put your hands up high above your heads!"

Our escorts released their iron grips, and we all thrust our hands skyward. Three uniformed police officers popped out of the cruiser with service weapons in hand. One of them shouted, "Which of you are Mister Mitchell and Mister Al?"

We both waved our hands fast enough to create a hurricane and we were ordered to step forward. "You got any ID on you?" asked the officer. Thanks to being required to dress ourselves, we both had our wallets in our pockets and we both produced our press credentials and driver's licenses. While we were doing this, our six captors were being frisked and handcuffed by the other two officers. Jutern Boch was relieved of his revolver before the handcuffs were snapped on his wrists.

We were joined by four officers from the other two police vehicles, who marched Boch and company to those cruisers and crammed three of them into each of the back seats. The officer who'd examined our credentials escorted us to the back seat of his cruiser and got into the front seat beside the driver. He introduced himself as Officer Johnson and as the vehicle began to move, I finally got to ask the question that was burning up my brain.

"How on earth did you know we were here?" I said.

"We got a 911 call from a woman in the Reservation's hotel saying that Mister Mitchell and Mister Al from the St. Paul newspaper were being kidnapped and taken to the lake to be drowned," Johnson said.

"A woman in the hotel on the Reservation?" Al said.

"That's where the signal came from," Johnson said.

"When I tried to get a room there, I was told that the hotel was closed for the season," I said.

"I think they close it for tourists but keep some of the ground floor rooms heated because a few people live there year-round."

"Did the caller say what her name was?" Al asked.

"No, she didn't. Dispatcher said she had an accent that sounded like she was calling from some other country."

"Can you take us to the hotel?" I asked.

"We need to take you to the station first and get your statements about what's been going on this morning," Johnson said. "Where are you staying if you're not at the hotel?"

I told him where we were staying and that our car was out there, but said that we very much wanted to go to the hotel and find out who the caller was and how she knew what was happening to us. "This has me totally baffled, in addition to being extremely grateful," I said.

"I figured that she'd heard a ruckus in the hotel when those guys grabbed you," Johnson said. "But if you weren't in the hotel, how did she know that you were in trouble?"

"My question exactly," I said. "That's why we need to go there."

At the Rez's small police station, Al and I were taken to separate rooms and questioned verbally, after which we were asked to write statements about our experience. Then we were driven to the hotel, where we thanked Officer Johnson again for the rescue.

In the hotel lobby we got another surprise. Standing in front of the register desk to greet us was Chief Raymond Hardshell Turtle. "Boo-Zhoo!" he said. "I hear that you had quite an interesting morning."

"You might say that," I said. "We got a free ride to the lake here on the Rez and we would have had quite an invigorating swim if your troops hadn't showed up when they did."

"I'm sure that our troops, as you call them, were happy to have been at your service," the chief said.

"Not half as happy as we were to have them," Al said. "We're just wondering who the mysterious woman is who called them from here and how she knew what was happening to us."

"That's why I'm here," said Chief Raymond. "I will escort you to that woman's room. Come along, gentlemen, and meet your guardian angel."

We followed the chief out of the lobby and into the first-floor corridor and walked past the vacant breakfast room, which reminded me that all of a sudden I was hungry and could really use a cup of coffee. The chief led us all the way to the end of the corridor and stopped in front of room 101. Chief Raymond knocked on the door and I was stunned to hear a female voice that I'd heard many times through closed room doors call out, "Who eez eet?"

"It's Chief Raymond with some visitors," the chief said.

The door opened, and beside it stood the slender and shapely form of Gigette, clad in a form-fitting blue turtleneck sweater and faded blue jeans. Behind her, wearing what looked like an extra-large plain brown bag, I saw the imposing figure of Lady T. "Please to come in, gentlemen," said the Lady.

Chief Raymond greeted the women and excused himself, leaving Al and me alone with Lady T and Gigette. After we'd both verbally drowned Lady T with our thanks for saving us from being physically drowned in the lake, I asked, "How on earth did you know we were here and that we were in trouble this morning?"

"Lady T can answer that with a question of her own," Lady T said. "When was the last time that Mister Mitchell checked the pocket of his large winter coat?"

I said the standard, "Oh, my god!" before I put my hand into the left side pocket of my big winter coat and felt a square hard object. I wrapped my fingers around it and pulled it out. It was the listening device that Gigette had planted there two weeks earlier, upon which Lady T had heard the attack on Martha Todd and me in our home and sent St. Paul police to the rescue.

I held the little box up and said that I'd put it back into my pocket and forgotten about it.

"Lady T is very pleased by your forgetfulness," she said. "It has allowed Lady T to send help to you once again."

"You've been listening to us talk all this time?" Al said.

"Ever since you arrived at the cabin in which you are staying," Lady T said. "Your accommodations are close enough for Lady T's receiver to capture the signal from the device in your pocket."

"You've heard everything we've been saying?" I said.

"Either Lady T or Gigette has been aware of the sound of your conversation at all times but have not usually paid attention to what was being said," she said. "However, this morning Lady T was most fortunate to hear the disturbance in your cottage when the group of men crashed in and made you both prisoners."

"Thanks for paying attention to all that happened to us this morning," I said. "I'm surprised that you were even awake at the hour we were attacked."

"For many years, Lady T has been arising at five o'clock to begin her morning meditation, no matter what time zone she is in when she is away from Budapest. This morning, the high volume of the voices and the sound of a motor vehicle on the listening device, which is normally quiet at that hour, drew Lady T's attention while she was brewing her first cup of tea," Lady T said.

I asked Lady T why she was on the Reservation, and she said that she'd been ordered by her superiors to stay there as if she were a year-round resident of the hotel and quietly watch for activity at the site of the proposed nickel mine. She said that she had neglected to turn off the receiver that was tuned to the listening device in my coat pocket and that she was startled to hear our voices suddenly break the silence when we got within range of the receiver Thursday afternoon. She began paying attention to our voices so that she could follow our progress as we interviewed the copper miners.

"Lady T was not surprised to learn that Mister Mitchell did not accept her advice to wait for information from official investigators," she said. "Naturally, Lady T was pleased to discover that she was able to hear everything that Mister Mitchell was learning from his talks with the mining crew."

"Did Lady T ... uh ... did *you* learn anything from my interviews?" I asked.

"Lady T heard confirmation of things that she already knew," she said. "Lady T is almost ready to call upon her supervisors to bring an end to the threat of the proposed mining project by making some arrests."

Whoa! This was a bombshell I hadn't seen coming. "Who will be arrested?" I asked.

"The man who led the group that kidnapped you and threatened your lives this morning will be the first."

"Jutern Boch? He's already under arrest for that."

"He will soon be under arrest for planning and facilitating the international sale of stolen material—namely a small cache of cadmium—to a forbidden foreign power."

"Is Jutern Boch the man who called himself Bigdigger?"

"Lady T cannot discuss this situation any further with the news media, Mister Mitchell. Lady T has already said too much and asks that Mister Mitchell refrain from publishing any of what she has disclosed."

"Oh, please don't stop now and leave Al and me hanging in suspense," I said. "We'll keep it all off the record and won't print or speak a word about the impending arrest or any of the juicy details until you authorize it."

Lady T bowed her head and thought for what seemed like hours before replying. While she pondered, I held my breath, hoping that my plea had sounded passably professional and not pitifully pathetic.

At last Lady T spoke. "Very well, Mister Mitchell. On the condition that you will not print a single word until I authorize you to do so, I will tell you what I have learned about the plan to mine cadmium in your state of Minnesota and transport it to the country of Iran."

"Which used to be called Persia," I said.

"Precisely," Lady T said. "The person who identified himself as Actionman is located in the country formerly known as Persia, hence the email address ending in PPower.com."

"And again, I'm asking, is Jutern Boch using the email address Bigdigger?"

"He is. But his real name isn't Jutern Boch. His true name is Mohammed Yuseff, and he is not from Germany as he claims. He really immigrated to the United States from Iran."

"So, both Actionman and Bigdigger are Iranians?"

"That is correct, Mister Mitchell."

"Okay. How did he go from being Mohammed Yuseff to calling himself Jutern Boch?"

"By stealing the identity of a deceased German citizen named Jutern Bach from Mister Bach's website and changing the 'a' to an 'o.'"

"Why did the late Mister Bach have a website?" I asked.

"In life, he was a square dance caller," Lady T said. "His real name was Hans Scharfenbach, but he changed his own identity as a caller to Jutern Bach, which apparently mimics a popular square dance call."

"Of course it does," Al said. "*U-turn back* is a call you hear twenty times a night at a square dance."

"Mister Bach had been deceased for two years, but his square dance caller website was never taken down by his survivors and Mister Yuseff, who was looking for name that wasn't Arab to steal, found it. No square dancers look at this website anymore, so it easy for Mister Yuseff to take deceased owner's identity without it being noticed."

"The change from Bach to Boch after the theft explains why Jutern Boch never shows up on Google," I said. "He doesn't exist in the electronic universe."

"Too bad he exists in the flesh and blood universe," Al said. "He came altogether too close to hitting the delete button from that one for the two of us this morning."

I took the little black box out of my coat pocket, waved it back and forth above my head, and said, "And just think about this. We'd be at the bottom of a watery trash bin right now if I'd ever cleaned out my coat pockets. This little gadget could be a piece of junk sitting on a shelf in our basement in St. Paul if I hadn't just put it back in my pocket and left it there forever."

"Whoever said cleanliness is next to godliness had it all wrong," Al said. "Being a slob has life-saving rewards."

I had more questions to ask. "Boch—Yussef—said that his boss had ordered him to take us fishing this morning. Is his boss some executive at Coordinated Copper and Nickel, Incorporated?"

"No," said Lady T. "Mister Yussef employed by mining company as Mister Boch, but boss who ordered him to drown you is fellow Iranian, who use email address of Actionman."

"Now I'm really confused," I said. "How did Yussef-slash-Boch get under the control of Actionman while he was working as a miner for CCNI?"

"Mister Yussef cannot find job in Iran, so he come to America to look for job. He have to leave family behind in Iran because they have not enough money for trip. Wife and two small children—one boy, one girl. When Mister Yussef, using name Jutern Boch, get job with company that owns nickel mines, which sometimes also have cadmium with the nickel, Iranian officials arrest wife and children and hold them in prison. Officials tell Mister Yussef that if he ever hope to see his family go free, he must do whatever Actionman tell him to do, which is to look for cadmium at nickel mines without American bosses knowing that he doing this. Mister Yussef did find cadmium here in Minnesota nickel mine and make report to Actionman. Now mining of cadmium just wait for Minnesota government to approve nickel mining permit."

"How could Boch get the cadmium out of the ground without his American boss discovering what he's doing?" I asked.

"Lady T does not know details, but associates believe Mister Boch has formed small group to get cadmium without telling others in mining crew what is being removed from mine or where it will go. Lady T's associates know that Mister Boch has purchased special safety equipment for himself and four others."

"So some of the miners that we've interviewed might be in that foursome and have lied to us about not knowing of anything other than copper being mined here?" I said.

"That is possible, Mister Mitchell."

"Okay," I said. "Do you know how the cadmium would get from Minnesota to Iran after it was out of the ground? I mean, they can't just throw it on a truck and drive it to a port somewhere and load it on a boat, can they?"

"No, they cannot do that, Mister Mitchell," she said. "But they can put safe container of cadmium in large delivery type van and drive it to airplane with skis on ice of very large lake just few miles from where they dig it up."

"Won't a ski plane landing on the lake attract the attention of neighbors who might call their local police?"

"Seven ski planes already sitting on lake. Belong to owners of homes built all around lake. One more plane on lake not going to be what you Americans call 'big deal.'"

"What about loading the cadmium onto the airplane?" I asked. "Won't some of those homeowners have questions about that when they see it going on?"

"Lady T's associates believe plan is to load airplane without making noise late at night. Mister Boch already has van with electric engine that makes no sound. Plane can wait to take off first thing in morning so not cause problem with neighbors at night."

"Pretty slick plan," I said.

"Slick as a turtle's wet belly," Al said.

"Tricky as a really cool shell game," I said.

Lady T looked puzzled, so I explained that we were only cracking silly jokes.

I thanked Lady T for her lengthy explanation and asked if a time had been set for the arrests.

"No exact time set," Lady T said. "Presence of Mister Mitchell and Mister Al cause time to be set back because you asking miners questions about what other things might be mined after nickel put Mister Boch and Actionman on what you call 'alert.'"

"So we screwed up your agency's arrest schedule?" Al asked.

"You did," Lady T said. "But you have no way to know this, so are safe from arrest."

"Arrest?" I said. "What would we be arrested for?"

"For interfering with action by law enforcement agency," she said. "Lady T had to speak for you to keep you from being arrested."

"That would have been awful," Al said. "Being in jail would have kept us from going on that wonderful trip to the lake with Jutern Yussef and his jolly band of fisherfolk this morning."

"Thank you for keeping us from being arrested," I said. "What did you say to save us?"

"Lady T say you are ignorant."

"O-o-okay. Thanks so much for that description," I said.

I heard Gigette giggle before Lady T said, "Lady T means ignorant of law enforcement agency plan to make arrest. I tell them you not guilty of interfering with something you know nothing at all about."

I unruffled my feathers and said, "Ah, yes, that makes sense."

Al was looking at his watch. "We should get going if we want to make it back home in time for tonight's school board show."

I agreed, and again thanked Lady T for everything she had done for us, including preventing our arrest.

"Remember, you make promise to wait for word from Lady T before you print anything that Lady T tell you."

"I won't forget," I said. "As a reporter, I've never broken my word on keeping off the record information to myself until the proper release time comes."

I turned toward the door and had just put my hand on the knob when a voice behind me said, "Monsieur Mitch-*ell*."

It startled me. Was Gigette, who never spoke to us unless requested to do so by Lady T, calling my name? I turned around and said, "Yes?"

Gigette was smiling. At me. She said, "Monsieur Mitch-*ell*, are vous a Tur-*tell*?"

I was so surprised that I stood in open-mouth silence for a moment before the words came out, "You bet your sweet ass I am, Gigette." On that frivolous note, Al and I made a swooping exit, laughing all the way.

"I'm ready for some breakfast after all that," Al said as we walked down the corridor toward the hotel lobby.

"I'm way past ready. We can stop at the first open restaurant we see on the way back to Corrie's," I said.

"Whoa!" Al said. "How are we going to get back to Corrie's? Our car is parked out there in front of our charming cottage."

"I'd forgot about that," I said. "We got a free ride away from there with Jutern and his friends. But how *do* we get back? I doubt that Uber is selling its services up here on the Rez."

"Do you think Corrie would come and get us if we called him?" Al said.

"Worth a try." I looked up the number for Corrie's Charming Cottages as we continued walking and was just about to punch it into my phone when we entered the lobby. I stopped in mid-punch because there on a sofa in the lobby sat Chief Raymond Hardshell Turtle, who greeted us with a smile, stood up, and said, "Boo-zhooh, gentlemen. Can I give you a lift somewhere?"

Not only did Chief Raymond give us a lift to Corrie's Charming Cottages, but he also stopped at the first open restaurant and bought us breakfast, which was, as he put it, "Just compensation for your morning's discomfort on behalf of the endangered turtles that reside beside the Ojibwe Nation."

"Discomfort is a very interesting way to describe our adventure with that quartet of nasty nickel miners," Al said.

"The leader, Jutern Boch, was the only nickel miner in that bunch," the chief said.

"Who were other three?" I asked.

"Goons sent up from the Cities," Chief Raymond said. "Ordered to get you by whoever's been trying to keep your stories out of the paper."

"Actionman," I said.

"You know him?" the chief said.

I thought of my pledge of secrecy to Lady T and said, "I've heard of him back home."

At our charming cottage, Al and I got out of the car and thanked the chief for the ride and the breakfast. Then I asked, "Chief Raymond, are you a Turtle?"

Chief Raymond looked at me in wide-eyed surprise, burst out laughing, and said, "You bet your sweet ass I am."

31

OFF WE GO

We packed up as fast as we could toss our stuff together and walked to the office to check out.

"What the heck was all that racket at five o'clock?" Corrie asked as Al slid the cottage key across the counter.

"Some guys we met out here picked us up to go ice fishing," Al said. "They were kind of noisy. Sorry if they woke you up."

"So how was the fishing?" Corrie asked. "Any luck?"

"Hooked a big one, but we gave it away to a guy on the Rez," Al said.

"If we'd caught one more, a really nice walleye, we'd have left it with you," I said.

"Just my luck," Corrie said. "Always playin' second fiddle."

"Maybe next year," I said. No way that would happen, but it didn't hurt to schmooze him a little bit.

One the way home, we stopped for lunch—deep-fried walleye and apple pie—at a family-owned restaurant in Sauk Centre and sent text messages to our wives to inform them that we'd be home in time to join them for supper and get to the school board meeting. I also sent a text to Don O'Rourke, saying that we had completed our mission with the nickel miners and would be returning the company car to the *Daily Dispatch* garage and picking up our own cars at about four o'clock.

"Will you have any copy for us?" Don texted in reply.

"Nothing today," I responded. "Both of us will be at the Roseville school meet tonight."

"Good. I was looking for someone to cover that. Get story and pics in tonight and come to office tomorrow. You are on Saturday schedule," Don texted.

"After going through all this crap, we don't even get a day off tomorrow because of the school board meeting," I said to Al.

"Timing is everything," Al said.

The timing of my arrival at home was good. Martha was already there, and she greeted me with a long hug and half a dozen welcome home kisses. Sherlock Holmes wrapped himself around my ankles and allowed me to scratch behind his ears. What more could any man ask for?

The school board meeting was scheduled for 7:30, but it was already a standing room only scene when Martha and I arrived at 7:15. There were dozens of young faces in the crowd and up near the front I saw the back of a head that I thought belonged to Sarah Nordstrom. Some people came bearing homemade signs urging either the rejection of or the reinforcement of the previous book ban decision. It was easy to pick out the members of the Sensitive Materials Under Trial committee. Their signs all urged the preservation of decency and godliness in the schools, while the other side advocated preservation of the First Amendment for all.

Al had wormed his way into a spot in front, from where he could shoot pics of both the board members at the front table and the people in the crowd. We spotted Carol in a chair near the back, but there was no polite way to get near enough to talk to her. The noise level in the room was equal to that produced by two jet airplane engines revving for takeoff.

The five members of the school board filed in at 7:35, with looks of surprise and awe at the size of the crowd facing them. Instead of turning around and running away, which probably would have been their first choice, they sat themselves down at the table behind their respective nameplates and pretended to study the printed agendas in front of them.

It took three poundings of the gavel and three calls for the meeting to come to order from chairman Hjalmar Nordstrom, who was seated in the middle, to reduce the din to a level at which his shouts for order could be heard. Nordstrom gave the gavel a fourth rap and this time everyone heard him say, "The meeting of the Roseville School Board will come to order."

Nordstrom looked quickly to his left and the woman at that end, whose wooden nameplate said Ms. Anthony, raised her hand and said, "Mister Chairman."

"The chair recognizes Amber Anthony," said Nordstrom.

Amber Anthony read from a note card in her hand: "I move that this board rescind the previous motion requiring the board to appoint a committee of volunteer parents to rule on all the books in all the libraries and all the books proposed for use in all the classrooms in all the schools in the district."

"I second the motion," said the man beside her, whose name plate said Mr. Walker.

"All in favor signify by raising your right hand," said the chairman.

The hands of Anthony and Walker went up.

"All opposed signify by raising your right hand," Nordstrom said.

The two hands on the other side of the chairman both went up. This made it a tie, which required the chairman to vote.

All eyes were on Hjalmar Nordstrom as he looked around the room. His gaze settled on the head that I was now certain was that of his daughter. He stared at her for several seconds, and then said, "The chair votes aye. This meeting is adjourned." Down came the gavel with a crash and out of the corner of my eye I saw Al's camera flash.

A thunder of cheers and jeers that would drown out a train whistle filled the room as the board members swiftly rose and vanished through the door behind the table. Some people in the crowd were laughing, some were shaking their fists, some others were weeping.

"Not much discussion of the motion," Martha said as we stood up.

"Very efficient chairman," I said. "Meet me outside; I need to talk to Sarah Nordstrom."

I pushed my way through the mob with a judicious use of elbows, shoulders, and "excuse me's" until I reached the person with the head that really did belong to the chairman's daughter. She saw me waving my hand and moved within shouting range.

"What have you got to say about your father?" I yelled.

"Best daddy ever," she shouted. "And best school board chairman in the world!"

Sarah raised her arms above her head in triumph, and again out of the corner of my eye, I saw Al's camera flash.

That image dominated page one of Saturday morning's *Daily Dispatch* as it appeared above my story. Pics of people in the crowd displaying messages on sign boards and a four-column-wide shot of the board members staring at their chairman as he pondered his tie-breaking vote took up most of an inside page. A boxed insert in my story directed readers to an Opinion page editorial (no doubt written before the vote was taken) praising the board's decision. I surmised that an editorial lamenting the defeat of the motion to rescind the ban had also been written but was now buried in the computer system's trash bin.

Don O'Rourke called Al and me into a huddle over coffee and doughnuts in the lunchroom at mid-morning Saturday. After giving us each an attaboy for our coverage of the school board meeting, he asked if we had learned anything about the nickel mine other than that the lay-about nickel miners weren't very interesting people.

"You'd be surprised how interesting one of them is," Al said, and between us we rattled off an expurgated version of our kidnapping and nearly fatal ride to the lake.

"So, the guy who led the fishing party is involved in the cadmium thing?" Don asked when we'd finished.

"He's the leader," I said. "There's a big deal from law enforcement coming down on his head any day now, but I can't tell you more."

"Why not? Don said.

"Everything I have is off the record. On my honor as a Turtle, I have sworn not to give it away until my very reliable source authorizes it."

"What do you mean by your honor as a Turtle?" Don asked.

This was not the proper question, so I did not have to give the proper answer. "It's just something personal that I'm involved in," I said. "Anyhow, we've been promised advance notice of when the lightning strike will hit, and I think you'll want us to be back at the Rez when the arm of the law comes down on the cadmium diggers."

"Is this the guy who called himself Bigdigger in the emails that T.J. had on her thumb drive?"

"It is."

"Does he work for Coordinated Copper and Nickel, Inc.?" Don asked.

"He does," I said. "But he also works for somebody else, and I can't write about any of this until my source gives me the go-ahead."

"Why is this so hush hush?"

"The good guys don't want to tip off the bad guys that the hammer is coming down."

"Okay, I'll buy that excuse," Don said. "Any idea when this might happen?"

"I'm guessing it's a matter of days and not weeks," I said. "You should expect us to zoom out of here on a moment's notice. It's a five-hour drive to the miners' motel."

"We're keeping our bags packed, ready to roll," Al said.

"Don't forget to say goodbye," Don said.

We adjourned from the lunchroom, and I decided to look for an answer to another question. I called Brownie's number on the chance that he might be in his office on a Saturday morning. For once, my luck was good.

"Homicidebrown," he said.

"Dailydispatchmitchell," I said.

"Of course it's Mitchell," Brownie said. "Nobody else expects me to answer this phone on Saturday. Where've you been all week?"

"Up north," I said. "Did you miss me?"

"Like I'd miss an aching tooth after it was pulled."

"As a reporter, I consider that high praise. Have you turned over any stones on the turtle-jack killings while I was gone?"

"As a matter of fact, we have," Brownie said. "We checked into the rental records of the house that burned on Summit Avenue, the one called Tall Timbers that your wife was held in, and discovered that the tenant was something named P.Power.com, which we can't find anywhere on the Internet."

"Actionman!" I said.

"What do you mean?"

"I mean that the house was rented by the person or group that called itself Actionman on those emails that were on our reporter's thumb drive. That's huge!"

"Why huge?" Brownie asked.

"It means that the gang that killed two members of our staff, trashed Al's house, kidnapped Martha Todd, and invaded our home were hired by someone in Iran, and not by anyone at Coordinated Copper and Nickel, Inc., as I suspected. It wasn't CCNI that was looking for the turtle with the thumb drive, it was Actionman, whoever the hell that might be, over in Iran."

"This is very important to you?"

"It is. I've been telling the CEO of CCNI that someone on his staff hired the turtle-jack killers, and he has been insisting that I was wrong. Now you're telling me that he's right and I'm wrong."

"So now you're saying that the mining company is completely innocent of everything?"

"Not completely. Some of his company's employees are involved in a major crime, but they've got nothing to do with the goons who were operating out of Tall Timbers."

"What major crime are they involved in?"

"I can't talk about it yet, but I can tell you it has nothing to do with the homicides."

"This PPower.com that rented the house is located somewhere in Iran?" Brownie asked.

"*Was* located somewhere in Iran might be a better way to say it," I said. "If you can't find it on the Internet, they must have taken the website down. The first P in PPower.com stood for Persia, which was the previous name for Iran. Thank you for telling me all of this."

"Thank you for the info about PPower.com," Brownie said. "This means that I can close the book on those two homicides and go ahead with prosecuting the bums that we have in custody."

"A mutually beneficial conversation," I said. "Not bad for a Saturday's work."

"Not bad at all. Have a good day, Mitch," Brownie said, and he ended the call.

For once, his wish for a good day for me had been granted. Unfortunately, Corrine Ramey was not at her desk to hear my low-volume whoop of triumph.

32

THE TURTLE CALLS

The call came while Martha and I were clearing the supper dishes from the table that night—and it came from Lady T herself. "Mister Boch is to be arrested by Interpol for planning to steal and sell cadmium to banned country at 6:00 A.M. tomorrow in Reservation jail, four men working with him in cadmium mining scheme are to be arrested at same time in motel where they stay, and identity of man who calls self Actionman is known and he is to be arrested at same hour at home in Iran," she said. "Mister Mitchell and Mister Al have to be early rise Turtles if want to witness arrests."

I laughed, and said, "Early rise Turtles won't make it to Iran but they will be at the jail and the motel. Tell me one more time, Lady T, are you a Turtle?"

"You bet your sweet ass I am," she said. Her first-person response to this question always makes me laugh because it's the only time that she ever breaks her third-person schtick as Hungary's most popular TV personality.

I called Al and told him that we had to be on the road by midnight. "I'm gassed up and ready to go," he said.

"I hope all the gas is in your tank," I said. "Anyhow, I'll be waiting with bated breath on the porch."

"If you bait that breath with garlic, I'll make you sit in back."

"Martha says that I'm a pain-in-the-ass backseat driver, so you'll want to keep me up in front no matter what kind of bait is on my breath."

Our plan was for Al to drop me behind the jail with a camera to wait for the Interpol agents to march Jutern Boch out the door, and for Al to return to the motel and wait for Interpol action he could photograph there. We arrived at the jail a few minutes after five o'clock and found that all was dark and quiet on that scene. I leaned against the side wall near the front corner of the building to wait in the darkness after Al rolled away. Ten minutes later my phone beeped, and I found a text message from Al saying that he was in position at the motel and that not a creature was stirring, not even a louse.

I was feeling drowsy enough to take a nap standing up when the parking lot was illuminated by the headlights of two black SUVs and the outside lights of the jail popped on. The Rez's police chief emerged from one of the vehicles and two burly men in plain-clothes got out of the other one. All three men went into the jail, and I hung cautiously behind the corner, watching and waiting for them to exit with Jutern Boch.

I waited. And waited. Five minutes went by and nobody came out of the jail. A minute later another vehicle, this one an ambulance, rolled into the parking lot. My curiosity climbed higher than a cat's when I saw two medics carrying a gurney go running into the jail.

This was too much; I couldn't wait any longer. I trotted to the door and stepped inside, where I was stopped immediately by a uniformed police officer whose name tag said Wendell. I told Officer Wendell who I was and why I was there, and offered to show him my press credentials. "Stay right there," he said. "This is an emergency situation. I will speak to the chief."

Officer Wendell turned and was gone before I could ask what kind of emergency was occurring. When he returned, he said that I should step outside and wait beside the door. The chief, he said, would speak to me at the appropriate time.

What else could I do but obey? I stepped out into the darkness and checked my phone. Nothing from Al. I hoped he was having better luck than I was. I wondered how long it would be until the time was appropriate.

The door beside me opened and the EMTs came out wheeling the gurney, upon which an adult-size figure lay stretched, covered completely with a sheet. I clicked the phone into the camera mode and took a shot as the EMTs slid their package into the back of the ambulance. Then they closed the rear doors, climbed into the front seats, and drove away toward the first glimmer of daylight in the sky.

Curiouser and curiouser, I thought. Should I go back into the police station or should I keep waiting for the chief or whoever the chief was sending to deal with me at the appropriate time? The question was answered a moment later with the appearance of Officer Wendell. "Chief Rogers will speak to you now, sir," he said.

Chief Rogers met me just inside the door and held out his right hand for shaking. "I assume you were here this morning to observe the arrest of one of our guests," he said.

"That's correct," I said. "I was notified by a representative of the arresting agency."

"You're dealing with some pretty high-powered people," he said.

"I've been very lucky to have met this representative," I said.

"You're not so lucky this morning," Chief Rogers said. "The guest whose higher-level arrest was to have occurred this morning went away in the back of that ambulance."

"Is he sick?"

"He is dead."

It took a moment for that reply to register. When it had, I said, "Dead? How?"

"We thought we'd searched him thoroughly when we tucked him in for the night but apparently he had a cyanide capsule or something of that nature hidden somewhere. We found him stretched out and unresponsive on the floor of his cell this morning and the EMTs couldn't restore any sign of life. They said that he apparently had ingested something highly toxic, probably cyanide."

"That's a whole different story than I was planning to write," I said.

"It's a whole different story than I was planning to tell," Chief Rogers said. "I'm taking it as a guilty plea and closing the case we had against him. Are you one of the guys that he and his crew took out to the lake for a swim under the ice?"

"I am," I said. "Gives me goose bumps to think about it. I guess I won't have to come back here to testify against him."

"We've still got his buddies in custody. You might be called to testify against them."

"Whatever," I said. "Right now I'm stuck here until my photographer, who is at the motel to get pics of the arrests that are happening there, comes back to pick me up. Is it okay to wait inside?"

"Be my guest," said Chief Roberts. He smiled and added, "You'll have to wait out here, though. I won't be offering you a private room." He waved me toward a chair beside the front desk, wished me a good day, and left through a door behind the desk where Office Wendell was sitting.

I saw that I had a text from Al. "Crazy here. Rooms of intended arrestees were empty. Owner is royally pissed because they bailed out without paying their bill."

"Intended arrestee here also bailed out. Permanently," I replied.

"What do you mean by permanently?"

"Ate something that disagreed with him 100 percent. Permanently means dead. Come get me."

"I'm on the way. Helluva story."

"Not quite what expected."

I watched through the window and waved goodbye to Officer Wendell when I saw Al's car pull up in front of the station. He waved back and said, "Have a good day, sir."

I refrained from commenting on the unlikelihood of my having a good day and trotted out to the car. "Let's go get a response from Lady T," I said as I fastened my seatbelt.

"That should be a hoot," Al said. He drove to the hotel, and we went in. The reception desk was vacant when we went through the lobby. When we arrived at Lady T's door at the end of the hall, I knocked and waited for Gigette's usual query, "Who eez eet?" When I heard it, I told her who it was, and the door opened.

Lady T was seated in the big chair, wearing an orange bathrobe that made her look like the great pumpkin. Gigette was less spectacularly garbed in a deep blue bathrobe that hung to the floor. Laddie T, wearing a light blue doggie sweater, was asleep on the carpet at the foot of the bed.

"I assume you know everything that happened this morning," I said.

"Lady T is most disappointed in this morning's results," she said.

"I hope things went better in Iran than they did here," I said.

"Lady T is sorry to tell you that they did not. Iran officials not cooperating with our agency. Actionman not arrested. He is safe from arrest there forever."

"Oh, no," I said.

"No way," Al said. "Can't we send him a bomb or something?"

"I know; let's send him an exploding turtle," I said.

"Lady T thinks that most appropriate," Lady T said with a smile. Gigette just giggled.

"Will you give me a comment on the morning's action if I quote you as an anonymous reliable source?" I asked.

"You may say that anonymous reliable source is disappointed by the failure to arrest suspects at motel and is saddened by self-inflicted death of suspect being held in local jail. The anonymous source's sympathy goes out to that suspect's wife and children in Iran."

"Thank you," I said. "Too bad your people in Iran couldn't bring in Actionman. He's responsible for a couple of murders in St. Paul. He should be in prison for those, as well as for trying to steal the cadmium, instead being free to cause more trouble."

Lady T smiled and said, "Lady T reminds Mister Mitchell that serious accidents sometimes happen to people, even in seeming safe places like Iran."

"So Actionman isn't entirely safe, even though he wasn't arrested?" I said.

"As Lady T has said, serious accidents sometimes happen to people, even in Iran."

"I'm hoping that Actionman is accident prone," I said.

"That would be a bang-up finish," Al said.

"Lady T will keep Mister Mitchell informed if any serious accident happen in Iran," she said.

"I guess we're done here," I said. "I need to write my story and send it to St. Paul along with the non-arrest pics that both of us took this morning. Will you two be going back to Hungary now that the cadmium caper is over?"

"Lady T and Gigette will be on first possible flight to Budapest," Lady T said. "It is farewell from both to Mister Mitchell and Mister Alan."

"Farewell to both of you," I said.

"Likewise," Al said. "May you have a very boring flight."

We sat down in the hotel's vacant breakfast room and I wrote my story, incorporating notes that Al had taken at the motel, and emailed it to Sunday City Editor Gordon Holmberg. His response was: "Wow! Hope this finally kills the nickel mine and saves the turtles we've been rooting for."

"Time to wake up the PCA," I sent back.

"'Tis a consummation devoutly to be wish'd," he replied.

"Gordy's quoting Hamlet for the preservation of the turtles," I said to Al.

"I'm sure the turtles are shellabrating his performance," Al said.

We were almost back to St. Paul when I realized that I had not made my ritual Sunday phone call to my mother and my Grandma Goodie. I punched their number into my cellphone and Mom answered with: "Good morning, my wayward son."

"What's with the wayward bit?" I asked.

"I'm betting that you'll have to tell your grandmother that once again you have failed to attend a church service," she said. "I'm sure of this because we are just walking out of ours."

"You're right. Al and I had a very early start on the day and our schedule didn't allow any time for a worship service," I said.

"Good luck selling that alibi to Grandma Goodie," Mom said.

"You can read all about it in this morning's *Daily Dispatch* if you don't believe me."

"I'll look at the online edition as soon as I get home. I hope nobody tried to kidnap you or worse this morning."

"We were in no danger, but we were a long way from home." I gave her a quick rundown of our morning, omitting our visit to Lady T, and she expressed her shock at the suicide of Jutern Boch and the escape of his fellow cadmium seekers.

"Are the turtles safe now?" she asked.

"They won't be safe until the drones at the PCA wake up and deny the mining company's permit request."

After a couple of minutes, Mom passed the phone to Grandma

Goodie, who immediately asked if I'd been to church. I gave her my answer and my alibi, and she said, "Your boss should not be sending out to deal with criminals on the Sabbath. The salvation of your soul is more important than the capture of a petty criminal."

"This was an international dangerous substance thief, not a petty pickpocket," I said. "This was a man who tried to do away with both Al and me a few weeks ago."

To change the subject, I asked her how the Minnesota Wild hockey team was doing. It amazed me that a gentle, peaceable woman like Grandma Goodie would go gaga over a violent sport like hockey, but she was a wildly vociferous fan of the Wild. We finished our conversation in agreement that the team's major weakness was its goalie, and that management needed to make a trade for someone who was better at stopping speeding pucks.

"Good move, getting her out of church and into hockey," Al said when our discussion was finished.

"Thank God for the Wild," I said. "The only things she loves as much as her church are her Minnesota sports teams."

33

THE DECISION

"**B**ig story coming from the Capitol this morning," Don O'Rourke said Monday morning as I passed his desk on the way to mine.

"What's happening in the citadel of our political gods?" I asked.

"Bernie says the PCA is going to issue its decision on the nickel mining application this morning." Bernie was Bernard Benchley, our state government reporter who covered everything that happened in the Capitol.

"Did Bernie have any inside dope on what the decision will be?" I asked.

"No. None of the board members would talk about it, but Bernie can't imagine how any of them could vote in favor of the permit after all the crap that's gone on up there."

"Stranger things have happened," I said. "I'll be sending my thoughts and prayers to the turtles until I've heard the decision is in their favor."

"They'll need your thoughts and prayers even more if the decision isn't in their favor," Don said.

"Thoughts and prayers won't stand a chance against sulfide mining procedures once the miners start digging," I said. "While I'm waiting, I'll put in a call my buddy in Pittsburgh, the CEO of Coordinated

Copper and Nickel, Inc., for a side bar on his reaction to the PCA's decision and to the crap that went down at the Rez yesterday morning."

"Why don't you wait until after the decision is announced?"

"Because it will probably take that long to get through to the gentleman. This lord of metallic ore digging never just picks up a call. We mere earthlings have to schedule a calling time with his intrepid guardian of the telephone gates."

I called the number for Kurt S.C. Turner and, as expected, got the husky voice of the mighty Madge. I explained my reason for calling and she transferred me to Caroline, who said she would schedule me for 11:35 CST.

"That's way too late," I said. "I need his reaction to the PCA's decision, which is only minutes away. I don't think he'd like to have me write that the CEO couldn't be reached for comment on this big of a deal."

"I'll tell Mister Turner what the situation is and get back to you," Caroline said.

Three minutes later Caroline called and said that Turner would be issuing an official statement via email to all news media as soon as the decision was announced.

"I will still need to talk to him at 11:35," I said. "I have a special question that nobody else on his email list will be asking."

"I will tell him of your special request so that he will be prepared for your call," she said.

While I waited for the news from the Capitol, I wrote the ledes for two stories—one the response to an approval and the other the response to a denial. I was ready for both and hoping for the right one as I sat waiting for the word from Bernie.

Every one of us in the newsroom jumped up from our chairs and ran to the city desk when Don shouted, "Here it comes!"

Don opened the attachment to the email that he'd just received, and we all leaned in to read it over his shoulder. It said:

___

"By Bernard Benchley

"*Staff Writer*

"The Minnesota Pollution Control Agency (MPCA) today denied a request by Coordinated Copper and Nickel, Inc., of Pittsburgh, PA, to mine for nickel at a wetlands site in northwestern Minnesota."

A collective cheer went up, several cries of "the turtles are safe" were heard, and we all started high-fiving each other on our way back to our desks. The lede of Bernie's story was all that we on the staff needed to know; Don could read the rest of it without a crowd of spectators jostling for space behind him.

The outburst drew Al and all the other photographers out of their den, and Al asked me what the mass shouting was about.

"The nickel mining permit has been denied," I said. "We've swamped the would be wetlands wreckers, and the turtles that live there are safe."

"That *is* worth shellabrating," Al said, and we exchanged high fives."

"Hey, get this everybody!" Don yelled. "The reason it has taken the PCA so long to make the decision is that one board member has been holding out, demanding approval, and today that member has been charged with accepting money from a foreign power in exchange for his favorable vote."

On my computer, I delightedly deleted the lede that said the mining permit had been granted and went to work filling in the sidebar story under the lede that said the permit had been denied. At 11:35, I received my scheduled call from Kurt S.C. Turner, who sounded like a very unhappy CEO.

"Are you going take this call as an opportunity to gloat over the denial of the permit, Mister Mitchell?" Turner asked.

"I am taking this call first as a reporter without prejudice who is asking for a statement about the permit denial and second as the claimant of a debt," I said.

"My statement is that I am terribly disappointed in the agency's unfair action, and we will be withdrawing all of our employees from the state of Minnesota immediately. Now what the hell is this debt that you're talking about claiming?" he said.

I had decided to take the proverbial bull by the tail and look the situation squarely in the eye one more time. "You said that you'd give me one month's worth of your pay if I identified the person who called himself Bigdigger and was attempting to mine cadmium in addition to nickel at the site here in Minnesota," I said. "I have successfully identified that person and I stand ready to give you the bank account number into which you may deposit a month's worth of your pay. Or I can give you my home address if you'd prefer to mail me a check."

After a moment of silence, Turner cleared his throat and said, "I'm sorry to inform you that that statement was only the proverbial cliché, Mister Mitchell. Only the proverbial cliché." Then he hung up.

Bummer. I wasn't going to harvest a financial windfall as a reward for my brilliant reportorial coup.

But what the hell? The turtles were safe.

The End